INSIDE THE WALLS

K.M. Tomkinson

DEDICATIONS

With thanks to my husband, Luke.
Without his consistent support, I never would have found the courage to follow my dreams and end up as accomplished as I am today.

To my beautiful children, Scarlett, Rubey, and Seth, may this publication prove to you that if you set your mind to something, anything is possible.

And to my mother and sister, Colleen & Charisse, for being there for me not only during my writing journey, but my life, in times of need.

Contents

Inside the Walls

Chapter One

"You're actually serious about this aren't you?" I groaned as the car I'd spent the last several hours curled up in gradually slowed and came to a halt beside the curb.

"Of course we're serious, Olivia," my mother chuckled from the front passenger seat. "You know perfectly well we didn't make this decision overnight."

I rolled my eyes and slumped my head backward as I proceeded to unbuckle my seatbelt. Completely dreading what the new house was going to be like, considering I knew how tight my parent's budget was, I took a short breath and leaned forward. Glancing out the window across an unsightly, overgrown front lawn, I was pleasantly shocked. To my utter surprise, it was *huge*. If I had to guess, I would have categorised it as a mansion.

I pushed the car door open and stepped out, picking my jaw up off the ground and taking in every detail. Granted, it was fairly rundown, and the yard obviously hadn't been looked after during a lengthy absence of owners but even in its neglected state, the house itself was gorgeous. Spiky brambles grew up each side of the front path, the lawn was more than a meter high and the hedges looked about ten years overdue for a trim but still, it had potential. Overlooking the whole street, it was the only two-story house on the block and boasted a giant wooden porch, double front doors, big bay windows, and a lock-up garage large enough for at least three cars to park side by side. I focused in on the finer details, picturing what it must have looked like before hell swallowed it up and spit it back out.

Upon gazing into the first story window by the front door, my heart palpitated and I found myself holding my breath momentarily. For just a few seconds, I caught a glimpse of a tall figure standing in the shadows, partially hidden by the dark curtains. I leaned forward ever so slightly and squinted, trying to decide if there was actually a figure standing there, or if it was perhaps just a bunch of random shapes and shadows that looked like a person. Though I couldn't see his whole face, I concluded that it was definitely a man. The height of the figure alone was enough to determine that much. He stood as still as ever, leaning against the window frame, and was staring, fixated on our car, as though intently watching our family move in.

As soon as he noticed that I had seen him, he tilted his face to the side, further into the shadows and gave me a cold, unfriendly smirk. Then, robotically and still without much emotion, he raised an arm ever so slowly to wave at me. I frowned, turning my head to look back at my parents in the hope that they had noticed the creepy, brooding stranger inside our new house.

"Hey parentals, is there supposed to be someone waiting inside for us?" I asked nonchalantly. I rolled my eyes when I realised they weren't even paying attention, instead choosing to argue loudly over the correct technique and order to unload our belongings from the car. I repeated my question, slower and louder this time, directly aiming my voice at my father. Still nothing, they were oblivious to the world around them. I sighed, nodded to myself and whispered sarcastically, "It's cool, focus on yourselves. I mean, is he a realtor, is he an axe murderer, who knows? It's not important…"

Completely unaware that I'd even spoken to him, my father's head emerged from the boot cradling a large cardboard box. Forcing me to grab onto it by shoving it into my chest, he exclaimed chirpily, "Well off you go Livvie, take your brother inside and fight each other for the best bedroom!" He glanced wearily around the car, lowered his voice and spoke with clenched teeth, "Just make sure you hurry back to help unload the car, otherwise your mother's brain might explode for real."

I shook my head in disbelief and frowned. "Uh, Dad…did you seriously not hear me? There's a man watching us from inside the lounge room."

He peered over my shoulder inquisitively, then looked back at me with a stupid grin on his face. "Well, I can't see anyone there now, but I tell you what, if you happen to come across a squatter, tell him he can stay if he's willing to pay board." I checked the window again myself, gave him a sarcastic half-smile and made way for the front door, carefully avoiding being spiked by dead plants along the way. My little brother Noah, being much smaller and fitter than me, made it up the path in half the time and quickly disappeared into the house.

As much as I hated myself for it, I was somewhat looking forward to seeing the interior. Once I got closer to the house, I cautiously surveyed the whole area where I'd seen the man standing. There was no one in sight, nothing but an empty living room. I concluded it must have been shadowing after all, relaxed a little and picked up the pace, even more eager to get inside. I wanted to hate the new house, but I needed to know if the inside was as gorgeous as the exterior portrayed it to be.

It was in much better shape than the outside, to say the least. Though it smelt dank and musty, like an old house usually does after being sealed for years, I couldn't help but admire the house's attributes. The polished wooden flooring, tear-shaped crystal chandeliers, and vast size of the living room alone was enough to drop my jaw. The main lounge area even had two entrances and everything! I had to take a moment to silently punish myself. By liking the interior design, I somehow felt like I was cheating on our old house. That house, the house I'd grown up in, was back in Armistice, Northern Australia, which was now a long drive of four hours away. It was my first ever move, frustratingly enough right in the middle of my final year in high school, and I was finding it rather hard to adjust. Even worse, I'd been torn away from my long-term boyfriend, Sam, and I had no idea how I was supposed to go from seeing him every day to not at all.

I peered down the hall and made my way towards a large, decorated archway, which turned out to be one of several entrances to the kitchen. Ultimately, my sense of direction paid off, as there were curved stairs leading upward out of the kitchen to the second story where I only assumed the bedrooms would be.

I was in awe once I got to the top of the stairwell.
Five bedroom doorways all lined up in a row perfectly spaced along a long narrow hallway before me, with the middle doorway situated immediately across from the top of the stairs. There was even a small balcony overlooking the kitchen below, which
was positioned proportionally across from the first two bedrooms. The rest of the second floor seemed to wrap around the corner down the end of the hall and I could see more doorways opposite the bedrooms.

My seven-year-old brother came charging out of the bedroom right across from the top of the stairs, almost knocking the box I was carrying out of my arms. "Too late, I got the best one!" he declared happily, thundering down the stairwell.

"No way!" I called out after him, a little flustered. Hitching the box back into a comfortable spot on my hip, I began to explore the remaining choices.

The bedrooms with the balcony did seem to be the largest, however, I decided against them. The first one due to the lack of built-in cupboards and the second because it smelt like something very dead had rubbed itself all over the carpet. Upon inspecting the room to the left of the stairwell, I was sold. I couldn't put my finger on it, but something was telling me this room was meant to be my new bedroom. I dumped the box I'd been carting along on the centre of the floor, which sent a cloud of thick dust into the air and my former school's senior's jersey flying out onto the ground. Coughing and swatting away the dust, I crossed over to the singular window in the room to see what kind of view I had. Making a face at the ratty, moth-eaten curtains covering the glass, I carefully picked them aside with two fingers and had to give the panes a shove with my shoulder to get the window open.

Poking my head out, I was filled with an unfamiliar ache and soon realised I was missing my old room. As much as it had used to annoy me, I longed for the smell of my perfume scented carpet and the sound of constant street traffic. It wasn't all bad, looking around gave me a decent view of the street and the trees in the distance, but beyond that, it was all wide-open spaces with a hint of countryside. I really hated the thought of being surrounded by a country atmosphere. Sighing, I decided I'd better head back to the car before I got in trouble for "trying to get out of helping." I couldn't help stopping in the living room on my way past and positioned myself in the same spot I'd seen whatever it was in the window. Looking out towards the curb, I could see my mother and father standing by the boot of the car, inaudibly arguing as they lifted out boxes. At least some things don't change, I reassured myself. I rested my knees on the low bay windowsill, put my head in my hands and watched as my older sister's car turned onto the street, closely followed by two moving trucks.

It was really sinking in now; our old house was long gone. And it wasn't just the new house we all had to get used to; it was also a whole new town. Bellicose was small and seemingly in the middle of nowhere. Yet, it was apparently a popular tourist location, famous for its magnificent ghost tours and masses of haunted houses.

As my sister's car pulled into the driveway and the trucks parked out front, my family swiftly gathered around and began to help the movers unload the smaller items. After a few minutes, I noticed my mother getting flustered and looking around, visually searching for something. Me. Bugger. She'd noticed I hadn't come back out to help. After conversing briefly with my father, she suddenly looked over towards the house and swept her head across until her eyes met mine. Putting her hands on her hips, she continued to stare at me and mouthed angrily, "get out here." I did not need to be told twice; Mum was scary enough when she was in a good mood. Moving house was really starting to suck. It was going to be a long weekend.

It took hours for the movers to bring all our furniture into the house and get it all positioned. We barely stopped for lunch or dinner and yet my parents were adamant we would still have time to unpack our essentials before bed. As the sun went down, the house made a profound change from beautiful to creepy. The general atmosphere of the place sent chills up my spine every time I entered a room without the lights on. It got to the point where I was constantly checking over my shoulder, unable to shake the feeling that someone was watching my every move. I wasn't usually the jumpy type, but there was unquestionably something off about the entire place now.

Once the streetlights came on, there were several occasions where I spotted the neighbours from down the street sticking their necks out and trying to catch a peep of us moving in. They were not discreet about pointing at our house whilst communing with each other over their fences. Due to the multiple layers of dust throughout the house and the state of the overgrown yard, I figured new neighbours were somewhat unheard of and exciting to them. It had without a doubt been a long time since anyone had lived in the house at all. Or perhaps we were simply drawing attention because the house stood alone at the end of a dead-end street, with only shrubbery on either side and the nearest houses a good hundred metres away. However, whatever their reason for staring, they were very quick to duck out of sight any time one of my family members spotted them and made no attempts to come down the street and introduce themselves.

Whilst I was unloading the last few boxes out of the removalist vehicles in the dark, a middle-aged couple came strolling down the street walking a giant, nasty-looking dog. Usually, I was a dog person, but with the teeth baring scowl it flashed at me, I did not want to be anywhere near this dog. Though they were coming straight towards me, I pretended not to notice the couple and continued shifting boxes out of the back of the truck and onto the grass. They came to a halt unexpectedly in front of the mailbox and after staring at the house for a few moments, the woman passed the dog's leash to her accompanying partner and approached me. A little cautious, I stopped what I was doing and subtly stepped around the other side of the boxes I'd stacked, creating a wall between her and I.

She didn't seem to notice and leaned in, speaking softly with a sincere tone. "She won't be happy you're living here. We see her cry all the time you know."

I frowned. "I'm sorry, I don't understand. Who cries?"

She didn't respond and looked over my shoulder at the house, standing in silence for a long while. When she hadn't moved at all for several minutes, I turned to follow her gaze, glancing back and forth between her and the house. Then, just as she finally opened her mouth to speak, my father came striding out the front door, faster than I'd ever seen him move. Shaking her head, the old lady hurriedly turned and shuffled back to the curb, taking the dog's leash back from the old man's hand. "Shouldn't have sold it to you people," she muttered as they began to walk away.

A little irritated, I screwed up my face as Dad stopped beside me. He watched the old woman walk away for a few seconds with a curious look on his face, then asked, "Everything ok? What was that all about? What did she say to you?"

I shrugged. "I literally have no idea. Just some random old lady commenting on our house."

He nodded slowly, "Yeah don't worry about her, worry about us right now. I had to get out of the house. Your mother is driving me to the brink of insanity. Even though this place is double the size of our old house, she can't decide where exactly she wants the furniture and I've moved the couches four times already!" He paused to wipe a trickle of sweat off his brow. "Oh, and to make matters worse, the moving guys were taking some bedroom furniture upstairs and lost control of Mum's antique vanity dresser. It's scattered in pieces on the stairwell and they're refusing to take responsibility. I strongly recommend avoiding her for as long as you can."

It took all my strength not to giggle and I managed to contain my highly inappropriate smirk. "Sounds about right. Thus why I volunteered to come out and get the last of the small stuff out of the trucks."

I turned and bent over, intending to pick up a rather large box. The thick layer of packing tape across the top appeared to have ripped open when something else had jabbed through the side during transport and torn a large hole, somewhat revealing the contents. It looked to me like photo albums.

"Oh, I'll take that one!" Dad half-tackled me out of the way and wrapped his arms around the box, causing me to stumble and trip over my own feet in the process. I only just managed to catch my balance before face planting the grass. Cradling the box in his arms, he shot me a weird grin and took off at record speed back into the house without saying another word.

"Ok…," I muttered, grabbing a carton labelled "small kitchen appliances" instead.

Trudging back inside, I tried to make myself scarce as I passed through the living room. Thankfully, my mother was nowhere to be seen. I wasn't keen on being chewed out over the broken dresser. Unfortunately, when my mother was mad at something or someone, she was mad at everything and everyone, and punishments were dished out without a second thought. Still on edge, I took the package of appliances through to the kitchen, which was, to my dismay, where Mum had ended up. She was bent over the basin swearing to herself indiscreetly and twisting the taps vigorously as a cascade of water sprayed her in the face.

"Ooh, broken sink, huh," I said sarcastically.

She rotated her head robotically and glared at me with a look that made me regret my comment instantly. "Just be useful and go get my phone so I can call a bloody plumber! My handbag's sitting on the floor just inside the front entry!"

I sighed, dumped the box I was carrying onto the nearest counter and jogged back down the hall to grab her bag. When I returned to the kitchen, the plumbing situation had become much worse. A jet of water was now shooting out of the pipes below the counter as well as from the main tap. Soaked from the neck down and more frustrated than ever, Mum snatched the bag from my hands without mercy and pulled out her mobile phone, along with a travel-sized emergency phonebook. Before the move, she'd written out a list of all possible service numbers she'd need in case of complications with the new house. At the time I thought she was being a bit over prepared but as it turned out, it was a good thing she had thought ahead.

Oddly enough, it took a few attempts to find a plumber willing to accept an emergency callout, due to it being after six in the evening. Pacing the kitchen out of stress, Mum explained the situation to the plumber who ended up accepting the job in an attempt to get a rough quote. She began to calm down a little once she teed everything up for an immediate fix. A smile forming on her face, she slumped onto a stray dining chair in the corner and continued nodding along for a few moments whilst he talked. Once she gave them our address, however, her facial expression morphed into a scowl.

"What do you mean you won't come here?" she spat angrily, jumping to her feet to resume pacing again.

Curious, I crossed the kitchen and leaned in behind her, trying to hear what he was saying also.

"I'm sorry ma'am, but we just can't service that house," the man on the phone said bluntly, before hanging up abruptly.

"Time wasting idiot!" she exclaimed, tossing her phone onto the dining table.

I hurriedly took a few steps back, casually leaning against the closest wall before she turned around. "What was that all about?" I asked.

Clearly frustrated, she ignored me and rubbed her forehead a few times, staring blankly at the spray of water still escaping the sink, clearly deep in thought. As I watched the water begin to form a pool on the floor along the base of the counters, I waited in silence hoping she was actively trying to come up with a solution. Once the water had pooled up so much it started trickling across the floor towards us, I figured it was time to say something. "Uh, Mum the kitchen's flooding…"

As though only just noticing the ever-growing puddle of water, she gasped and rushed towards the basin. Jiggling the tap handles furiously, she snapped, "Go to the basement and retrieve some tools for me would ya, I think that's where your father would have put them!"

I wrinkled my nose, somewhat annoyed. Whilst I was unimpressed at having to play fetch for her, I found it pretty cool that the new house had a basement and was keen to check it out.

Unfortunately, the entrance to the basement happened to be in the floor at the far corner of the laundry, which had now been mostly blocked off by carelessly dumped duffels of clothes. Fighting my way through the mounds of bags, I eventually cleared enough space to be able to open the basement door. It took a few attempts as the door was quite heavy, but I managed to wrench it open and started down the stairwell into a pitch-black abyss. I paused for a moment once I'd gotten halfway down when I heard what sounded like someone whispering behind me. I rotated my head slightly, but there was no one in sight. Thinking nothing of it, I continued and started feeling the walls for a light switch.

I found a pull chain light at the bottom of the stairs, which stupidly enough, only lit up about a quarter of the room. From what I could see, the basement was small and clammy, only just larger than the size of the laundry above, with ancient-looking brick walls and jagged pieces of stone layered together to make acceptable flooring. Squinting through the dimly lit centre, I spotted a small stack of cardboard boxes against the opposite wall and made a beeline towards them. Luckily, the tools were sitting in an open crate on top, so not a lot of digging was required to access them. Out of the corner of my eye, I noticed the box of photo albums my Dad had taken off with beforehand and curiosity got the better of me. Perhaps there was something hidden inside the box underneath the albums that he didn't want me to see?

Just as I reached for it, someone behind me blatantly cleared their throat. Startled, I twisted around so fast that I kicked my toe on a stray hammer lying on the floor in the process. It was my Dad. As my toe throbbed in pain, I took a deep breath, trying not to swear aloud at him.

He narrowed his eyes at me and reached around, picking up the crate of random tools. Glancing across at his album box he murmured firmly, "Your mother sent you for tools, she said you were taking too long."

I rolled my eyes. "I swear I only just got down here." I then proceeded to leave the basement hastily without seeing his reaction.

It took my parents over an hour to fix the broken faucet and pipe network together while the rest of us continued shifting our stuff inside and setting up what we could. Neither of them had a clue what they were doing, but they still managed to repair whatever it was that was broken without killing each other in the process and before the kitchen fully flooded. We then used every towel we could find to soak up the water because no one could find the mop and bucket. With tempers running high, we managed to get through the rest of the evening without too many arguments. Mum and Dad managed to send the removalists off a little after eight and they finally let us call it a night about an hour after that, allowing us to stop sorting and unpacking. Since most of the beds hadn't been assembled yet, we all crashed on the living room floor in random bedding piles. I was somewhat grateful, the idea of sleeping alone the very first night in a brand-new house was very daunting.

The next morning, my father left the house before sun-up after receiving a call from his new boss stating he was to come in and commence his role immediately. Apparently, he needed to be up to speed for the beginning of the work week. Mum was not happy and as usual, took her frustration out on anyone who crossed her path, which was almost impossible not to do when being forced to shift furniture with her. I loved my mum, but she was extremely hard to deal with in high stress, busy situations.

It took nearly the rest of the weekend to sort out all of our belongings, organising the house room by room, with my mother breathing down everyone's necks the entire time. Dad managed to get out of all the unpacking drama, spending both days working from the crack of dawn right through until sundown. The house was starting to come together by Sunday afternoon. I was relieved when Mum eventually allowed us to take an hour's break in order to rest and have a late lunch. Noah, of course, had been allowed to eat earlier and went off to his bedroom to play instead. As the three of us girls gathered together in the kitchen, I flopped into a chair at the dining table and glanced across at my sister with a smirk as she struggled to squeeze into a chair comfortably.

Isabelle had just turned twenty-one and she was pregnant with her first baby. She had eight weeks left to go and had come to stay with us temporarily, on Mum's orders, because her boyfriend, Carl, had been sent out of town for work. Since the baby wasn't due for a while, his boss assumed that everything would be dandy during a four-week-long business trip. Personally, I thought he was being rude and I was mad at Carl for accepting. Isabelle was too pregnant to do a lot of heavy lifting, so she'd been put in charge of sorting and unpacking what she could manage. I looked Isabelle up and down and scrunched up my nose as she jammed a peanut butter and avocado sandwich into her mouth as fast as she could. She was eating as though she hadn't for days, but she was growing my first niece so I still thought she was beautiful, even when she acted like a pig. I smiled at her as she got up to take her plate to the sink and examined the kitchen, finally able to take a moment to appreciate the décor.

My peaceful moment was ruined abruptly however when a shattering sound echoed through the kitchen, followed by a high-pitched scream. Both Mum and I jumped, whipping around to see what had happened. Isabelle was standing stiffly by the kitchen sink, her hands and arms outstretched in horror, surrounded by piles of broken glass. She was covered in light gashes and shaking with fear. It appeared as though the window above the basin had shattered into hundreds of pieces, which were now strewn across the bench and floor. Bewildered, I dashed to her side to see if she was alright.

"The damn window just burst for no reason!" she cried out hysterically.

I patted her shoulder in comfort whilst Mum brushed her off from the other side, working quickly to remove a few stray pieces of glass that were sticking in Isabelle's skin.

Highly confused as to how the window had spontaneously exploded in the first place, I started cleaning up the glass while Mum guided Isabelle to the bathroom to find a first aid kit. Grabbing the broom from beside the fridge, I began to sweep the main chunks on the floor into a pile at the sink's base. I stopped in my tracks for a moment when an eerie reflection in a large slice of glass on the bench caught my eye. For just a second, I could have sworn I saw a woman in a pale nightgown standing behind me. As I leaned forward to get a better look, she was gone. I picked up the shard of glass to double check and even physically scanned the kitchen, but there was definitely no one around. I shook my head and continued to sweep, putting my hallucination down to overexertion from moving.

A few minutes later, my mother returned to the kitchen to examine the damage and take measurements of the window space. Waddling close behind was Isabelle, who was covered in tiny bandaids that she claimed Mum had insisted on dressing her wounds with. Scouring her little contact book, Mum soon found a window repair company and phoned for a quote. So she could tidy whilst she spoke, she put the call on loudspeaker. She became annoyed instantaneously when they also told her that they "couldn't service our house."

"We must live in a bad area or something," she remarked, hanging up with frustration. "I'll just have to go get a panel of glass from the shop and replace it myself after I drop you kids to school tomorrow."

Whilst I felt bad that things were going wrong with the new house, I couldn't help but smile on the inside at the same time. I felt like the house was on my side, proving to my parents that we shouldn't have moved in the first place. Our old house was a lot smaller, sure, but at least it wasn't falling apart.

By that evening, I was beyond exhausted, both mentally and physically, and for the first time ever, I was glad to be sent to my room. That is of course, until the real-life nightmare started later that night.

Chapter Two

From somewhere nearby a floorboard creaked and the sound of heavy footsteps echoed through the hallway. A chilly breeze whistled through the holey curtains that hung over the window in my new bedroom. Had I left the window open…? No, I could have sworn I'd shut it when I had come back from the bathroom. I pulled the blankets tighter around me and cautiously lifted my head off of the pillow, peering through the darkness.

The window was still closed and yet, mysteriously, the curtains continued to flutter as though caught in a gentle breeze. Could I hear someone whispering? No. I sighed and lay my head back on the soft, inviting pillows. If I kept worrying about every tiny movement and sound, I would never get to sleep. Reassuring myself that it was an extremely old house and that old houses made eerie noises all the time, I rolled over and buried my face in the pillows. Unfortunately, that only slightly muffled the weird sounds, but thankfully did reduce the awful musty smell in the air.

Soft rattling noises had started up now, which sounded as though they were coming from the bottom of my cupboard, causing a shiver to run down my spine. I began to wonder if anyone else in my family had any problems getting to sleep. We were all in unfamiliar territory after all.

It was getting hard to breathe as my pillow wasn't providing any source of oxygen, so I rolled over onto my side and tried to force the annoying, eerie sounds from the room out of my mind. From the moment everyone went to bed, I'd been hearing strange noises and the curtains never seemed to stop fluttering. It was pretty creepy, but I just assumed there was a gap between the windowsill and the glass where the wind was entering through. I'd had difficulty getting any shut-eye the previous night also, but the commotion hadn't gone on all night long the way it was now.

Adding to my misery, a scratching sound had now begun, coming from somewhere close to my head. Scarily enough, it seemed as though it was coming from inside the wall that my bed was pushed up against. Like something inside the wall was trying to scratch its way out using long, razor-sharp claws.

My heart rate increased slightly as mental images of all the possible creatures who could be trying to claw through the wall flickered through my head. I forced myself to relax and tried to stop letting my imagination get the better of me. Bloody rats in the walls. Reassuring myself didn't stop the tingles running up and down my spine though; I was beginning to feel alone and afraid in an unfamiliar, unwelcoming room.

I shuddered. Tomorrow was Monday, which meant my first day at a new school and I didn't particularly want to show up with red, puffy eyes from a lack of sleep. Knowing what I needed was a distraction, and feeling like a total idiot doing so, I started singing nursery rhymes. It must have been hours later but somehow, I eventually managed to drift off.

It felt as though I'd slept five minutes, when my very loud brother flung himself onto my bed and shook me awake.

"Hey, Livvie!" he yelled in my ear, "Get up, Mum says it's time to get ready for school!"

I groaned, covered my ears with a pillow and waved him away with a flick of my wrist. Squinting, I watched as he turned and ran full speed ahead out of my room. The sound of his footsteps thundering down the stairs could have easily matched the decibels of an elephant stampede and it rattled my poor, tired brain. I frowned, and pushing the blankets off of me lazily, sat up shaking my head at the empty doorway.

I reached over and grabbed my hairbrush off the bedside table, running it through my long, fluffy blonde hair before dodging a few unpacked moving boxes as I dragged myself across the room to grab my new uniform from the cupboard. As I pulled it out and studied it, I cringed as I thought to myself that whoever had designed this school's uniform must have been blind. Or perhaps they got enjoyment out of watching students suffer. It was just *so* ugly.

The skirt was knee length and moss green in colour with thin horizontal brown stripes. The button-up shirt that went with it was a muddy brown colour and had green vertical stripes and the logo on the pocket read "Harriet Brown High School." Why would anyone force teenagers to wear something like that? I screwed up my nose as though the uniform had an awful stench to it and groaned. What was wrong with this place?! I missed my old school already and I had never even used to like it, I was never exactly the teacher's pet type of person. Holding the shirt up against my body in front of the mirror, I sighed, shrugged and started to get dressed.

"Aww darlin,' that looks just gorgeous!" said my mother sarcastically as I emerged at the bottom of the stairs into the kitchen. She was buttering Noah's toast and clearly thought the same of my uniform as I did.

I rolled my eyes and gave her a sarcastic smile before sliding in next to my older sister at the table. It was just past seven-thirty in the morning and as I looked around, I figured with his favourite coffee mug upturned in the sink, my father had already left for work. Likely at the crack of dawn again for the third day in a row. His stupid job was the reason we had to relocate in the first place. But, as my parents had said repeatedly when they were convincing us that moving was a good idea, it was a huge promotional opportunity for my father and the paycheck was better. According to them, so was Bellicose. On our drive through it, however, I had serious doubts about that part. The town was tiny and seemed to be one of those "everybody knows everybody's business" kind of places. Having come from big city living, this was going to be a huge change. I was trying to be happy for my dad, but so far, I was not liking the idea of a new beginning.

Realising that I didn't feel hungry, I hastily left the kitchen and headed for my room in order to get started on finding my new schoolbooks and packing my bag. When I opened the door to my bedroom, the rather gross and musty smell found my nose. It seemed somehow that the room had been even more deprived of air since the day before.

I crossed the room to the forever fluttering curtains and forced the window open with a slight grunt. They instantly stopped moving and became dead still against the window frame. Frowning, I pushed them aside and stuck my head out the window. A beautiful breeze washed over my face. I moved back and as an experiment, shut the window again. The curtains began to flutter once more.

Examining the windowsill with my fingertips, I found no gaps between the window and the frame of any kind. I narrowed my eyes, shook my head and then opened the window again. I jogged over to my bed and looked back at the unmoving fabric. There was something very weird about that window, but I tried not to care, the feel of fresh air entering the room was nice.

I walked over to the wardrobe, grabbed my new textbooks from the drawers with one arm and threw my bag on the bed with the other. Briefly looking at each book, I stuffed them into my school bag. Just then, something on the wall caught my eye. I paused and lightly dropped everything I was holding onto the bed. As I moved closer, I noticed that it wasn't something on the wall; it was something *in* the wall. It was a small hole, about the size of a large coin, which I soon realised as I studied the paint chippings closely, looked as though it had been made from the inside.

My heart began to pound faster as I remembered the scratching I had heard the night before. The sound had come from inside the wall, I was sure of it. And this hole proved that it hadn't just been my imagination, it was real. I backed away from the wall and stared at it. Now I really was starting to freak out. I felt like an idiot for panicking. Before we'd moved here there was nothing that scared me. I had recently turned seventeen and being afraid of a little hole in the wall seemed to me like something a child was supposed to fear. I ultimately decided to ignore it, it had probably been there when I'd moved my stuff in and I just hadn't seen it. On the other hand, if it was fresh, did rats chew through random places in walls?

Just as my mind began to create a series of vivid images explaining how the hole had come to be, heavy footsteps sounded from the hallway outside my bedroom, stopping seemingly near my door. Confused, I paused for a moment and listened. The footsteps sounded much too heavy to be anyone but my dad, who I knew was still at work. I froze and waited for whoever it was to knock or burst into my bedroom. When no one did, I crept towards the door, peered out onto the landing and took my time to check up and down the hallway. I couldn't see anybody at all. My stomach clenched when I saw there was, however, a trail of large bloody footprints leading from the top of the stairwell through to my brother's room.

My heart began to race as I studied them further, inevitably deciding to follow the trail into Noah's room. His door was ajar, and I could see the shadow of a figure standing just inside the doorway. I pushed it open slowly, expecting to see Noah standing there with blood covered shoes, perhaps from a scraped knee or something. To my surprise, his room was empty and the footprints ceased a few steps short of his bed. I almost jumped out of my skin when someone suddenly popped up beside me. It was Noah.

"What are you doing in my room?" he asked quizzically, pushing past me to grab his schoolbag from the top of his dresser. I held my hands up in frustration and gestured to the floor, wondering how he hadn't taken notice of the bloody footprints.

When he stared blankly at me with confusion, I looked down and immediately discerned the footprints had vanished. I fixated on the ground, wide-eyed, trying to figure out what was going on. Taking a few steps back, I glanced out into the hall to double check but there was no trace of blood left in sight out there either. I decided a lack of sleep was getting to my imagination. It seemed I had become capable of dreaming whilst awake.

Mum's voice called out from somewhere downstairs and while I couldn't make out the words, I guessed it was time to leave for school. Noah pulled on his schoolbag and poked my arm, obviously waiting for a reaction of some kind. I pulled myself together and playfully punched his arm, "Eh, thought I caught a glimpse of the monster under your bed. Let's just go."

Almost an hour later, Mum pulled up at my new high school shortly after dropping off my little brother. Apparently, he needed extra love and care to settle into school, whilst I was offered the "drive-by" treatment. I got out of the car, slung my schoolbag over one shoulder and looked up at the worn and battered sign bearing "Harriet Brown High School." Glancing past the semi-rotted boards, I noted that the lack of upkeep on the sign was misleading. It was such a fancy school, so clean and proper looking. The buildings almost sparkled in the sun, except for one or two at the front which appeared slightly charred.

Mum called out, "Remember to make friends, not enemies. How about you walk home this afternoon and get to know the area. Have a good day!" She then hit the accelerator and was gone.

I sighed and headed across the empty, leaf-strewn front oval for the big building declaring "Administration." I approached the blackened, run-down looking building but saw only windows, so I figured the entrance would be on the other side.

As I rounded the corner at a quick pace, I walked headlong into a girl around the same height as me. She stumbled, but managed to stop herself from toppling backward.

"Dammit, I'm sorry!" I cried out.

She looked surprised but smiled at me and hitched her bag back onto her shoulders. "Nah, don't worry about it," she said chirpily, "Say, I haven't seen you around before, are you new?"

I nodded. "Yeah, new to the school and the town."

She grinned and remarked happily, "That's so great, it's good to have new faces around here." Gesturing to the buildings, she asked "I suppose you still need to confirm your enrolment?" I nodded again and studied her. She was possibly around my age and quite pretty with smooth pale skin and silky, chocolate coloured hair that shone beautifully in the sunlight. I looked into her dark, brown eyes and was surprised by what I saw. Her smile was warm and portrayed happiness, but her eyes said different. They were almost hollow and swam with deep sorrow. She shook her sleek, straight hair off of her face and grasped my arm firmly, proceeding to lead me off towards the buildings situated in the inner part of the school.

I must have looked confused because she laughed and said, "Someone started a fire in the front administration block a few months ago, the inside is still mostly gutted. They moved the main office up the back near the staffrooms."

I raised my eyebrows. This school didn't seem so bad after all.

I felt my mobile phone vibrate in my pocket, so I stopped walking and pulled it out with the hand that wasn't being held hostage by my apparent new friend. Whose name, I realised, I didn't know yet.

"Hey, what's your name?" she asked out of nowhere. It was as though she had read my mind.

"Oh, Olivia Murphy," I shrugged, "but please just call me Liv. And yours?"

She grinned. "Grace Maker, but you can just call me Grace." She then burst out laughing as though she'd made some sort of hilarious joke. When I didn't laugh, she stopped herself short and looked at me as though waiting for some kind of acknowledgement.

Feeling awkward by the sudden silence, I gave her a little chuckle to let her know I wasn't a total jerk and checked my phone.

Smiling to myself as I read the text all I could think was, gosh I was going to miss him. Sam had sent a message saying, "Good luck at your new school, don't forget to wreak havoc. Miss you heaps, xx."

"What are you smiling like a goober about?" Grace asked with a smirk.

I laughed, "Oh just my boyfriend being the sweet guy he is."

Startling me, a bell rang out through the buildings and kids of all heights and ages poured out of classrooms, babbling incoherently. "Did we miss class?" I asked as I shoved my phone back into my pocket.

"No, just form, which is only attendance marking, it's not overly important to go." Grace said calmly. "We can fix it up at the office in a minute. So, does your boyfriend live back where you moved from?"

"Uh, yeah," I replied with a sigh, "Yeah, Sam was just one more thing I had to leave behind."

Grace nodded stiffly. "I know what that's like," she said softly. I observed that her eyes had filled with tears and now even her cute smile had been affected by the pain they encased. Grace shook her head, wiped her eyes and said hurriedly, "Sorry. Anyway, how come you moved here and where are you living now? I know Bellicose may seem like a ghost town with nowhere to go but maybe sometime I can come over to your place and we can hang out, I'll even show you around the neighbourhood."

I found myself wondering if this girl had any other friends, she seemed awfully eager to make a new one.

We dodged a crowd of students as we started walking again in the direction of the new administration office. I thought about my response a moment and then began to ramble without meaning to. "Well, my dad was asked to transfer here as part of a promotion. They offered him an instant raise if he'd move to Bellicose because it's where the head office of his company is, which he's now kinda in charge of. Annoyingly enough, things seemed to keep falling into place for my parents. They got offered this cheap old property up on the end of Mason Street, which they bought—"

Grace cut my sentence short by gasping and throwing her arm out in front of me, smashing me across the chest and somewhat winding me.

"Olivia, please don't tell me you are living in the Mason Manor?" Her voice was hysterical and her eyes widened as her face contorted with nothing short of terror.

I felt my heartbeat start to speed up as I tried to catch my breath. I exhaled and replied, "Well yeah, we moved into the huge house on the hill at the end of Mason Street, I don't remember the number…." I trailed off as I watched Grace before me. She seemed to struggle with my words and was barely managing to stand on her own two feet. "Er, Grace, it's ok," I said quietly, patting her arm. "Is there something wrong? I mean, what's so bad?"

Grace's eyes came back into focus. She clamped her hand down onto my shoulder and her fearful eyes bored into mine. "Do you believe in ghosts?" She asked in a very stern voice. I let out a short burst of laughter and blurted out, "Yeah right! Oh wait, let me guess, this is the part where you're going to tell me my house is haunted or something, yeah?"

Grace's expression didn't change at all. I noticed she'd gone quite pale and her bottom lip began to tremble. I felt bad now and frowned at her until she proceeded to glare back at me, no longer looking frail and upset. "I'm sure you've heard by now that Bellicose is famous for hauntings. Well, the Mason Street manor is the worst of them," she said seriously. "You have to get *out* of that house. Before it's too late. People die there, that place isn't just haunted, it's downright dangerous…you're living in the house of bloody walls!"

Chapter Three

I frowned at Grace and tried to look concerned, but really, I felt like laughing. She looked so serious; I didn't think she would have taken it well if I had laughed at her. Unintentionally letting out a little giggle, I asked with a snigger, "The house of bloody walls? Grace, what are you talking about?"

Visually shaking, she replied with a break in her voice, "I'm talking about the fact that your whole family is going to end up dead. It's happened before. That house once belonged to a crazy woman who killed herself in the living room. Ever since, no one who has lived there has survived. You're in danger! She haunts the manor, killing anyone who moves in, then keeps their spirits trapped in the house and consumes their souls for power."

I cringed. I despised ghost stories. "Grace…"

I started to protest, but she snapped, "If you don't believe me now, just give it time. Ask your neighbours, ask anyone who lives around here. It's a small town, word travels fast and everyone knows that house is haunted. Everyone avoids it at all costs. I mean, look up the house's history in old newspapers if you want! You shouldn't be living there. No one should be living there."

I held up a hand to interrupt her, slightly frustrated. "Look, I'm not saying the house's history isn't true, Grace. I'm just saying it's a load of crap that a bunch of ghosts are still roaming around and I'm not going to buy into haunted stuff about a deadly ghost. It's an old house, it's creepy, it's big and hey, maybe in the past it's had some bad luck run through it or something, but that doesn't actually mean my family is in any kind of danger." I paused to roll my eyes. "Even if they do exist, which I highly doubt, ghosts can't just go around killing people."

Grace pursed her lips, obviously annoyed with my disbelief. "Agatha *will* be biding her time, waiting for the right moment to come for you, soon enough you'll realise that. So, when you want to believe, come find me and I might be able to help you get out before you perish. I'm *always* going to be around." Looking slightly agitated, she then turned on her heel and stormed off in the opposite direction.

What a strange girl. She'd made me somewhat irritated. I didn't like the way that Grace had emphasised the word *always*. There was something about her tone that sent a chill down my spine.

Not quite understanding what had just happened, I shrugged it off and continued to head for the school office. After clarifying multiple times that I was in fact Olivia Murphy, the administration clerk handed me a timetable and map. She was a rude, pompous woman who seemed to have it in for me already as she waved me away from the desk staring down the nose of her hideously large spectacles. I gave her a single nod, as some form of thanks, checked my timetable and made a beeline for my first class, English.

I found myself to be a spectacle of entertainment all day. Students were staring at me throughout classes, during lunch breaks, and even in hallways as I walked to change lessons. No one spoke directly to me, but I could hear them talking behind my back, I caught the whisperings of my name and words like "haunted, ghost, manor, and Clayton." I was somewhat creeped out by all the attention. Had the school *never* had a new student before or something? Or worse, did people actually believe my house was haunted?

I started thinking about what Grace had said and for a brief moment, found myself wondering about the past weekend and the strange, somewhat creepy things I'd seen. There was the man inside the house, the window that randomly busted, the reflection of a woman in the kitchen and the vanishing bloody footprints. Could there even be a remote possibility my house was full of actual ghosts? I wasn't sure what to think.

Deciding I was being silly, I brushed it off and continued trying to get through the day. School had always been hard for me. I felt naked without my old crowd, but I was now somehow able to focus. It was weird, but I felt like without my friends, I finally had nothing to do except schoolwork. I'd spent much more of my time in the past messing around with Sam, Jenny and the others than I ever did on studying. We used to cause all kinds of havoc. My mother always said I'd fallen into the wrong crowd and the more I thought about it, the more I wondered if they chose to move halfway through my final school year on purpose to give me a chance at qualifying for graduation.

I kept an eye out for Grace all day as I navigated my way around the school between class changes, but I hadn't seen her at all and found myself wondering where she'd gotten to. Harriet Brown wasn't that big, and she hadn't been in a single one of my classes. I was hoping to run into her and find out more about the tall tale she was spinning about my new house. Even though I wasn't a believer in ghost stories, she sure had me curious about my house's history. Besides, Grace Maker may have been a weird one, but she was the only person in the whole school who had attempted to make conversation with me, rather than behind my back.

Hours passed, and by the time the final bell of the day rang out through the school, I had given up on finding Grace. Figuring if she really cared, she would come and find me since I apparently couldn't find her anywhere. I stuffed my textbooks into my bag and made my way out the front gates. I had a fairly good memory when it came to direction, a fact I hated my mother using against me, and managed to find my way back to the new house with ease.

Ten or so minutes later, I stood on the front lawn of the manor with my bag slung off of one shoulder, the way I liked it. I found myself studying the house carefully, wondering why Grace seemed so scared of it. In a way, I could understand people calling it haunted. I gazed over every inch of the exterior, examining the peeling, faded blue paint, studying the fancy spiral bars that held the windows on the second story in place and……my thoughts trailed away and my heart skipped a beat.

A strange boy was sitting, frozen, on my brother's windowsill, looking out onto the front lawn. I blinked, closed my eyes and shook my head. When I opened them, I found that he was still sitting there and hadn't moved an inch. He definitely wasn't Noah. My brother had blonde hair, just like me, and he was tall for his age. This little boy was small, with dark eyes, brown hair, pale skin, and looked as though he was only around five or six.

The peculiar boy was sitting on the outward ledge of the window with his knees pulled up to his chest. He appeared sad and as he stared out onto the street, one could almost call him lonely. My heart began to beat faster when his head suddenly turned, and his eyes stared into mine. It was hard to read his true expression at this distance and suddenly I had the urge to know who he was and what he was doing in my brother's room.

I hesitated for just a moment before dropping my schoolbag on the front lawn and sprinting into the house via the double front doors. As I ran down the front hall, I heard my mother's voice calling out to me, presumably from the laundry room. She was most likely wanting to know how my first day at school had been. I paid absolutely no attention to her and started quickly up the stairs, two at a time. I slowed to a fast walk as I reached the top and rounded the corner onto the landing where Noah's room lay straight ahead. As I pushed open his door in one quick motion, I half expected the mystery boy to be gone. Or perhaps I just hoped he was.

The bedroom door swung around on its hinges and slammed into the wall behind it. I stared across the room and was unable to take my eyes off the little boy who was still sitting there. He hadn't even looked around at the sound of the door and was still curled in the same position; it looked almost as though he was hugging himself.

Now that he was right in front of me, I suddenly didn't want to be standing there anymore. I wanted to get as far away from this kid as I could. But I figured I was here now; I couldn't just walk away. Plus, my legs were frozen in place so I probably couldn't have left even if I wanted to and if I didn't get rid of him, one of my family members would discover him anyway. My mum probably wouldn't have taken well to a strange little boy trespassing in my brother's room. I found myself wondering how he'd even wandered into our home without anyone noticing.

Taking a large breath, I cleared my throat loudly.

The boy did nothing for a few seconds, but then he turned his head slowly and his body swivelled around to face me. His eyes were deep, sunken, and full of cold emotion and as he stared into my eyes, I felt a wave of sadness wash over me like a cold wind hitting you in the face as you step outside in a harsh winter. He placed his feet on the floor and leaned forward as if waiting for me to say something. I felt like it would be ok to speak now so I inhaled deeply to calm my nerves and said quietly, "Hey, little buddy, what's your name? Are you lost?" I noticed his bottom lip quiver slightly and then, like the flip of a switch, suddenly he wasn't upset anymore, he was angry.

His eyes became fiery and as he stared daggers at me, he screamed, "Get out!"

Frightened and startled, I took a step backward, but didn't leave the room. The boy didn't seem so lonely and helpless anymore. I could almost see the steam escaping from his ears as he slid down off of the windowsill and stood upright. He moved forward a few steps and then yelled at me once more. "I said get out, so go away! This is *my* room!" And with that, he suddenly rushed at me.

I screamed and stumbled backward, tripping over my own feet and landing on my tailbone. But just as he was about to crash into me, I blinked, and he was gone. He'd simply vanished into thin air before my very eyes.

I collected myself off the floor and backed into the door frame, using the wall to support my body weight. My legs felt weak and I wanted to scream out again, but I bit my tongue and held it in. I wasn't sure what had just happened, it had occurred too quickly. Little boys didn't just disappear into thin air. Who was he? It wasn't his room, he didn't live here, we did. And this was Noah's room, right? I had to convince myself for a few moments that Noah was in fact, my brother. I could feel my throat burn slightly, but I refused to cry. Admitting to myself that I had momentarily been scared for real, I swallowed down my feelings and sat on Noah's bed, going over and over possible explanations.

Then my mind clicked together and it felt as though someone had poured ice-cold water into my chest as I finished piecing together what I had just seen and suddenly realised something. That little boy was a ghost. Oh great, was that Grace girl right? Was I seeing ghosts for real now? Did they exist?

Unable to move, I could barely even turn to look as my brother came into view out of the corner of my eye.

"Livvie, are you ok? Why did you scream?" he asked me. He walked around and stood in front of me, waving a hand in front of my face when I didn't answer him. I knew I couldn't tell him about what I had just seen, so I shook my head and pulled myself together.

Sounding as casually as I could I replied, "Oh, yeah everything is fine buddy. I just came in here to tell you something and…." I trailed off. What could I say? I ran my hand through my hair and said slowly, "And a big thing…uh, winged-bird…uh, I mean a pigeon bird thing flew onto the windowsill suddenly and it really scared me, so I screamed and…and it flew away."

Noah raised his eyebrows at me. He wasn't going to buy that.

He looked over at the window suspiciously, then back at me and said, "Wow, sissy, you're really weird. So, what did you want me for?"

I didn't know how to respond to that either, so I quickly mumbled, "Don't worry, I forget." Without waiting to see his reaction, I turned and sped down the hallway to my own bedroom.

Once I'd passed through my doorway, I turned on my heel and clicked the lock. I needed to be very much alone right now. I felt like sliding my back down the door and sitting on the floor in a ball, but I resisted the urge and crossed the room to my bed instead. I collapsed onto it face first, then turned myself over, so I was staring at the ceiling. What a day it had been!

The more I pondered over it, the more I realised that the rumours about the house being haunted could very well be true. But another part of me said that it was stupid to think so, that I should hold onto my belief that there was no such thing as ghosts. My brain began to hurt as I closed my eyes and concentrated with all my might, trying to wipe the little boy's face from my mind. Seconds later, my eyes shot open when a loud series of thumps followed by a spine-tingling scream rang through the house. After fumbling to unlock the door, I dashed out onto the second-floor balcony, trying to figure out which direction it had come from, locating the source of the noise quickly when a second scream pierced my ears from below me in the kitchen.

My mother lay sprawled on her stomach, seemingly unconscious on the floor at the bottom of the staircase whilst Isabelle knelt beside her checking her pulse. Gasping, I flew down the staircase as fast as I could manage without tripping over my own feet.

"She fell down the stairs, but she's breathing," Isabelle declared as I reached her. Mum groaned and started trying to roll over, struggling to pull her arms out from underneath her body. Isabelle shuffled out of the way so I could use my arms as a scoop, locking underneath Mum's armpits to pull her up off the ground into a sitting position. I could see bright purple bruises forming already under the skin on the areas she'd used to break her fall.

"Mum, are you alright, do you want to go up to the hospital?"

She shook her head and stood up slowly, groaning as she stretched out her legs. "No, I'll be ok, just a tumble. I have no idea what happened, though. I didn't even trip, I wasn't even…I mean, it honestly felt like I was pushed. I swear I felt hands on my back, they shoved me and I lost my balance."

I frowned and felt my stomach sink as I imagined the little boy ghost creeping up behind her and shoving her down the stairs. I shook it off quickly, however, telling myself that kid sure didn't seem to want to leave his room.

Mum shook her head again and stretched out her back, then began to mutter to herself as she walked away. I looked at Isabelle, hoping she thought it was odd too, but she just shrugged, following Mum down the hall. I, however, trudged back up to my room and locked the door behind me, trying my hardest not to think about it too much. So, Mum fell down the stairs, that had to be a common occurrence in homes with staircases, right? Maybe she just felt like she was pushed because she didn't want to admit to us, or herself, that she tripped.

I sunk back into the comfort of my bed and closed my eyes to rest, wanting nothing more than to forget the whole afternoon. I was just tired; I knew I wouldn't be bothered by ghost nonsense if I could just get a decent night's sleep.

A few minutes later, I felt a strange warm sensation spread across my chest and my arms began to tingle as something thick and wet trickled down them. I began to feel sticky and uncomfortable and once I was unable to ignore it anymore, I opened my eyes, raising an arm in front of my face to see if there was something on me. I had to clamp the other hand around my mouth to prevent myself from screaming out loud once I confirmed that there was truly a liquid substance coated across my skin. My whole body was soaked from top to tail in fresh blood.

Chapter Four

I shot upright, flinging my legs around and leaping off the mattress in one quick motion. Horrified, I darted over to the mirror. Lo and behold, I was as clean as a whistle with not a drop of blood to be seen anywhere on my body, or on the bed behind me. No evidence at all. In disbelief, I held a hand over my eyes for a few seconds, half expecting that when I removed it, I'd be covered in blood again. But I wasn't. I started to hyperventilate uncontrollably as I patted my body down, section by section, grabbing at my very dry, clean clothing. Trying to calm my breathing, I asked myself repeatedly what on earth was going on. Was I going insane? Suffering mental episodes as a result of my brain lashing out over the move? What was with all the hallucinations?

I suddenly had a strong urge to run and ask my mother for her opinion, but I had to stop myself. I knew that would get me nowhere. She'd surely think I was just making it up for attention, or setting up some kind of prank to scare everyone. I suddenly regretted having been a trickster and mischief maker all my life.

Wanting to crumble into a million pieces, I dragged myself back to bed and this time curled up into a ball. I closed my eyes tightly and after laying there for a few minutes, accidentally slipped into a dreamless sleep.

When I awoke, the first thing I noticed was that it was dark. The second thing I noticed was that there was something weighted lying across my feet. I panicked. What if it was the little boy ghost, watching, waiting for me to wake up so that he could get me? I sat up quickly and pulled my knees up to my chest. The weight slipped off my feet and fell to the floor. I crawled forward and relaxed when I saw that it was only my schoolbag. Someone must have retrieved it from the front lawn.

Kicking myself for being a worrywart and freaking out over a bag being on my bed, I pulled my phone out of my pocket and checked the time. It was just past nine-thirty in the evening. I was surprised that my mother hadn't woken me for dinner. Opening my notification bar, I noticed an unread goodnight text sitting there from Sam, from an hour prior. I felt bad that I'd fallen asleep without wishing him goodnight back. Although, with the number of times he'd done it to me in the past, it was about time I did it back.

By the sound of the silent house, I gathered that everybody had already gone to bed. I was a bit bummed when I realised I'd missed seeing Dad at all today. He would have gotten home, had dinner, gone for a shower and then straight to bed. Now that I thought about it, I didn't think I'd seen him for more than an hour since the day we'd moved here, and I was beginning to miss hanging out with him. Though I looked more like my mother, I was a lot closer to my father. We'd been like two peas in a pod my whole life. Mum was hard to get along with at the best of times, whereas Dad, he was easy-going and understanding. More down to earth like me.

Annoyed at myself for sleeping all afternoon, I got out of bed, making as little noise as possible and turned on the light. My whole body felt heavy and if I didn't know better, I would have said my head was going to roll off my body any second. I was still so tired that unfortunately one afternoon nap wasn't enough to catch up on three nights of missed and broken sleep. Smelling my armpits, I decided I could afford to wait to take a shower in the morning. I wasn't desperate enough to wake everybody up now, the plumbing rattled like crazy through the walls whenever the shower or washing machine was used.

Out of the corner of my eye, I noticed a little piece of paper sticking out from under my door. Inquisitive, I walked over and slid it out from between the door and the carpet. Unfolding it twice, I recognised my mother's handwriting. All she had written was, "Figured you were dead after knocking for ten minutes. Seriously though, don't lock the door next time you nap. Dinner's in the fridge. Love Mummy." I pretended to retch. She'd referred to herself as "Mummy," really? My stomach began to growl at me, and I wasn't surprised that I was suddenly extremely hungry.

I crumpled up the note and tossed it over my shoulder, quickly ripped off my hideous school uniform and hurried to change into a pair of boxer shorts and loose T-shirt. I kicked my uniform behind the door and flicked open the lock. I was about to move forward into the hall, but I stopped suddenly in the doorway when I realised something. If I had just unlocked the door, how had my schoolbag been placed on the end of my bed? I was sure I had left it on the lawn. Who had gotten into my room without unlocking the door?

My door didn't have a keyhole, so nobody could have used a key to get in and besides that, Mum had said in her note that she couldn't even get in when she wanted to wake me at dinner time. I imagined ghostly hands floating my bag up through the window and dropping it onto my bed trying to make me jump whilst I was sleeping.

This led to my head being filled with a vivid replay of the mysterious little boy ghost charging at me and I wasn't so keen to go downstairs and get something to eat all of a sudden. I wanted to turn around, jump into my bed and hide under the blankets until morning. But my stomach growled again and this time it was painful, so I closed my eyes and braced myself. Taking a deep breath as I reopened them, I stepped out into the hall and headed for the stairs.

It took almost ten minutes to make my way down the staircase as quietly as I possibly could. Every few steps I found myself looking around, making sure I wasn't being watched or followed. I shivered as I peered carefully through the darkened kitchen. Not because I was cold but because, admittedly, I was pretty afraid. I could feel goosebumps covering my body as I walked out further into the room. Feeling my way along the wall, I bumped into several things before I finally found the light switch near the refrigerator.

It wasn't as creepy when the light was on, but I still had chills running down my spine at the thought of a dead little boy roaming around. I almost jumped out of my skin when I spotted my father sitting hunched over at the dining table, clutching a mug of coffee in his hands. He, however, didn't jump at all. "Erm, Dad, how long have you just been sitting down here in the dark?"

He shrugged and rubbed his eyes with an open palm before taking a large swig of obviously cold coffee. I'd never seen my dad looking so rundown before. His face was unshaven and ungroomed, brown curly hairs had almost overtaken his lips and dark circles surrounded his eyes like a beaten up, homeless man who hadn't slept for a month.

Concerned, I sat down at the table beside him and stared him down until he felt forced to speak.

"Don't worry Livvie, I've just had a lot on my plate since the move. I just finished replacing the exploded window for your mother and didn't feel ready for bed yet. Although, what time is it? That may have been a couple hours ago." He paused and gave a weak chuckle, "So, you finally made it down for dinner, hey."

I smiled, "Yeah, sorry I fell asleep this afternoon. I, uh, haven't been sleeping so well since the move."

Nodding apologetically, he raised his eyebrows and murmured quietly, "Me either."

There was something off about the tone in his voice now and I suddenly wondered if maybe I *wasn't* the only one seeing and hearing strange things. Curiosity got the better of me and I blurted out without thinking, "Dad, have you noticed anything odd about this house? Like, have you seen or heard things you can't quite explain?"

His eyes grew wide and he was silent for ages, staring past me into space. He was nervous, I could tell that much. "N….no," he finally said, with a break in his voice. "Of course not! Have you?" He leaned towards me and lowered his voice even more, "If you have, don't worry, it will go away in time. I'm sure it's just your mind playing tricks on you."

"Err, sure, I know that," I said, narrowing my eyes and frowning, observing his shaken manner. "I was just wondering…do you know anything about the history of this house? Did they tell you anything about it when you bought it? I mean…this weird girl at school told me the house is haunted."

Shaking his head, he stood up, resting clenched fists on the table and answered abruptly with a forceful tone, "You know you shouldn't believe everything you're told; people make up all kinds of stories about haunted places throughout this whole town. There's no ghosts in this house. I don't want to hear you mention this nonsense again."

I could feel my mouth hanging slightly open. That escalated quickly.

Dad sighed loudly, relaxing his face and his knuckles simultaneously. "Sorry, kid. I'm off to bed now, got an early start again tomorrow. Goodnight, Livvie." He tousled my hair, placed his mug into the sink and wandered off up the dark stairwell.

For several minutes I was left alone, confused, and bewildered with a heap of unanswered questions burning inside of me. His behaviour towards a simple question made no sense at all, making me believe he was in denial. I jumped slightly when a soft groan sounded from nearby. Analysing my surroundings, I relaxed slightly once I reassured myself that I was still alone. The noise had to have been just the house creaking. Feeling confident and much more like my usual self all of a sudden, I scoffed out loud at the eerie-looking shadows cast along the wall.

Tiptoeing across the kitchen to the fridge, I opened it and leaned down to scan the shelves in search of Mum's not-so-often tasty cooking. Just as I spotted a plate covered with plastic wrap on the bottom shelf, a wave of fear rolled over me, causing my body to shudder involuntarily. I suddenly felt like I was being watched. Feeling silly, I glanced behind me and surveyed the kitchen. It was still empty. Relieved, I turned back around and started to reach out for the leftover plate until I heard a soft, sad, moaning sound behind me.

My body froze and I wanted to disappear on the spot, but I forced myself to turn around slowly. The blood in my veins turned ice cold when my eyes rested on the figure now in the kitchen with me. She stood by the sink in a lacy, white nightgown with her head slightly tilted to the side and was staring, expressionless, at me. I swallowed and tried to take off, but for some reason was quite literally unable to.

Frozen in fear, I studied the woman who stood ever so stiffly before me and realised it wasn't the first time I'd seen her. She was the same figure I'd seen briefly reflected in the shard of glass from the exploded window. Strangely enough, it made me feel saner knowing that I *had* seen a woman's reflection in the glass when the kitchen window had busted. It was her. What I hadn't noticed the first time was that the material covering her chest was heavily bloodstained and so was the slightly see-through skin on her shoulders. She blinked for the first time, moving her arms to cradle her stomach and the hairs on the back of my neck prickled. It was then I noticed that this woman was also heavily pregnant. As I focused my eyes closer on her person, I realised that the reason her head was tilted to the side was because she had a large piece of glass wedged in the side of her neck.

She was attractive, but her sullen, dark eyes were watery and excessively depressive, causing her to have a very sinister glow about her. I knew in an instant that this woman was a ghost, though her transparency was minimal. I suddenly wished I was able to teleport at will. After we stared at each other in total silence for a minute or two, the woman opened her mouth to speak to me. I cowered against the fridge door, as I found myself incapable of doing anything else. Her voice was so soft that I almost missed what she said. "Can you help us?" She paused to rub her belly bump affectionately and sighed, waiting momentarily like she was listening for something and then without warning, spat out forcefully, "She is always watching us…but my baby is out there…got out alive…can help us. You can get my baby to come home and get rid of her…can save us all."

She was barely making any sense to me. My heart thumped away loudly within my chest and I gritted my teeth as I allowed myself to accept that my new house was in fact haunted, by multiple ghosts it seemed. I had no idea who this woman was, but she didn't seem to fit the profile of the apparent crazy woman who committed suicide…but from what I *could* make sense of, perhaps that was who she wanted help to get rid of. I rolled my eyes to myself, feeling ridiculously moronic for even thinking it. I was torn between wanting to run for my life or sarcastically telling the ghost that I was sorry for her losses, including herself. But then, making my mind up for me, she slowly began to drag herself towards me. Her legs appeared to be so stiff that she had to hold onto the kitchen benches in order to limp her way over to me.

That did it. My legs powered into gear as I sprinted out of the kitchen. My feet pounded up the stairs and I reached the door to my bedroom in no time, not caring at all who I woke in the process of fleeing. Flinging open the door, I darted into my bedroom and screamed at the top of my lungs when I saw the gloomy, pregnant ghost standing beside my bed.

Chapter Five

My legs felt like jelly. Never before had I experienced or even known fear like this. The ghost of the mourning, expectant mother stared across at me more solemn than before, if possible, and shook her head in disapproval.

"You can't escape from anyone who remains here, dead, in this house."

Her words cast a chill over me, and the ice feeling ran through my veins once more.

"Don't be ignorant. Everything in this world happens for a reason. It's not a coincidence that you're here." As if she had just given her final word, she took a step backward and looked down at the floor.

I blinked and she was gone.

I stood for a few moments, bewildered, and then, realising I was standing in the middle of a dark room where ghosts could apparently appear whenever they felt like it, I charged forward and leapt into my bed. As I buried myself in the blankets, I could feel my bottom lip start to tremble. No, I told myself firmly, you are not going to cry over this. The warmth of my quilt, combined with the fluffy sheet, comforted me to some extent and I was able to relax a bit.

I felt like I was actually being driven insane. This was a madhouse. I took a few deep breaths, trying to remain strong whilst in an argument with my own brain. Part of me wanted to forget everything I'd seen and heard so far, but the other part of me, the stronger part, told me I had to find out everything there was to know.

Forming a step-by-step plan in my head, I realised the first thing I had to do was find and talk to Grace. She had said I could come and talk to her when I believed, and I was definitely starting to believe. I wasn't thrilled by it, but her information seemed fairly accurate so far.

The second step, with or without her help, was to track down records of all the previous deaths that had occurred in this house. As my brain started to go into overdrive, I forced myself to slow down and breathe, realising I had to pull myself together if I had any hope of staying sane. For starters, I had to stop thinking about ghosts and rest for the night; after all, I would see Grace at school the very next day. She had some explaining to do, given that she seemed to know so much about my new house.

Unfortunately, Grace was not at school the next day. She didn't show the following day either. Then, on Thursday morning, just as I was beginning to believe she was a figment of my imagination, I spotted her as I was coming out of science class to begin a lunch break.

"Grace!" I cried out.

She looked up, seemingly startled by my presence.

"You're ok!" she exclaimed.

"Uh, yeah I guess..." I said slowly, thinking I was about as ok as anyone could be by the end of a school week after being the spectacle of other students' gossip every day. Then, without warning, she grabbed me with both arms and pulled me into a bear hug. Awkwardly unsure what to do, I patted her back using only the wrist I could bend and waited for her to release me.

When she finally did, she locked her gaze into my eyes, as if analysing my soul and said softly, "Have you noticed anything odd about your house yet?"

I took a moment to think about my response, wishing I could tell her that nothing was wrong with it, that I had seen nothing unusual. Although, other than being insanely tired from a consistent lack of sleep due to the never-ending sounds throughout the night, I hadn't seen any apparitions or weird things happen since the woman in the nightgown showed up in the kitchen. I had been back and forth debating with myself every day whether or not the semi-transparent people I'd seen were just a part of my imagination all along. Things had been almost normal for days.

As I pondered over Grace's question, my heart jolted a little as I remembered something from the previous evening that I had initially thought was a dream. Joining the strange noises throughout the night had come a series of whispers in my room and shadowy figures pacing the hallway. As much as I wanted to discuss the house and its apparent inhabitants with Grace, I had decided that morning to go back to being as determined as ever that none of it was real, it couldn't be. I knew hallucinations were a normal part of adjusting to moving house for the first time ever at seventeen, especially when the new house was a large, creepy mansion. Besides, no one else in my family had mentioned anything at all about seeing ghosts so if they were in the house, they would surely have seen something by now and someone would have said something. It had to be all in my own head.

I hadn't been bothered to look up the history of the house like I'd originally wanted to either, given that everything seemed to settle and I chose to forget rather than worry about things I didn't need to. If I mentioned to Grace now that I did initially see and hear things that weren't really there, I'd be admitting defeat and I wasn't really sure I wanted to do that. Instead of opening up and grilling Grace for information like I'd intended to earlier in the week, I closed up and found myself shrugging my shoulders and casually replying, "Nope."

I knew in an instant Grace didn't believe me. She folded her arms and stared at me for a few moments, then said with a sigh, "Well then, I guess I'll have to tell you myself what you're in for."

Without warning, she latched onto my arm, tugged on it and started running. I had no choice but to run with her, or I'd trip and fall on my face. We passed the front school oval in no time and yet she continued to sprint down the road, well past the school gates. A small part of me wanted to turn back, I'd been caught and punished heavily the last time I had wagged school by both the principal and my parents and wasn't so keen on it anymore. This seemed to be important to Grace though and she was my only friend here. I couldn't let her down, right?

It took only a few minutes running at Grace's turbo-charged pace to reach my new block, only slowing to a walk as the sign declaring Mason Street came into our view. She stopped halfway down the street and her eyes fixed on the large, looming house at the end. My house. I grabbed my stomach tightly as though trying to hold my insides together and breathed heavily. I didn't realise how unfit I was until that moment.

Puffing, I stepped up beside Grace, who didn't appear out of breath at all, and started to ask what we were doing here, but she turned to face me and held up a hand to silence my words.

"Liv, that house has an awful history behind it," she said bluntly. Tears were brimming in her eyes again as she continued to speak in the same flat monotone. "Within its history, there is nothing but death after death. You're in danger, so you need to know *everything*. No one is supposed to be living there. I honestly thought all the realtors in town had that manor barred off their sale lists."

I was now very confused. We had to leave the school so Grace could tell me a horror story? I wasn't afraid, but curiosity was now eating me alive. I did want to know what had happened in the house I was currently residing in that everyone seemed so intrigued by. So, still panting heavily, I turned and sat on the grass beside the footpath and she followed my lead. Nothing could tear her eyes away from that house so she spoke facing away from me. I listened as best as I could over the whistle of the wind and the pumping sound of my heartbeat in my ears.

"It was a fair while ago, more than thirty years I think, when that house was owned by an elderly couple named George and Evelyn Clayton. It was, once upon a time, quite a beautiful manor, and the Claytons were like the town's royalty back then, they were very loved and quite wealthy. When the Claytons were suddenly murdered, their daughter, Agatha, inherited the house from her parents. Destroyed by grief from their sudden death, Agatha didn't want anything to do with the house at all, having previously moved out, but she moved back home anyway as it had belonged to her family for many generations and she couldn't bear anyone else to have it. After she moved back in, she made herself scarce and the street residents would only occasionally catch a glimpse of her in the garden at night, surrounded by candles and chanting to herself over mounds of books.

After a while, the neighbours started up nasty rumours about her. The townspeople had heard that Mr Clayton had some sort of falling out with Agatha before he and his wife were murdered and that's why she'd initially moved away. Some people declared her mentally ill and insisted she'd killed her own parents and was going insane with guilt. Others said she was driving herself crazy trying to find out who her parents' killer was and using witchcraft to do so. They nicknamed her the Bellicose witch and made fun of her because she made it clear she never wanted to get married or start a family and instead chose to live alone in a mansion, never making an effort to do anything with her life. Especially mean to her were all the mischievous kids of the town. They caused havoc and played tricks on her just for fun.

Eventually, Agatha kept to herself completely, showing a great hatred for the world and all the people in it and before long, she stopped coming into town at all. It seemed she couldn't stand it anymore when the police were officially unable to catch her parent's killers. On the day their murder case was declared cold, she went around door-knocking, telling all the neighbours within a four-block radius to come to her house at midday as she had a big announcement to make. Curious as to why she was suddenly out and about, no one objected to coming to the manor. Before everyone arrived, Agatha smashed out the huge bay window near the front door in the loungeroom to allow more people to see clearly into her house. She waited until people started flocking onto her property and gathering across the front lawn, then simply stood in front of the wall opposite the smashed-out window, pulled out a knife and announced to all the watching neighbours that her death was the only way justice would be served and she could have her revenge."

Grace paused momentarily and furrowed her eyebrows, like she was trying to remember every tiny detail of information.

After a few painstakingly slow minutes, she tucked her hair behind her ear and began to speak again, nodding to herself as she relayed the story. "To the horror of the townspeople, she then stabbed herself to death. Her blood was spattered everywhere across the floor and on the wall behind her, and she died a slow, painful death. Everyone panicked of course and ambulances were rushed to the scene, but she had made sure to hit vital organs and there was nothing anyone could do for her. After her body was removed and the incident declared an official suicide by police, the crime scene cleaners were sent in. They were baffled by the fact that no matter how much they tried, they were unable to remove the blood stains on the wall behind where Agatha stood. The rest of the living room was able to be restored, but that one particular wall would not come clean.

Once the press got ahold of that information, reporters had a field day with it and all of the townspeople soon began to believe that the blood was cursed. Those types of rumours began to grow when people noticed that even though the house was uninhabited for many years after Agatha's death, the lights always flickered on and off at night, people who passed the house could hear a woman crying loudly inside, the front doors would open by themselves whenever someone walked onto the front porch and the knife she had used to take her own life was, strangely, *never* found. It had vanished into thin air by the time the medics and police got to her and was never seen again. A lone removalist went in to clear out her furniture quite some time after her death and he never came out. After that incident, no one even went near the house for years, beginning to believe that an enraged Agatha still lived inside the house as a spirit. All the residents of Mason Street packed up and moved, afraid they'd vanish too if they stayed close by.

A few years later, after the publicity stopped and the heat surrounding Agatha's death had finally simmered down, a group of professional decorators were hired to do some repairs, remove the furniture and clean the house out. But that blood on the wall, no matter how much they scrubbed or how strong the chemicals were that they used, could still not be removed so they simply chose to paint over it."

I was starting to get anxious now. I'd never left school before only to stand right near my house. If my mother looked out the front windows, she'd easily see me. "Um, Grace, I really don't think we should have left school for story time," I interrupted hastily as Grace stopped to take a breath.

She glared at me and snapped, "The important part is coming up, please just listen!"

She crossed her arms, sighed loudly and continued, resuming her flat monotone. "It was a little over thirteen years after that, in 1987, that the Grayson family, new to the area, bought the house. By that point, the other houses in the street had only just become inhabited again, with most people still on edge about living near the manor. Arthur and Penelope Grayson, however, didn't believe the rumours and ignored the townies' stories. A trusted, local realtor had offered them a cheap price, just to get it sold and Mr Grayson didn't hesitate. This family was like any other, the mother was a pregnant housewife, the father was a successful businessman and they had two kids, Owen who was five and Mary who was fifteen. They were uptight and mainly kept to themselves, brushing off anyone who warned them the house was haunted.

After a few months of living there, however, Agatha's spirit began to contact Mary. Mary started to hear whispers in the night and scratching sounds coming from inside the walls of her bedroom. She tried to ignore everything for as long as she could, but one day found that an actual hole had been made in her bedroom wall, right near where she slept. This she could not ignore and freaked out, but told no one. That night whilst she slept, she awoke to find that the hole was dripping blood. The more she pretended not to notice, the faster the blood poured out. Not wanting to disturb her mother and father, who she knew would think she was crazy, she went downstairs to find something to plug the hole with and clean up the mess. It was then that a ghostly woman appeared right before her eyes and began to beckon her forward.

Mary was put under a trance almost instantly, like a controlled possession of some kind. Agatha made her walk over to the living room wall, where she had spattered her own blood at death and as Mary touched the wall, it began to bleed. Lost in the trance she was under, she didn't even notice and instead became calmer than ever, heading back to bed. Or so she thought.

The next morning Mrs Grayson got up as usual and went to check on her five-year-old son, who was usually the first awake. He was drenched in blood, possessed many stab wounds and had evidently been killed in his sleep. Panicking, Mrs Grayson screamed to her husband and hurried to see if their daughter was safe. They found her sound asleep, a bloody carving knife in bed beside her, and her hands, clothes and bedsheets stained with blood. Accused of murdering Owen, she swore over and over to know nothing about her brother's death and was in shock at the very thought.

Mr Grayson suddenly slipped into a rage and grabbed Mary by her hair. He tossed her down the hallway and, ignoring his wife's screams of protest, dragged Mary into the bathroom. It was there he plugged the bathtub, turned on the taps and pushed Mary's head down into the tub, swearing he wouldn't let her up until she confessed to murdering her little brother. Of course, the bath eventually filled up over Mary's head and though she fought and screamed until her last breath, her father was too strong and she ended up drowning."

I found myself autonomously biting my fingernails. As a person who usually didn't scare easily, I was surprised to find my arms breaking out in goosebumps. Staring at my new house and listening to Grace deliver a horror story, I assured myself it was only because I was caught up in the moment. Grace hadn't noticed how tense I'd become and powered on with her monologue.

"Mr Grayson then ordered his wife into the kitchen to discuss a plan, wanting help with covering up the murders. He was a very power-obsessed man with a terrible temper and she was too overwhelmed with grief to talk, which pushed his buttons. He ordered her to stop crying so he could figure out what to do with the children's bodies. She couldn't contain her devastation and to act like she was fine, turned away to face the sink, pretending to do the dishes like she would any other morning. Obviously in emotional agony, she was unable to mask her pain and cried louder than before.

Mr Grayson, overwhelmed himself by that point and with a different way of handling grief, marched across the kitchen and seized his wife, pushing her head straight through the kitchen window. She was sliced up and collapsed to the floor, seemingly dead. Suddenly awakened, with no memory of doing this to her and in disbelief of what had just happened to his family, Mr Grayson then stabbed himself to death in the living room, *right in front* of the original stained bloody wall. The neighbours had heard all the screaming, loud crashes and ruckus, soon calling the authorities without hesitation.

Police and paramedics arrived shortly after Mr Grayson's suicide and Mrs Grayson fought to stay alive just long enough for the paramedics to work miracles, passing away almost immediately after they managed to cut out her baby. The Grayson infant was adopted a few days later by a local widow who'd been having difficulty getting a baby due to being single. After that day, the house was sealed off and declared not suitable to sell until thorough investigations were carried out. After five murders and two suicides within sixteen years, I'm sure you can understand why. I honestly thought they'd never try to sell it again."

Grace took a deep breath and paused to wipe a few tears from her eyes. "Don't you understand, Olivia? It was all Agatha's doing. She set the whole thing up and played it like some kind of twisted game. She was the one who possessed Mary to kill Owen. She was the one who possessed Arthur to kill Mary, then Penelope, before making him kill himself right where she did, like she did. Agatha isn't going to just stop, she's pure evil. She's in there and she's going to come after you and your family now."

Grace's tone had stayed flat and quiet the whole time she was speaking and when she finished, she stood up rapidly and turned away from the house, fixated on the concrete with her head held down. I noticed little droplets sliding down her cheeks and felt terrible for her. For some reason, I felt like she had to be more connected within the Grayson's story than just knowing about it. The flood of emotion across her face displayed more depth than just a history buff's knowledge about an old house. Did I think she was partially nuts? Absolutely, but my heart still went out to her. There had to be something from her own past that had caused her brain to become so dysfunctional to believe in a story like that. Better yet, how did she know any of that information? Perhaps she was the one to make it up. I got up and reached an arm out awkwardly intending to console her, but just as I did, she clapped a palm to her forehead, began to sway back and forth rapidly and within seconds, collapsed.

Chapter Six

"What the hell, are you ok?" I cried out, attempting to grab ahold of her arm as she fell and swiped air instead.

As soon as she hit the ground, she threw her arms out wildly and scrambled back up as fast as her legs would let her. "I'm so sorry, I, um, just got a bit dizzy. No big deal," she said, blushing from embarrassment.

"Uh, it's ok, you don't need to apologise for almost fainting," I replied, confused.

Once stable, Grace began to stare intensely at my face, as though waiting for me to say something. Feeling like I'd been put under a microscope, I slowly turned to look back at my new house, deep in thought.

I barely heard Grace when she asked, "Olivia, you have seen something in the house, haven't you? Do you believe me yet? You can keep pretending it all doesn't exist if you'd like, but it's not going to go away."

I really didn't want to believe the history about the things that had previously happened within the house I now lived in. I wanted to laugh at Grace and say, "Nice one, you nearly got me," but I knew deep down there had been one too many strange occurrences to not give her story some thought. Not only was I fairly sure I'd seen the ghosts of who I now assumed were Penelope and Owen Grayson, but some of the things that the girl, Mary Grayson, had seen…I had seen them too.

"Grace," I asked, deliberately ignoring her questions, "how do you even know for sure that this information about my house is true? That these Grayson people died in it the way they did. I mean, how do you know what they saw or felt or any of it, even newspapers aren't *that* detailed."

Grace scratched her nose nervously and stared directly through me, like she got lost in thought trying to choose her next words. "Because I was there," she replied with a casual shrug. Before I could react fully, her voice broke as she corrected herself quickly. "I mean, I um…I watched it happen through the windows."

I raised my eyebrows in disbelief. That couldn't be right, this had happened about eighteen years ago. I didn't know exactly how old she was but unless Grace was some sort of ninja infant at the scene, she couldn't have watched any of it unfold in real time. Yet, there was a strange gloomy quality in her eyes I couldn't explain any other way and she did have an awful lot of emotional depth in her tale.

Still, all in all, I couldn't bring myself to accept that there was a murderous ghost running around with the intention of hurting people. I wasn't going to let myself immediately panic because of a local legend. I felt like I could admit I'd seen a couple of dead people in the house, which was a weird enough concept on its own, but no "evil spirit." I didn't believe the part of the story that involved possession, it was ridiculous. So what, maybe a long time ago a whole family had died in that house, and a shut-in woman and her parents before them, but that didn't mean anything bad would happen now. It seemed to me like Mr Grayson had been a psychopath all along and had just snapped at his family after a tragic incident triggered an emotional outbreak. The teenage girl seemed a bit deranged too. Who in their right mind would kill their own brother for no reason? As for the Agatha woman who inherited the house from her parents, she was clearly just depressed and from the sounds of it, very strange.

I felt a sense of accomplishment by summing up a normal, non-supernatural explanation for the series of events Grace had described to me. I was, however, even more anxious to look up old records about the manor as soon as I was allowed to leave the house outside of school hours; it seemed fascinating. My mother had been dismissive so far of the idea of me hanging out anywhere but home. I had even been waiting for the home internet to be connected, but apparently, my parents hadn't deemed it important enough to do so yet, so it seemed like I was going to have to research the old-fashioned way. At the library.

Grace crossed into my view suddenly, wiped her eyes and fixed her hair. She gave my house one last fleeting look and sighed, "Just be aware, okay? Not only does Agatha still exist within the house, but the whole Grayson family does too. Not that they'll hurt you. They're just all stuck, unable to move on because of Agatha. You'll see."

I waited for a moment, not wanting to be rude and interrupt her. The desperation in her voice was clear and I felt like I should reassure her I believed her to some extent, so she'd know that I wasn't just dismissing her altogether. Unable to look her in the eye, I turned my head and spoke to the ground instead. "I'm sorry Grace, I did lie to you before. I admit it okay, I have seen…people…in the house. I assume they were the Grayson mother and her little boy. But I swear I haven't seen anything that would lead me to believe my family is actually in danger."

When she didn't reply, I looked up, expecting her to be glaring at me in silence, and was instead shocked to find she was gone. I turned a full circle on the spot searching for her, but gave up quickly as I realised she was long gone. I was left standing alone like an idiot in the middle of the street, wondering why and when she'd taken off.

Lost in thought for a few minutes, I suddenly came to my senses when I realised that I couldn't stand around in the middle of the street for much longer; I was surprised my mother hadn't already spotted me. I quickly started jogging, heading in the same direction that Grace had originally brought me. I wondered whether or not I should go back to the school. If I didn't, I'd probably end up in trouble, but I'd be in trouble anyway if I did go back and got caught for sneaking back onto the school grounds. So, I decided what the hell, I was likely in trouble either way and by not going back, at least I avoided schoolwork and being gawked at and whispered about all day. I thought I should probably try to find Grace and comfort her, she couldn't have gotten that far. There was more to her than I knew about yet, more that went into her fear of the house.

I turned into the next street I saw that I partially recognised and casually strolled down the footpath alongside the road. From where I was, I could see a guy at the end of the street on an aggregate driveway, messing around on a skateboard. As I got closer, he looked up, saw me, and a split second later, landed on his face. Gravity claimed his skateboard also and it landed by his side with a thump. I jogged over to ask if the guy needed some help, but he was on his feet by the time I got to him.

"Thanks for that," he mumbled, rubbing his cheek a few times.

"Like it was even my fault!" I protested, annoyed.

He arched his back until I heard a cracking sound.

I crinkled my nose thinking ouch, but he simply said, "That's better." He smiled at me and held out his hand. "Name's Matt."

Still a little ticked off at being placed at fault for his fall, I placed my palm in his reluctantly and as we shook hands stuttered, "I'm Oliv...ah, Liv."

"Interesting name, I like it," he chuckled, grinning as he let go of my hand. "If it helps, I'm technically Matthew, but *please* just call me Matt."

I couldn't help but smile back, a little embarrassed.

"So, why aren't you at school little lady?" he chuckled, playfully punching my shoulder.

My ears burned and I could feel my cheeks flushing. Little lady? How old did he think I was? Trying to sound cool, I stuck out my chest slightly and remarked, "Maybe I just didn't feel like going, school's such a drag. How about you...big gentleman?"

The second I said it, I regretted it. How stupid must that have sounded?

He smirked and shook his head. "I'm eighteen Oliv-Ah-Liv, I've already graduated."

I half smiled. "Well then...Matthew, I'd better keep moving. Got loads to do with my free day and all. Actually, I was trying to find a friend of mine, do you know her? It's a tiny town after all. Her name is Grace Maker."

Matt rolled his eyes. "Yeah actually, I kinda do know her. She's my little sister and a bit of a loner, I didn't actually think she had any friends."

I was a little surprised; Matt was Grace's older brother? It really was a small town after all. "Don't be nasty Matt, she seemed really upset when she ran from me and I have no idea where she went."

"Lately, she's always upset though," Matt said, shaking his mousy-brown hair out of his eyes. He flipped his skateboard, so it was the right way up, before speaking again. "She's also become obsessed with the old Mason Manor, the one on the end of Mason Street that's supposedly haunted. It drives me and Mum crazy."

I nodded, "Yeah, I know the one, uh, do you happen to know why she's so obsessed with it?"

Matt grabbed my shoulder and pulled me closer to him. I was about to protest, everyone in this town seemed a little bit crazy or something, but he whispered loudly, "I think she was born there."

I was extremely puzzled for a moment, but then remembered a piece of the story Grace had told me; the Grayson baby was saved from the dying, pregnant mother and taken from the house to be adopted. Maybe it was all true.

Matt continued to whisper, "All I know is, my Mum adopted her when I was like two or something, I mean she's been my sister as long as I can remember. I think she somehow figured out who she was and must have spent months looking up all the old stories and records about how her family was killed and she hasn't left it alone."

Now I truly did feel awful. The poor girl. I knew there was an unexplained sadness behind her eyes.

Having clarity on this made me desperate to go and find Grace all of a sudden. "Thanks, dude!" I exclaimed. "Bye!" I tugged my shoulder out of his grip and started walking away, fast.

"Olivia!" Matt called out.

I stopped in my tracks but didn't turn around.

"Please don't tell her I know who she is and definitely don't mention you suspect it either. You don't want to get her started on it; she won't ever talk about anything else. I, uh, hope to see you around."

I sighed and kept walking. Why did someone always have to stop you and tell you not to say anything before you had the chance to get away? Not that it mattered, I'd already been sucked right into the middle of it anyway. I had no choice but to talk to Grace about it.

I spent the rest of the day wandering around in search of Grace. By the afternoon, I'd become familiar with most of the neighbourhood after spending so much time walking the streets, which was good in a way. My mother did want me to get familiar with the town after all, perhaps I could use that as an excuse when she eventually discovered I'd skipped school that day. I couldn't find Grace anywhere and I was sure I'd almost been around the whole town. It seemed to me like she didn't want to be found. The only place I hadn't looked was at the school and I was not going to risk going back there. I glanced at my watch quickly. If it was correct, then it was just past three and I was safe to start heading home. Grace would hopefully be at school the next day, I could always talk to her then. I turned around and made my way back to the manor, dawdling along at the pace of a snail. Getting home too early would be a dead giveaway.

Eventually, I made it back to the manor in a convincing timeframe. Unsure I would be able to cope if I looked up and saw Owen sitting on my brother's windowsill, I stared only at the ground as I made my way up to the front doors. Eerily enough, as I stepped onto the porch I heard a creak and both doors swung open on their own accord.

I stopped in my tracks, peering cautiously into the hallway. I suddenly didn't want to continue inside and began to question how much longer I could pretend every creepy thing that happened involving this house was normal. Putting on a brave face, I puffed out my chest and filling myself with false confidence, marched inside. My main goal at the current point in time was to get to my bedroom and avoid my mother in the process. As I marched down the front hall, I could hear her calling out to me. Perhaps it was a good thing that I was in a hurry to get upstairs, I thought guiltily. I needed time to prepare my lying face in order to get through dinner conversation.

A few hours later, I sat in a ball on my bedroom floor sorting photos of all my old school friends into albums and reminiscing on some of the awesome memories we'd shared over the past years. I'd been texting Sam back and forth for hours prior to pulling out the photos, but once he'd fallen asleep, I had to find something else to keep my mind occupied. I was supposed to be going to sleep myself, but now that I had an indication of just how many deaths probably happened in the house, fear had set in once everyone else went to bed.

It was long past midnight and yet I found myself wide awake, unable to wind down enough to attempt sleep. I kept wondering if anyone else had noticed anything strange and freaky about our new house yet. Why me, why did I have to be the one who heard the weird noises and whispers every night? I knew at some point, if not just to ease my own sanity, that I was going to have to speak up and tell my parents what I'd been seeing and the story I'd been told about the history of the house. Who was I kidding though, they would never believe me…or would they?

Based on my father's weird and nervous dismissal of it, I remembered why I was sure he'd seen or heard something at some point. Was I really the only one who had seen two of the Grayson ghosts, or was Dad also living the same real-life nightmare? Maybe he *had* been warned about the place when it was sold to him and he just didn't want any of us to find out.

I stopped turning pages when I heard a shuffling sound just outside my bedroom door. I felt the contents of my stomach churn as the butterflies set in, nervously waiting for whomever or whatever was at my door to make itself known. I could hear whispered arguing now and unclenched slightly when I recognised my parents' voices. Whilst crawling towards the door so I could hear better, I heard the word ridiculous being uttered repeatedly by my mother, who sounded incredibly frustrated. Pressing myself against the door, I could hear what they were saying, just.

"Scott, I'm telling you, it was a dream!"

"Explain the burns then, look—my whole arm is singed!"

"Well, then it was just an accident."

"Yeah, well that seems to happen a lot in this house, doesn't it?! It was him, Mags. His face was pretty clear before he went up in flames. He was trying to warn me we're in danger."

My curiosity peaked and I leaned forward a smidge, unfortunately causing the floorboard under my knee to creak. The landing fell silent for a few seconds before footsteps carried their voices back down the hall. Bugger. So, my Dad *was* seeing things too, he just didn't want to admit it to me. I racked my brain and started going over Grace's story in my head. I couldn't recall her mentioning anyone who'd burned to death, so who was my father talking about? He even spoke as though he knew him. As far as I was aware though, Dad had never been to Bellicose before and certainly hadn't ever mentioned knowing anyone from here prior to the move. Nothing about it made any sense at all.

If this mystery male ghost was warning Dad though, who or what was he warning him about? Agatha? Although, if the Agatha woman was supposedly so dangerous, wouldn't she have shown herself by now? I'd seen the Grayson's, but not the woman who was supposedly going to try to possess and kill us. Was I really supposed to believe a deadly spirit was coming after my family? What on earth was I actually supposed to do about it anyway? Move out? Convince my family to move out? I couldn't talk to Dad about it, even if he was seeing them too, he certainly made it clear to me he didn't want to discuss it. I got up and crept across the room, starting to gather and pack away my albums, my mind a blur of mixed emotions. I felt a strong urge to talk to someone and the first person I'd usually turn to, if not my father, was Sam. I felt an ache deep in my chest thinking about him. It wasn't like I could sneak out and go see him like I used to be able to and the more I thought about it, the more I realised this wasn't exactly a conversation to have over the phone.

Just then, my body went rigid and my heart began to race as a seemingly familiar voice suddenly whispered directly into my ear, as though she were standing right behind me.

"Olivia, she's going to kill you."

Chapter Seven

Almost jumping out of my skin, I dropped the photo album I was holding and flung myself onto the bed without hesitation, reefing the quilt up over my head in one swift motion whilst the sincere voice continued, "You have to listen to me, you have to help us so we can help you."

My hands autonomously clenched tighter around the section of blanket that was covering my face, causing a pool of sweat to start beading across my forehead. As hot as I was getting, I refused to pull the blanket back, not wanting to encounter whoever it was.

"Help us or you're going to die," the voice persisted while I wished harder than ever that I could melt into the mattress and vanish. "Agatha is going to come for you, one way or another. So, you can either help us stop her or perish."

Tears began to form in the corners of my eyes, but as terrified as I was, I was determined not to let them fall. I'm braver than this.

"Go away!" I called out forcefully. "Just leave me alone, I don't understand exactly how I'm supposed to help you!" I paused for a few moments, waiting for a response. When none came, I figured it would be safe enough to re-emerge from my cocoon. Peeking out and scanning the room, I decided the area was ghost-free once more.

Relieved, I ripped back the blanket and took several long breaths, fanning my face with the back of my hand. Shaking my head at myself, I flipped over onto my belly and pulled the pillow over my head. I was so conflicted. I had spirits begging for help, Grace telling me to get out, Dad telling me not to believe in ghosts, but seeing them himself. I scowled into my mattress. My father had never lied to me before, or kept secrets, so why would he start now? Then, I remembered the box of albums he'd been so secretive over when we were moving in. He'd sure gotten weirdly overprotective over a box of photos.

As much as I wanted to confront him all of a sudden, I decided to keep my mouth shut for now. If Dad didn't want to hear about it, or talk about it, then fine. But that didn't mean I couldn't go snooping through his secrets in the meantime. I had to know what was in those albums. It certainly sounded like he knew the ghost who'd come to "warn" him. For some reason, I had a strange feeling that there was some sort of answer in Dad's photos, like a missing piece of the puzzle I needed to know. I knew I was being nosy and curiosity had gotten the better of me, but enough was enough, I had to start somewhere.

As I got out of bed, I had to give myself a pep talk. I found myself constantly checking my surroundings, just waiting for someone or something to pop up. But I stayed strong and kept walking, somewhat forcing one foot in front of the other upon each step through the darkness, like I was walking an invisible tightrope. In the old days, I would have been in the basement rummaging through my father's things in seconds. I had no idea what it was about this house that had changed me so dramatically and made me feel so powerless.

Whilst tiptoeing out onto the landing, I tried again to remember every detail of each death that had occurred in the house, but my mind was tangled, caught up with playbacks of the afternoon I'd had. Struggling to push haunting images of the Graysons' faces aside, I squinted, attempting to pull threads of memory from the back of my mind. Fighting myself over what was the top priority at that moment, I forced my brain back to the mission at hand. I had to see what my dad was hiding in that box.

Without spending too much time in one place, I edged ever so quietly down the stairs, across the kitchen and into the laundry. Checking over my shoulder quickly, I tiptoed down each stair to the basement cautiously, picking my footing carefully as to not cause any creaking. I fumbled briefly for the light, turned it on and snuck across the room, fearful I would be caught any moment. I just couldn't shake the feeling I was being watched. I finally reached the box of albums and, squatting down beside the pile of junk they were strewn amongst, began to pull them out onto the floor. Opening up the first cover and flipping through a few pages, I was a little disappointed to see nothing overly interesting. They were just regular old photos of my dad, perhaps a young adolescent at the time, with another young man I didn't know, possibly a childhood friend.

As I continued turning pages, however, the pictures became somewhat more intriguing. The first thing that caught my attention, was a seemingly regular photo of my teenage Dad and the other man standing in front of a birthday cake. However, standing behind them, was the old lady who'd tried talking to me the first day we'd moved in. She was a lot younger, sure, but it was definitely her. Frowning, I turned a few more pages and noticed she appeared again, several more times. The most surprising in what seemed to be family gatherings with my grandparents.

I'd never seen these photos. I guessed it had to be a few years before any of us kids were born, possibly even before my parents met, but I still found it strange that these people had never been brought up. My father obviously had no intention of mentioning them either, given the fact that he'd chosen to hide the albums away instead of keeping them with the rest of our family photos. I wasn't sure what I'd been expecting, but I felt a little more let down than I'd hoped. Perhaps I was expecting to see photos of the house or something, but I felt like these pictures, though interesting, revealed nothing useful.

As I went to pick up the next album, I tilted my head in curiosity as a thick, brown folder sitting underneath the albums caught my eye. It looked like it was full of paperwork. I reached for it immediately, but froze when a creaking sound projected through the room from somewhere near the top of the basement stairs. Unsure what I would say if someone came down suddenly, I listened carefully for a few moments before ultimately deciding to leave as quickly as possible when another creak sounded even closer.

I shoved the albums back into the box as quietly as I could manage whilst making sure they were placed exactly how I found them and made a beeline for the exit. Squinting up the stairs, I made sure I couldn't see anyone in the laundry before I leapt up the stairs two at a time. I figured if I could just make it to the kitchen, I could pass off not being in bed as though I'd just come down to get a glass of water. I successfully made it out to the kitchen without seeing anyone in the process and decided that it had probably just been the house shifting creakily.

Taking a deep, calming breath, I headed for bed as fast as I could, without looking around too much. I'd never been so scared of being caught by either of my parents before. Getting revved by my mother was fairly normal, and I was used to that, but I wasn't sure how mad my father would be if he'd seen me snooping in his private stuff. Crawling into bed, I went over mental images of the photos in my mind, trying to remember if I had ever been told about the people in them before and maybe I'd just forgotten.

I wondered why my dad would want to hide a bunch of seemingly innocent photos from his past. Perhaps it was just a cover, something to hide the folder of paperwork underneath? I couldn't help but develop a bad feeling in my gut. It was hard to know if the man Dad was in the photos with was important without knowing who he was, but it couldn't be a coincidence that the old woman I'd seen on the day we'd moved in was someone my father had known from his past. Yawning, I realised I was getting too tired to think about it too much and was beginning to feel like my brain was a yoyo. The consistent back and forth second guessing everything was a nightmare in itself. I rolled my eyes as a persistent, annoying tapping sound started up, echoing loudly from underneath my bed. I sighed. Maybe I'd get up the courage to ask Dad about the photos eventually. For now, however, living in and navigating the house with its freaky ways had to become top priority.

Going over the encounters I'd had that week, and incorporating my father's suspicious behaviour on the matter, I accepted wholeheartedly that the Agatha ghost may, in fact, be real. There were too many people now who had warned against her. Why would a ghost even feel the need to mention her if she didn't exist? I revisited my parents' conversation in the hallway. There was another ghost, someone I hadn't seen yet, who had tried to speak to my Dad. I shuddered. I had never been one to even believe in supernatural beings and yet I was suddenly forced to live in a real-life haunted house, flagged down by the inhabitants apparently needing help to be free.

Taking a big breath, I tried to will the courage from deep inside me to resurface. The old me would have never been scared of ghosts, if I'd even believed in them back then that is. I would have laughed the whole scenario off with my friends and joked about how silly it was.

Half an hour passed without me realising time was slipping away. I finally decided that if I was going to be forced to hear their cries for help, I was going to have to figure out what they wanted me to do to help them before the rest of my family was caught in the crossfire.

I had to get a grip. Ghosts were no trouble, right? All I had to do was get them to "cross over." That's what all the characters in movies about ghosts seemed to do, no stress. And if Grace was truly the Grayson's biological child, like Matt said she was, then according to Mrs Grayson, she was supposed to be able to help and I was going to have to tell her I believed. That's what she seemed to want me to say, whenever she actually decided to stick around. My body wouldn't even cooperate with me when I tried to curl into a ball, it seemed like I'd finally run out of energy.

The next morning, I awoke to the sound of a familiar voice in my ear. A warm hand touched my shoulder and I was disappointed when I realised it was probably time to get up and go for the day. I opened my eyes and let out a screech as big blue eyes filled my entire view. I sat up quickly and pushed myself away from the person who, I realised now, had been bent at my side trying to wake me up.

"Bloody hell, Olivia," Isabelle laughed, "Bit jumpy this morning, honey?"

I breathed out heavily and flung myself off the bed.

Hugging my sister, I chirped, "Yeah, just had a bad dream, that's all." I bent down, kissed her tummy, and hurried over to my wardrobe, pulling out my awful school uniform.

Isabelle stared at me in disbelief. "Ok, so on the day Mum needs you to stay home from school, you want to go desperately?"

I turned so quickly that my skirt created a wave of wind across my legs. "Why aren't I going?" I demanded, perhaps a little too harshly.

Isabelle raised her eyebrows at me. "Mum didn't tell you? Today you, me, and Noah have to help clean out the previous owner's junk from the back shed to fit all of our stuff in it. Whoever lived here last must have moved out and forgotten to check the shed beforehand." She gave a slight nod towards me and added, "Hurry up and get dressed in old clothes, Mum wants to start by ten." She then left the room, waddling as fast as her baby belly would allow her to.

I gaped at the doorway for a few seconds. Grabbing my phone to check the time, I discovered that it was already nine-thirty. Sam had sent me a good morning message two hours prior. I hoped he didn't think I was ignoring him. Hastily, I texted him back with a loving good morning and an apology. I hurried once more to my wardrobe and chose a pair of old jeans and a singlet. So, no one had gone down to the shed after the Grayson family had died. The house had been cleaned out, obviously, but the shed still remained full of their things. I slid on my jeans and brushed my hair roughly, not really caring what I looked like.

I wondered why Mum couldn't just wait until the weekend for our help. Sending us to our new school for four days and then keeping us home the day before the weekend made no sense at all. In saying that though, my mother was a little obsessive when it came to cleanliness. Having a junk-filled shed wouldn't have sat well with her and it would probably take all weekend to clean out. As I woke up more, I remembered the events of the previous night. Had it all been a dream? I was pretty tired after all and vivid dreams were part of an exhausted mind. Thinking intensely trying to separate the week's dreams from reality, my body had caught up to my head, and, realising that I was officially awake, my stomach began to growl. The pain was unbearable, so I threw on a pair of shoes and headed straight for the kitchen.

I ended up shovelling three pieces of toast, two eggs, and several rashers of bacon into my mouth for breakfast. Once my stomach was finally satisfied, I collected my dishes and carried them to the sink. Whilst quickly washing up my plate, I stared out of the window at the neighbouring houses down the street. A few houses down the road, I could see a middle-aged man mowing his front lawn wearing nothing but a pair of leopard-print underwear. I automatically closed my poor eyes; I didn't do anything to deserve a peep at that view. What a freak! Who in their right mind mows the lawn in their undies?

Then suddenly, my body gave a jerk and I gasped as the image of a pregnant woman in a nightie jumped into and filled my mind. It was like watching a film in slow motion. She was bent over the bench, crying into the sink. After a few moments, I was no longer just watching. The sensation was completely taking over my body, like being sucked into someone else's dream. I no longer felt like myself. There was a weird weight in my torso and little wiggles coming from inside me. I heard a huffing sound from behind me and as I turned around, an angry man came charging at me. I was afraid, but stood my ground, knowing he would never actually hurt me. Screaming rang in my ears as he thrust his hand at me and, grabbing a fistful of hair, jerked my head forcefully into the window.

Chapter Eight

I screamed out loud and the world around me returned to normal just as a huge pain jolted through my head and neck. My hands immediately shot up to feel my face and I swallowed deeply once I confirmed there were no wounds. Isabelle and Noah were both at my side instantly. I heard voices saying things like, "Are you ok?," and "What's wrong," but I couldn't answer. I couldn't focus properly. All I could do was nod and dry my shaking hands with a tea towel.

My brother and sister still looked worried and confused so, to let them know I was perfectly fine, I said as normally as I could manage, "Okay, let's go and help Mum now."

They hesitated briefly, Isabelle especially lingered with concern, but eventually agreed and the three of us headed outside to find our mother at the shed.

I wasn't sure I knew exactly what had gone on in the kitchen, but I had an idea. It had been some kind of vision, an insight into what Mrs Grayson had seen and felt just before she was murdered. I shuddered. I didn't think I could handle anything like that happening again, it was the worst feeling I'd ever endured. I pushed it out of my mind for now and focused on the angry, living woman who stood before me, leaning on the shed door.

"It's about time you three got down here," Mum snapped. "There's more crap in this shed than I thought."

I wasn't keen on being near my mother if she was going to be in this type of mood, but I was curious to know what kind of things the Graysons had kept in this shed many years ago. Before long, Mum had allocated a section of the shed to each of us. We had to sort through all of the possessions, see if there was anything that we could use, and throw the rest of it into a pile in the middle of the backyard so it could be disposed of at the dump later on. I looked around at the dusty, dirty tin walls and then plopped down beside a large box that had almost completely fallen apart.

I started to paw through some of the objects it contained and felt a little disappointed as I realised there was nothing interesting to look at. I tried to lift the box but felt as though I was going to snap my backbone, so I dragged it out into the backyard instead, kicking it along for the last few metres. Then I made my way back into the junkyard with walls we were calling a shed and found another box to examine.

Four ruined boxes full of useless junk and two torn bags full of foul clothes later, I dusted off my pants and stood up once more, stretching out my stiff legs. The bones in my knees cracked and I regretted kneeling for so long.

I stood with my hands on my hips for a minute or so, watching my mother swear at a table she was trying to move, which was wedged in between other furniture. I bit my lip and tried very hard not to laugh at her. Clearing my throat, I turned back to my "section" and immediately spotted something shiny lying on the ground that I hadn't noticed previously. Had it even been there a moment ago? I frowned, stepped forward to pick it up, and was surprised to find that it was a little handheld mirror, not broken or anything. The reflective glass was lined with a hard silver casing, which had an interesting pattern. The handle was thick and the heaviest part of the whole object. I ran my fingers along the cool glass and then straightened it up to look at my reflection.

I almost dropped the mirror when I saw the person staring back at me. That wasn't my face, it was the face of another teenage girl. But when I blinked, so did she. Every movement I made, that the mirror could see, was copied by the face of the mysterious girl. I was extremely confused and slightly creeped out by this point. What was going on here? I lowered the mirror and couldn't think of anything else to do but shake it. Then I slowly lifted it once more, hoping it was going to show me my own face.

This time when I looked into it, I was so frightened, I actually did drop the little mirror. The glass shattered across the ground and I had to jump back quickly to avoid my toes being stabbed by flying shards whilst turning my head in every direction, anxiously checking to make sure the horrid face I'd seen wasn't standing anywhere around me.

Everybody looked up to the sound of the shattering mirror and stared at me as if waiting to hear why I had dropped it.

"Does your face scare you that much Livvie!" Noah joked, poking his tongue at me.

I just glared at him. I didn't even have it in me to fight back. "Yeah, something like that," was all I could think of to say back. This answer left everybody laughing at me, but after a few seconds, they all went back to what they were doing.

I grabbed a fistful of hair on both sides of my face and tugged, at the same time sitting down right where I was. I let my hair go and allowed the profile of the face in the mirror to float back into my mind. It had been the morbid face of a gaunt and ghostly-looking woman, but it wasn't Mrs Grayson. This woman I hadn't seen before. Her eyes were sunken-looking, bloodshot and bulged out of their sockets, straggly white hair hung loose across her forehead and worst of all, her mouth had been open, and blood leaked from between her teeth. The look she gave me terrified me above all other things I had seen while living at this residence. I couldn't explain it, but somehow, I sensed that she was much worse than any Grayson spirit I could come across. Knowing in my heart her identity, and hoping it wasn't true, I tried as hard as I could to shake her face out of my mind.

I pulled my knees up to my chest and rested my chin upon them. A terrible idea I soon realised when Mum spotted me and yelled out, "Get off your butt Olivia, there's too much work to be done in here!"

"Sorry," I called out quickly and turned to another old box close by. This one was not cardboard, instead it was made of a thick wood-like material with a metal latch. Etched deeply into the top was the name "Arthur Grayson."

Now this one I was eager to go through. I was intrigued by what kind of things Mr Grayson had stored away. Opening the box, I rummaged through the contents, which seemed initially to be nothing but a bunch of random possessions and old newspaper clippings. I was about to pick it up and transfer it to the dump pile when something caught my eye. A headline declaring,

"COUPLE VICIOUSLY MURDERED INSIDE THEIR HOME"

Curious, I picked up the faded old piece of newspaper and started to read the article.

<u>May 28th, 1971</u>

Bellicose has been rocked this morning by a tragedy that occurred in the late hours of yesterday evening when two of Bellicose's most loved residents, George Clayton, 55, and Evelyn Clayton, 52, were found brutally murdered inside their home in what appears to be a violent break and enter. Police have sealed off and are currently investigating the scene and hope to provide answers as soon as possible.

Agatha Clayton, the couple's 22-year-old daughter was notified shortly after the incident occurred and after being pursued as a suspect, has been released. Miss Clayton, now sole owner of the infamous Mason Street Manor, will be holding a public memorial service for her parents next week at the Harriet Brown Church. Further information will be released to the public once investigations have been finalised.

Bellicose police officers are appealing to the public for anyone with information regarding the alleged murders of George and Evelyn Clayton to step forward.

Curious, I scrounged through the other clippings. I found several articles updating Clayton's murder case saying no new leads had been found, then one that announced that the case had been declared cold after three years of no leads on the murderer. Then came another interesting article.

"PERFORMED PUBLIC SUICIDE STUNS BELLICOSE RESIDENTS"

<u>May 28th, 1974</u>

Agatha Clayton, the 25-year-old daughter of George and Evelyn Clayton, a beloved couple who were found murdered in their family home 3 years ago, has shocked and scarred residents of Bellicose by publicly taking her own life this morning. Witnesses claim that shortly after 11:20 am, Miss Clayton invited residents from neighbouring blocks to her well-known manor, promising to deliver an important announcement about her parents' murder. Crowds gathered, curious for information, however, Miss Clayton instead proceeded to stab herself to death in front of more than a hundred bystanders.

The team at Bellicose's psychology facility is offering free counselling to those who witnessed this tragic event, feeling they will need extended help to move past the trauma. Investigators believe Agatha Clayton's suicide was triggered by grief due to the unfortunate news earlier this morning that the Clayton couple's murder case had been officially closed, pending new evidence surfacing.

Reading in disbelief, I realised that Grace's story was completely accurate. Although, she had probably read these articles at some point if she had been obsessing for years over this manor. I suddenly realised also that Mr Grayson wasn't unaware of the manor's former deaths. He knew everything about the Claytons, these clippings were stored away in a box that he owned. He'd known the whole time that people had died in the house and moved his family in anyway, and for some unknown reason, he'd obviously thought the articles were important enough to keep. Strange behaviour for a man who supposedly didn't believe the stories about the house being haunted.

I glanced across and studied the provided picture of Agatha Clayton in the article about her suicide. It confirmed what I had hoped wasn't true. The awful, creepy face I had seen in the little mirror was, in fact, Agatha. Although, in the photograph, she was quite beautiful, a little sullen looking perhaps, but much more human-like and with golden hair.

My heart skipped a beat. Maybe Agatha was making her presence known to me now so she could start killing us off. I sniggered silently at myself, trying to lighten the mood in my own head. Brushing off the frightening thoughts, I started digging again, anxious to read more newspapers. Seeing Grace's twisted tale written in print was helping my brain cope somehow, I felt like I was able to move past insanity.

Allowing my mind to drift towards the ominous side of things, I found myself hoping with all my heart that Agatha wasn't going to target my family the way she had the Graysons. Maybe she wasn't a threat to my family. There had to be a reason she did what she did to them. What if instead of fearing her, I could talk to her and find out why she had gone after the Graysons? Perhaps there was a simple way to go about getting rid of her. I could help her cross over. Then again, what if she wasn't evil at all? I found a sudden urge to read the articles on the Grayson's deaths. There was no evidence so far to suggest she was behind that tragedy, only a theory and proof she was a nutcase behind her own death.

Focusing on rummaging as fast as my fingers would let me, I was now desperate to know what the newspapers had to say about the Grayson family. Disheartened, I stopped digging when I remembered that this was Mr Grayson's stuff. I wouldn't find stories on their deaths in here.

I looked over at my mother to see if she'd noticed that I was not being overly productive. She was busy with her head in a bag sorting through mass amounts of clothing. Sighing, I closed the lid of the wooden box and silently asked myself why my parents had to choose such a confusing, haunted mess of a house. There had to be other cheap properties in town, surely.

I had just started to stand up when suddenly, a loud, wicked laugh sounded from nearby. I jerked my head around in the direction it came from. A figure suddenly materialised before my eyes and I was on my feet in a matter of seconds once I recognised who it was.

The bony, scrawny figure before me matched the terrifying, frightening face I had seen in the mirror. It was the dead, ghoulish, full-sized version of Agatha. She smiled at me and it felt as though a tonne of bricks suddenly hit me in the chest. I was completely mesmerised by her appearance. I felt woozy and warm, like I was fading away. I suddenly didn't want her to leave and if she did, I would follow her.

She raised a hand, stuck out her forefinger and beckoned to me. For a split second, I had the urge to step towards her, but the stronger part of me knew that was probably a stupid thing to do. It took a small amount of effort, but I broke the feeling she held over me by turning to glance over at my family members quickly to see if anyone had noticed the apparition of the gruesome ghost. No one had even looked up.

I turned my head back to look at the ghastly woman. Agatha looked slightly surprised that I hadn't come forth to her.

She then smiled cruelly and rasped, "It's only a matter of time, dear." She gestured towards my mother and sister. "Do you think they will believe you?" Her feet left the ground and she floated a few inches below the ceiling. Blood dripped sickeningly from her mouth, but it never hit the ground, instead disappearing into thin air once it left her chin. Her voice sounded as though her throat was full of nails, rolling around and slicing up the inside of her voice box.

I wanted to run over and shake my mother, to tell her that there was the spirit of a dead woman ten metres away from her who wanted to kill us all. But I knew there was no use, she would most likely just dismiss me and get cranky at me for pulling pranks. She was even firmer than I had been with not believing in ghosts.

Plucking up my courage, I asked Agatha softly, "What do you want with my family, what did we do to deserve this? Maybe…maybe I can help you move on?"

She shook her head slowly, smirking. Then in a moment, high-pitched cackles of laughter surrounded me and without warning, Agatha leaned forward and swooped with her arms outstretched, heading straight for me.

Chapter Nine

I gasped and tried to duck, but her long, bony fingers reached me before I was low enough to avoid contact. Her hands closed around my throat and for such a frail looking ghost, her grip was shockingly strong. I fell backward, startled that a ghost had even been able to grab me in the first place and landed on my tailbone with a thud on the shed floor.

Her awful laugh rang out through the shed as she attempted to strangle me, but it seemed I was the only one who could hear the horrendous cackle.

My hands found their way up to my neck, trying desperately to pry off the dead flesh that had a hold of me. I was now finding it hard to breathe and, as if she had read my thoughts, her fingers pressed down harder. Tears sprang to my eyes and I managed to let out a cry, hoping that my family would look up and realise that something was wrong. Seeing as I couldn't turn my head, I didn't see my sister coming to my rescue until she was right beside me. She started yelling out to my mother, but I couldn't understand the words. My brain was deprived of oxygen and could no longer function enough to work my ears properly.

I couldn't imagine how the scene must have looked to my family. To them, I appeared to be getting strangled by something that wasn't even there. Or perhaps it seemed like I was strangling myself. I could feel someone tugging on my arms and panicked voices communicating back and forth. It was then that I lost hope. How were they supposed to remove the spirit's hands from my throat when they couldn't see her? I felt weak and struggled with every movement my body made. I could barely think, breathe, or blink and I could feel my heartbeat start to slow down, like it was about to come to a stop. If this was what dying felt like, it was the scariest feeling in the world.

However, a few seconds later, that feeling changed. My vision became a white blur and a feeling of peace had started to work its way through my body. The voices of my family members had died out completely and I could no longer feel the touch of their hands on my skin. I felt my own arms drop to the ground onto the floor by my side. I wanted to call out, to say goodbye and to tell my family to stop trying to save me. I then lost the ability to hold up my head as my brain seemingly gave in as I shut off completely. I was at peace.

The next time I opened my eyes, I noticed I was lying on my back, staring at a very bright light hovering above me. I was warm and happy; maybe this was heaven. My body felt weak, but I started to roll over anyway and found myself crying out in pain as I rolled straight off the surface I was lying on. I sat up quickly and observed my surroundings.

This was my bedroom, in the Mason Street house. Or, as Grace had nicknamed it, the "house of bloody walls." I felt a surge of disappointment and happiness shoot through my body at the same time. Dying had been so peaceful, once you got over the pain, but I took comfort in the fact that I was somehow still alive. I raised my arms and checked them over, scanned my body to make sure it was up and running, then jumped up and tested my legs. I was just fine, apart from what felt like a bruised tailbone and crushed windpipe.

I looked up at the doorway just as my mother poked her head around the corner. "Olivia, you're up!" she cried happily. She then bustled into my room and gave me the biggest hug I'd received from her since I was a little girl.

I almost couldn't breathe again and had to push her away from me.

She stepped back and gripped my shoulders, standing an arm's length away from me. "I need to talk to you, Livvie," she said softly. I felt my stomach drop; I knew this wouldn't be good, she had that "you're in trouble" tone about her voice. She was going to want an explanation, something I couldn't really give.

My mother pulled me over to my bed, pushed me down and forced me to sit beside her. "After what just happened, Isabelle told me about the episode in the kitchen this morning with you screaming and nearly collapsing…would you care to tell me what has been happening with you lately? I was beginning to grow concerned when you started locking yourself off in your room, but now something seems very odd. Before we moved, I don't think I'd ever seen you act jumpy or closed off, it's like a switch has flipped in your head."

I stared at my knees, not knowing how to answer her. "Mum, to tell you the truth, I don't really know." And it was the truth…well, sort of. She stared at me for a long while, as though she was performing a lie detection scan. I tried to fix my facial features into a look that said I wasn't hiding anything, but it was difficult. It wasn't like I *couldn't* tell her what was going on, I just didn't *want* to. She wouldn't believe me.

Finally, she spoke. "Don't get me wrong, I'm not complaining when it comes to the toned-down behaviour, but I don't want you to feel alone. People who feel like they have no one to talk to usually end up acting out in the worst ways."

I inched slightly away from her, feeling too close for comfort. "I'm not alone, I made a friend. Or two. Things are just different here, I feel different."

"You may be coming down with some kind of illness then," she said slowly, "You do remember that you attempted to strangle yourself, right? Are you depressed?" She gasped. "Did you have a mental episode?" Her arm shot up to my forehead, placing the back of her hand across it as though measuring my temperature.

I smirked, "Yeah, I really don't think so, Mum. I'm not insane. Just the stress of the move I guess."

Was that seriously her conclusion? Perfect, my mother thought I was becoming mentally ill. Unfortunately, I suppose, looking at it from an outside perspective, I could level with her.

She patted my shoulder and gently said, "Well, you can relax for the rest of the afternoon then. I'm certainly keeping a closer eye on you, we almost lost you this morning." She stood up, kissed my forehead and left the room.

Glad that talk was over, I exhaled deeply and let myself fall back onto the bed. I checked the time after a few minutes of staring into space and soon realised it was now past three in the afternoon. Not wanting to waste any more of the day, I got up and made my way downstairs in search of something to do. After making a fruit salad and wasting half an hour shooting fruit peels one by one into the bin, I realised what I really wanted was to properly look up old newspaper articles on the Grayson deaths.

I also wanted to find out some more about ghosts in general and figure out how Agatha was able to grip onto me. Weren't spirits supposed to pass right through you? Why did she feel so solid? I was under the impression that spirits were supposed to be mostly transparent, yet all three ghosts I'd encountered looked almost like normal people with flickers of transparency in the light. Seeing as Mum and Dad still hadn't gotten the internet connected yet, the only way to find out anything was going to mean a trip to the library. I was pretty sure I had walked past it several times so I thought it wouldn't hurt to ask if I could spend the afternoon there, it was a "relaxing" environment after all. I figured I'd have a pretty decent chance of being allowed to go since it was nearby, especially if Mum didn't have to drive me.

Still not quite used to living in such a giant house, I set off in search to find her, calling out to aid my chances of locating her quickly. I managed to catch up with her in the laundry where she was sorting through endless piles of clothes from the moving bags.

"Hey Mum, do you think it would be alright if I head to the library for an hour or two before dinner? I asked casually.

Her head darted up at me, evidently shocked by my question. Pursing her lips, she asked quizzically, "Why? Planning to burn it down, are we?"

As though in retaliation, I found my hand automatically clenching around the lighter I kept in my back pocket. Being a gift from Sam, it had become somewhat of a habit to keep it on me. I'd only ever used it once, but wasn't surprised she should expect something like that from me. For starters, I wasn't exactly the perfect straight-A type student who'd use the library to study. Then there was the fact that back in the ninth grade, Sam and I had been caught in the act attempting to burn down the library at my old school on a dare. It was kind of fun, but thankfully, the building itself had only just caught fire when we'd been busted. I would have hated to see the consequences we would have been landed with if we'd actually succeeded.

"No, I learnt my lesson the first time Mum," I said confidently. "It's no fun doing that sort of stuff without my old friends anyway. I actually wanted to do some research. You don't even have to drive me, I know exactly where it is and I can walk it."

She paused for a moment, burning a hole in my face and finally agreed. "Home by six sharp, yes?"

I nodded, that was all the time I needed. I spun on the spot and jogged through the house. I'd almost made it to the front door when I heard a voice call out to me from down the hall. "Wait up!"

It was Isabelle. She came waddling into view around the corner, handbag strung over her shoulder and car keys in her hand. "Mum asked me to drive you, she doesn't want you walking alone in case you pass out again."

I rolled my eyes. Now I needed a babysitter?

It was a very uncomfortable drive to the library. I could feel Isabelle's eyes boring into me every time she glanced across, waiting for me to say something.

When I didn't, she finally spoke first, "Ok, spill. I know something is off with you. You were acting...well, for lack of a better word, *possessed* this morning. It was creepy."

I avoided looking directly at her and spoke to the floor. "Possessed, no. But I swear I was not trying to strangle myself. It was...," I trailed off. There was nothing I could say that didn't make me sound crazy. "Anyway, that's why I'm going to the library to do some research. I need to find out for myself what happened exactly."

Isabelle was silent for a minute and then asked the question I'd been dreading. "Research what?"

I sighed and decided to just power through the outlining details. I was going to have to tell someone eventually and she was probably the only person I knew who had somewhat of an open mind. I braced myself and spoke as fast as I could, without taking a breath.

"Ok, here's the thing. The new house, it's haunted. It belonged to this old couple back in the seventies who got whacked, then their weirdo daughter killed herself in the house, then she became like this evil spirit thing and when a new family bought the house in the eighties she possessed them for fun and had them kill each other off and now I think she wants to do the same thing to us and I have to stop that from happening."

Isabelle said nothing for a moment and then burst out laughing. "You're joking, right? Are you saying some old ghost tried to kill you this morning? Did you smoke something …odd…during the time you locked yourself in your bedroom last night?"

I rolled my eyes. I knew I shouldn't have expected anything else.

Defending myself, I said firmly "I didn't believe it either at first, this random girl at school told me about it. And for a while, I assumed she was completely mental. But I found newspaper clippings backing up her story about some of these deaths in a box in the shed and I've seen...things...in that house with my own eyes. I want to find the rest of the articles and see if I can work out what is actually going on."

Isabelle didn't respond for a moment while she pulled the car into a park outside the front of the library. Turning off the engine, she looked into my eyes and said, "This is meant to be a ghost run town, right? I bet every house is supposedly haunted. But if you believe ours is, I want to read these old articles too."

Relieved that she didn't think I was completely insane and was seeming to come around to the idea of ghosts, I rotated my body slightly to reach for the door handle and got quite a fright when I came face to face with an elderly woman peering through the car window at me. Taken aback and suddenly highly reluctant to open the door, I smiled at her awkwardly and waited for her to move to the side or at least back away from the door so I could open it.

She did neither, instead waving and flashing a warm smile, gesturing I should get out of the car. I glanced over my shoulder toward the driver's seat to see if Isabelle had noticed her but she was already out of the car. Turning my attention back to the old woman, I realised suddenly that I recognised her. It was the same lady who'd approached me outside the manor on the very first day we'd moved in. The one from Dad's secret photos.

Feeling a little less wary of her, and suddenly curious to see if she was going to try and resume the conversation we'd started that day, I started to open the door and gave a single nod to greet her. She barely moved and I had to edge out of the car sideways so as to not press the door into her or knock her over.

She smiled again. "Hello dear. How are you finding it, living in the manor? Any *problems*?"

A little weirded out, I narrowed my eyes at her and replied, "Uhhh, no it's fine thanks. Listen, I'm not going to lie, you're giving me the creeps a little, so is there something you wanted to say to me about the place? You started to tell me something when we were moving in and you seem very interested in it."

She nodded and looked down at the ground, biting her lip softly, as though thinking carefully about what to say. At that moment, Isabelle stepped up beside me looking slightly confused, clearly waiting for an introduction. For whatever reason, the woman wasn't scared off by her like she had been with my dad, smiling warmly at her instead.

Gesturing to Isabelle, I said quickly, "This is my sister, Isabelle. And Belle this is…" I trailed off, realising I didn't actually know the old woman's name.

"Eleanor," she piped up, extending her arm in an offer to shake my sister's hand. Isabelle accepted, but didn't look any less confused and kept making subtle gestures towards Eleanor with her head, as though wanting more information on how I knew her.

I ignored her and focused quickly back on Eleanor.

Isabelle scowled and gave me a slight shove with her shoulder.. "I'm sorry, you look really familiar to me, but I seem to be having difficulty placing you. Have we met?" Isabelle asked inquisitively.

"I'm sure I couldn't possibly tell you," Eleanor replied, her voice barely louder than a whisper.

Isabelle looked suspicious, but accepted her response gracefully and crossed her arms.

When Eleanor began to speak again, not making any effort to talk louder, I had to lean right in towards her, not wanting to miss what she said. "Anyway, I am sorry dear, I don't mean to be nosy, it's just that the manor means a lot to me and I like to keep up with its…current inhabitants. You see, I worked in the manor as a maid many years ago for George Clayton and his wife. I even nannied for their little girl, Agatha, for quite a few years before I eventually left town to start my own family. It's tragic, really, what ended up happening there. I moved back to Bellicose when my son died in the manor and I've been keeping an eye on it ever since."

"Wait, what do you mean? Who was your son?" I asked, a little bewildered. She paused a moment, like she suddenly realised she'd said more than she intended, before answering reluctantly, "Arthur Grayson."

Chapter Ten

My mouth hung open for what felt like forever before I was able to respond. "I don't understand. You're Arthur Grayson's mother? I don't get it, were you trying to scare us off or something when we were moving in? Am I missing something here?"

She frowned and looked at me, emotionless for a few moments. As we stood in silence, staring at each other, Isabelle hung in the background awkwardly for a minute, as though trying to be involved but invisible at the same time. After a few minutes, she started rubbing her back with her palms before seemingly giving up and walking over to a nearby bench to sit down.

Eleanor patted my shoulder in comfort before she broke the silence, "I'm sorry, I didn't mean to scare you. I only wanted to warn you. You see, initially, when I saw you and your family moving in, I suppose a part of me was a bit annoyed that Arthur didn't will the house to me and my husband in the first place. We weren't even allowed to purchase it after his death, so I was a little shocked to see people moving in. Back when the authorities first informed me that my son and his family had passed away, I moved back to town to take care of their funerals. I questioned who the house had been willed to and both the police and realtors dodged the question and simply told me it was none of my business and they couldn't sell the manor to me."

She paused briefly and stared off into space, as though trying to remember something. I continued to listen, even though I wasn't quite sure what her reason was for telling me any of this. "All I wanted was access to the house so I could see my son and reassure him that I didn't blame him for what happened to his family. Arthur and I had a big fight when he was a teenager, you see, and he shut me out, left home and ceased all contact. Do you know I never even got to meet my grandchildren while they were alive? I only saw a few photos of them. I had to wait until after they came back from the dead to see them."

I must have pulled a strange face, as she said hastily, in a completely casual tone, "Oh, right, I don't know if you've noticed anything odd yet dear, but they all stayed behind and still live in the manor. Sorry to be blunt, but I'm sure you've heard all about the manor being haunted by now? Maybe even met them. Anyway, I walk the dog with my husband every afternoon just to come and see my grandson sitting out on the windowsill. Haven't seen my darling Mary for years though."

I was getting somewhat worried by this point. She seemed way too casual about visiting her dead grandchildren, like it was something any normal grandmother did on a weekly basis.

Noticing I'd zoned out a little, I started paying attention again quickly when she started laughing like a maniac. Wiping little tears from the corners of her eyes, she continued, "Like I said I've been watching over the place for years. Now, one thing I have noticed, is that I used to hear Agatha crying pretty much every time I came by. The poor dear, she was such a sweet child."

I pursed my lips and almost said what I was thinking aloud. She's not a sweet adult.

Eleanor, unaware of my thoughts, continued, "That is, until your family moved in. Now, the vibe of the house has changed. Instead of upset, mourning spirits, I feel there's an angry aura surrounding the manor and well, truthfully, I've been concerned for your family's wellbeing. It's like everything is different now, somehow. I thought I should warn you to be careful. I don't think it's safe for your family to be living there. You should see if your father wants to sell, I'm happy to offer more than what it's worth. I think you'd be better off leaving them in peace."

I nodded, taking her words with a grain of salt. I was still in awe that she was Arthur's mother.
It really was a small town after all. Now I knew why she'd approached me though, she was annoyed her son didn't will the manor to her and just wanted to purchase it for herself. I wasn't sure if she was spinning the rest of the story for effect, or if she genuinely knew her son's family hadn't quite moved on.

"Well, thank you for your concern, Mrs Grayson, but we're okay. I am definitely aware that the house is haunted, but I'm going to try resolving the problem, and everyone will be happy again in no time. I don't think my parents want to sell the manor right now but I promise if I get a chance, I'll mention it to Dad."

I tried to keep a straight face. What on earth was I saying? I hoped she didn't detect the hint of sarcasm in my tone. I felt like she needed to hear it though, even if I didn't quite believe what I was saying. I wasn't certain she was mentally stable and didn't want to tick her off by telling her to just get lost.

She seemed happy enough and accepted my response with a simple nod of her head. "That's good to hear, dear. You keep that positive attitude up. How is your father handling the situation?"

I frowned, suddenly remembering she had some kind of past with my father. "Okay, that's it, I have to know. How do you know my dad? I saw you in some old family photos of his. Photos he's never shown me. That can't be a coincidence, right?"

She looked guilty all of a sudden and closed her lips tightly. With a grimace, she said, "He's not told you, has he?" She turned quickly and started to walk away.

I managed to stop her in her tracks by darting into her path and, somewhat politely, demanding, "Mrs Grayson, what do you know about my dad?"

She patted my shoulder. "If he hasn't told you, dear, it's not really my place. You should probably ask him. Also, you can call me Aunt Eleanor. Err, everyone around here does. I have to get going now dear, I'm sorry."

She proceeded to push past me, and I watched her walk away for a few seconds before turning and jogging over to Isabelle. What a confusing, yet somewhat insightful conversation. There was more to it, I knew that much. It was just going to be a matter of getting my father to open up about it.

My sister was slumped on a bench right near the front doors, almost falling asleep. "What was all that about?" she asked, sitting up as soon as she saw me.

I apologised and said with a sigh, "I'd love to know. And trust me, I'm going to find out later. But for now, where were we?"

We spent an hour pawing through the town records section inside the library, trying to find the records linked to the manor. As it turned out, there were in fact many houses, shops and schools deemed haunted. Surprisingly enough, and worryingly enough, more than half seemed to be derived from murders. I briefly left Isabelle alone to pore over the records while I searched through the shelves in the occult section at the back of the library. Bringing back a small stack of books detailing spirits and their unfinished business, I dumped them on the desk we were using, chose the thickest book and scanned through the main parts, trying to learn as much as I could without having to read the whole thing.

According to the book, it was theorised that violent or sudden deaths could result in more realistic type ghosts, caught after death in between the planes of existence, explaining everything I'd been wondering about why the ghosts in the manor appeared so alive. Unfortunately, it had no answers as to how Agatha was able to grab onto me, which was the subject I was more curious about. I searched through several books before discovering there was only a small section at the end of one of them offering a possible explanation. It mentioned that ghosts could eventually gain the ability to grab onto objects as they became more powerful, which would occur naturally over time, though manifested faster in vengeful spirits. It then concluded that angry or unsettled spirits could become more powerful if they chose to by harnessing the souls of other spirits, ultimately draining them from existence through a painful, torturous process in which they would absorb the target spirit's soul into their own.

That must be why the Graysons need help. It was beginning to make more sense. I racked my brain and could also recall Grace saying something similar about soul-sucking. I stared into space for a moment, deep in thought.

"Mason Manor deaths, I'm guessing that's what we're after?" Isabelle said suddenly, pulling out a thick manilla folder from a filing cabinet. Opening the file, we flicked through looking for the article on the Grayson family's deaths. All that was left of it was the headline.

"FAMILY TRAGEDY STRIKES MASON MANOR"

Unfortunately, the rest of the article had been ripped clean off the page. It was just gone. Isabelle checked through the rest of the folder to see if the page was loosely floating around, but it wasn't.

Completely bummed out, I said to Isabelle, "At least you can read the other articles about the first lot of deaths at our house."

She nodded and pulled them out of the file. We spent the next half an hour researching everything we could find that had to do with the manor. Interestingly enough, it turned out that Mr Clayton, the wealthy, original owner of the house, had been the founder of a major corporation. The same corporation in fact, that my father worked for now. I wondered if he knew.

After what seemed like an eternity of silence between us, Isabelle finally spoke. "So, you really think this Agatha woman is still living in the house, as a ghost?"

I sighed, "Oh yeah, it's definitely her. She threatened me before trying to strangle me this morning in the shed."

Isabelle opened her mouth, possibly to protest, so I quickly interrupted. "I swear I'm not insane, remember I didn't believe any of this until I saw it with my own eyes. She isn't the only ghost either, there's a woman in the kitchen and a little boy in Noah's room. If their article wasn't missing, I'd be able to show you the story about how they died there too."

Isabelle seemed to be thinking very hard. "Ok, well what do you think you're supposed to do about it?"

"Honestly, I have no idea. I can't even make sense of the whole thing," I said softly. "Grace, the girl from school, told me I should get everyone out, that Agatha was dangerous and anyone who lives there ends up dead. But the Grayson mother, she begged for help. I mean yes, she did warn me that Agatha was going to come for us as well, but I feel like there's more to it than that. Look, it's a long story, but Agatha has to be gotten rid of, I just have to figure out what the go is with that. Can you please just promise me you won't say anything to Mum?"

She nodded and gave me a half smile. I hoped that I could count on her silence.

That night, Mum cooked up a delicious homemade lasagne for once. Amazingly, Dad even ate with us. Mum had called him at work and told him of my awful morning and he'd been able to use it as an excuse to come home early. As I ate, I couldn't feel happier. My whole family was all together for dinner, just like we had been at our old house. Memories came flooding back to me as I glanced around the table observing everyone. I smiled to myself as I remembered the night that Isabelle had announced her pregnancy over dinner. We were eating roast chicken when Isabelle declared her news, just as my dad was chewing the last of his chicken off the bone. At Isabelle's words, he had choked and swallowed the bone whole. The rest of us had spent the night congratulating Isabelle in the emergency room at the hospital.

I couldn't help but stare at my dad, wondering what Eleanor Grayson knew about him that he hadn't told me. After he caught me staring intensely at him a few times, he motioned to the kitchen door and got up, indicating for me to follow him.

"Ha-ha, Liv's in trouble!" Noah taunted with a laugh.

I rolled my eyes at him and followed Dad out into the hallway.

"Ok, what's up?" he said, crossing his arms.

"Gee, Dad, I'd love to talk freely, but I don't know if it falls under your 'don't talk about it' category though," I said quietly and with as much attitude as I could muster whilst avoiding looking directly into his eyes.

He loosened his expression, unfolded his arms and said, "Try me."

"Okay fine, does the name Eleanor Grayson mean anything to you?" I asked. "Because she said—some things about you—and this house, and asked how you were 'handling the situation'."

The look on his face changed very quickly from relaxed and curious to straight-up worried. "Yeah, okay, that counts. Don't pay any attention to her, she went batty as she aged." He turned away and immediately marched back into the kitchen without a second thought. The more he tried to deny things, the more suspicious I was becoming about my father's prior knowledge of the house.

Tonight, it was Isabelle's turn to wash the dishes. Noah had to dry up and it was my job to clear and rinse the plates from the table. Once everyone had finished eating, I collected plates and took them to the sink. Glancing out the window, even though it was dark and hard to see, I noticed that it was raining. I was halfway through rinsing the dishes off when the phone rang.

Mum answered it and my heart leapt with joy when she looked at me and purposely said loudly, "Well hello there, Samuel." I sped up the rinsing process and dried my hands as fast as I could.

As I raced over to the phone, I laughed at myself when I nearly tripped over my own feet. As happy to hear his voice as he was to hear mine, we started babbling away to each other. We updated each other on how things had been going since I had moved away, almost a whole week ago. I told him everything that had happened at my end, leaving out anything that had to do with the house ghosts and the eventful history. And well, I found there wasn't much to tell him. It was so good just to talk to him though.

Mum and Dad left the kitchen to watch TV in the living room and once Noah and Isabelle finished the dishes, they followed. The rain became heavier as time went on and it wasn't long before it had become so intense that it pounded loudly on the roof, almost completely drowning out Sam's voice.

We had been on the phone for around an hour, when thunder suddenly sounded and a lightning strike lit up the darkness. Sam and I now had to yell at each other to be heard. Why did it have to storm on the night that I wanted to have a conversation? I let out a cry of surprise when the lights went out suddenly and the phone line went dead. Frustrated, I slammed the receiver down and marched across the kitchen to the window at the sink. I stared out at the rain and poked my tongue at it.

"Stupid storm!" I yelled. I could barely even hear my own voice and felt like such a child because of my actions.

Shivers ran up my spine as I remembered what had happened the last time I had been in this kitchen when it was dark. And I was currently standing at the sink…her spot. I whipped around and took a swift step forward, suddenly coming face to face with Mrs Grayson, almost bumping into her as she appeared. If I could that is, I didn't know if she was as solid of a ghost as Agatha was. Her watery eyes bored into mine and as she opened her mouth to say something, I dodged around her and hurried out of the kitchen and into the hall connecting the kitchen to the lounge room. I didn't want to deal with her tonight.

What I wanted was to find the rest of my family and stay with them. I refused to be alone when it was storming and ghosts were roaming the house. Since we had moved here, I was finding myself a lot lonelier than I liked to be. I looked up as the lights came on again and I felt a wave of relief wash over me, at least now I could see where I was going. But just as I headed in the direction of the living room, the lights flickered and went out once again.

I stopped in my tracks and waited for my eyes to adjust to the dark. They didn't even have time, because, without warning, the lights came back on again. What is this? The change in lighting was getting quicker and within a few minutes, it had turned into a continuous pattern. On for one second, off for one second. The flashing was starting to hurt my eyes. I made my way forward, with my arms stretched out in front of me and tried not to walk into a wall. I felt goosebumps form on my arms when I thought more about why the lights were flickering. Thinking back to what Grace had told me, I figured that Agatha was probably controlling it. She had done this after she died to scare people. If she was trying to frighten me, it was working very well.

My throat burned as I tried to stop myself from crying. I was so afraid. Continuing my slow movements forward, I nearly jumped out of my skin when a familiar rasping voice whispered in my ear, "Boo."

At that exact moment, the light in the hall that I was standing in gave out to the continuous flickering and blew up. Electrical sparks flew everywhere, making horrible buzzing noises and I had to run blindly forward to avoid being hit by falling glass from the exploded light casing.

I smacked my hand on the door frame as I entered the lounge area at a speedy pace. Wondering, or perhaps hoping that my family was huddling together in here, I nursed my hand and slowly moved past the couches. The flickering lights were really starting to hurt my head; I just wanted them to be either on or off, preferably on. I felt as though I was in some kind of olden-day horror movie with the haunted house, storm, and lights that flickered. If I wasn't so terrified of dying horribly, I probably would have found it rather exciting.

Scanning the large room quickly, I discovered that it lacked people. No one was in here except for me. They had all gone to bed early, like they always did since we'd moved to this stupid town. I didn't feel like I was fully alone however, the hairs on the back of my neck tingled as though someone was watching me. Just as that thought crossed my mind, my eyes found a rather petrifying sight.

In the centre of the lounge room, I could see the shadowy outline of a man holding a knife to his stomach. A few seconds passed before he pulled the knife backward, suddenly, thrusting it forward into his body, then instantly dropping to the ground. Blood began to pool on the floor from his mouth as I stared, frozen, wanting nothing more than to run away.

As I watched in horror, the flickering lights made the man appear and disappear from my view, which made the situation even more traumatising. I built up a little courage and managed to rotate my body slightly, preparing to run away. Before I could force my legs to work, however, the silhouette of Mr Grayson had disappeared altogether and, in his place, stood Agatha's spirit. I opened my mouth and gazed at her, knowing she would probably try to either strangle me or put me into a weird trance again. I cleared my mind and stood strong, I knew better than to let her get to me. Pretending I wasn't terrified, I stared daggers at her and waited to see what she would do.

She shook her head slowly and said in her rough, scratchy voice, "Got a bit of backbone there, hey. You're not going to make this easy for me, are you?" Grinning horribly, she turned her head to look at the wall that was opposite the large front window. The one, I realised, that she had spilled her blood over. With a wave of her hand, the paint that was covering her spattered pools of blood, crumbled. The wet, shining red blood could then be easily seen.

It really was some kind of cursed blood, for it looked as fresh as if she'd splattered it on the wall no more than five minutes ago. As I stared at it, my body and brain relaxed. I felt weightless and free, not even sure why I had been so tense a moment ago. I took several slow steps toward the bloody wall, eager to touch it.

Once I reached the wall, I held out a hand in front of my face. I looked my hand up and down, as though choosing the most appropriate motion to use. I felt a sudden desperate urge to get closer to the wall so, I pressed my palm against the cool surface and ran it in a downward motion. Surprisingly, though my hand felt sticky, when I removed it there was not a drop of blood on me. Turning around to face her, Agatha looked back at me smiling and beckoned me forth with a single finger. This time, I just couldn't resist.

<u>Chapter Eleven</u>

Once I had walked about half the distance to her, I was able to stop for just a moment. There was one tiny part of my brain that told me to turn around and run away. I couldn't think properly, which part of me was I supposed to listen to? Confused, groggy, and suddenly extremely dizzy, my brain fritzed and I uncontrollably started walking towards her again.

"That's a girl," she whispered, sounding as repulsive as ever. I felt wonderfully calm now, my head was as high as the clouds and suddenly, I felt as though I was floating.

The house began to disappear around me as I drifted off to a seemingly mystical place. I arrived in a small, brilliant white room where a large, comfortable-looking bed lay, all made up just for me. How peaceful. My mind was a swirling mess and just as soon as I thought about making myself at home in bed, I abruptly snapped back to normal, suddenly very worried. What was I doing here? And more importantly, where the hell was I?

As if eager to answer my questions, a loud voice echoed loudly through the white room, surrounding me. "You are trapped inside your mind whilst I have taken control of your body. The only place you exist while I control you, is where you are now." The distant voice then cackled loudly and after a few seconds, slowly faded away.

Though I presumed the voice belonged to Agatha, I couldn't help but notice how different she sounded and wondered just how far away I had faded. This was unreal. I closed my eyes tightly and tried to imagine going back home the way I had come here. It felt as though there was a thick brick wall wrapped around my head, blocking my way. Opening my eyes, I started to panic. All I could think about was Mary Grayson. Mary had killed her own brother and she hadn't even known she'd done it. I understood now exactly how that had happened, exactly how she must have felt.

Is that what was going to happen to me? Was this psycho spirit going to kill Noah using my hands, my body? I shuddered suddenly as what felt like cold water trickled down my back. A strange sensation swept through my brain and a few seconds later, a small window-like clearing opened on one of the walls of the room, allowing me to view the outside world through my eyes.

I could see what Agatha was doing, using my body, but was incapable of controlling my actions. Somehow, I'd ended up in the kitchen. I wanted to look around to see if I could call out to anyone but found myself fixed looking down upon open kitchen drawers instead. It was the strangest sensation, seeing what was in front of me through a window and not being able to move the way that I wanted to. After a few moments of rummaging, I watched and felt my hands close around a large carving knife.

My stomach churned and I felt a strong urge to vomit. Wildly attempting to throw my arms around to drop the knife, I became more and more frustrated as my body started to walk towards the stairs instead. It was the strangest feeling I had ever experienced. I saw out of my own eyes, felt my body move, but couldn't control my actions. Suddenly, it was like I could hear her thoughts as well, mixed in with mine, like a silent commentary I had no control over.

I looked down at my hands, turning the blade back and forth in my palm, admiring the large knife I was carrying.

I desperately wanted to stop her. I needed to be myself again, to take control. I knew exactly what she was planning to do. Everyone was going to believe I was a psycho murderer who had killed my brother. I jerked my attention away from the window for a moment and scanned the white room for some kind of door with an exit sign above it, or something similar. No such luck, but why couldn't it have been that simple? I was starting to feel completely helpless; I could feel my legs taking each step up to the second floor but as much as I fought, there was literally no way I could stop them from moving.

I reached the hall at the top of the stairs and was powering forward. There it was, the boy's doorway. I curled my hand around the handle, pushed the door open and closed it once more behind me after I silently edged myself in. I slowly shuffled my feet across the room.

I couldn't handle it anymore and started to throw punches at the window, in a hopeless attempt to smash myself through. I couldn't even make contact, my fists flailed around wildly through the air, passing right through the surface of the imaginary glass. It appeared as though it didn't really exist after all. I prayed with all my heart that Noah wasn't in his bed, that he was downstairs, or safe with Mum and Dad in their bed. I wasn't a very lucky person, obviously, for when Noah's bed came into view, there he was, fast asleep. Smiling peacefully into his pillows.

I screamed Noah's name as loud as I could, to warn him, even though deep down I knew that he couldn't hear me. My voice bounced off the walls of the little white room, ringing in my ears. I had known that it was no use, I was in some sort of other world and she was in my body. I had to do something, why hadn't Mary put up more of a fight? There had to be a way to take control again.

I raced over to one of the walls sealing the white room and banged on it, maybe hoping that it would collapse. To my surprise, it made my head hurt. Pangs of pain shot through my brain as though I had been pounding on it instead. Although, as I considered it more, it did make sense. Agatha had claimed that this room was some kind of chamber inside my mind. I clutched my head and waited for it to stop throbbing, then focused once more on my brother's room.

I lifted my arm, raising the knife above the completely oblivious child.

Tears streamed down my face as I braced myself for Noah's death. There was nothing I could do. I started screaming myself hoarse again trying to get his attention, but it didn't make a difference. My life was going to change forever. I'd end up in a psych ward or prison, the lost headcase of a girl who'd murdered her own little brother in his sleep just because she could.

That was of course on the assumption that I wasn't killed myself before I made it that far. It was apparent now that Agatha liked to follow a pattern and if that's what she was planning to stick to, then I was next to die. Presumably at my father's hand once she possessed him also. I clenched my teeth together as I felt my arm start to swing back down, aiming for Noah's heart. Fortunately, however, the sound of a door opening stopped my puppeteer just shy of Noah's body and my arm jolted sideways instead.

A familiar voice whispered, "Noah, sweetheart, I brought you some water—" until suddenly the words stopped short.

I swivelled around to look at the person who had interrupted the killing of Noah Murphy. It was the mother who stood in the doorway, a glass of water in her hand.

She had evidently been coming to check on how Noah was holding up throughout the storm. "Olivia Murphy!" she cried out dropping the glass in shock. "Just what do you think you are doing?"

The next moment was a swirling blur. It felt as though someone had squeezed my body through a tight tube…and then I was falling. Falling swiftly through a tunnel that had opened up in the floor of the white room. When I "landed" I was in Noah's room— and I was me again. Weak in the knees, my body fell heavily to the ground and the knife flew out of my hand, clattering noisily across the wooden floor. I hurried to sit up and look at my mother, who now stood amidst broken glass, fuming with a hand perched strongly on her hip. Her eyes were fierce, and fire danced in her pupils as she waited for my answer. Relieved to be in control of myself again and extremely happy that my brother was still alive, all I could do was grin.

I shook myself out of my happy state when she made a growling sound at me, crossing her arms in physical irritation. I picked myself up off of the ground in one quick motion. I needed to answer her—and fast. "Uh…," was all I could say at first. I racked my brain, searching for a non-mental explanation. "Don't worry, it was just a prank!" I exclaimed happily.

Mum widened her eyes at me with a mixed expression, like she was trying to decide if I was telling the truth. I reached to pick up the knife and held it up over my shoulder as though I was about to stab someone, moving it back and forth in the air with a stupid grin on my face. When she didn't say anything or react in any way in fact, I loosened my expression back to normal, lowered the knife and said, "I'm sorry, I know you'll be angry with me, but I was just playing a mean joke on Noah. With the storm and the freaky lights, I was just going to try and make him scream."

She looked a little relieved, but even a monkey could see that she was still livid. "How very awful of you, Liv! I'm glad to see you're feeling better and acting more like yourself, but I hoped you would have grown out of all that nonsense by now. He would have had nightmares for months!"

I rolled my eyes. After living in this house, *I'm* going to have nightmares for months. "Sorry, Mum," I said quietly, directing my feet towards the doorway.

She snatched the knife out of my hand as I walked past her and made a huffing sound. I flinched and kept walking, making a break for my bedroom. I could feel my emotions burring up, waiting to release a flood of tears, but I stayed strong right up until I curled up in bed. There, I let myself cry to my heart's content. I couldn't believe how close I'd actually come to killing my brother.

The weekend passed so quickly I barely noticed it was Sunday night until my mother pointed out at dinner that Noah and I should try to get an early night for school the next day. For the first time since moving, I'd spent all of my spare time the last few days out and about in the neighbourhood, attempting to make more friends so I could start fitting in with the crowd instead of feeling like a news piece. No such luck. The local parks of the town were hardly crowded, and anytime I did recognise someone from school, they made a point of ignoring me and leaving the area as quickly as they could. Eventually, I gave up on the idea and decided that just being out of the house was enough.

After having a shower and crawling into bed, I reached out towards my bedside table to flick off the lamp switch and got the shock of a lifetime when a hand shot out of nowhere, clamping down across my wrist. I gasped loudly and attempted to wrench my hand out of the grip of an unknown man squatting beside me. With his other hand, he held a single finger across his lips as though telling me to stay quiet and started to lean in towards me. I froze up in terror, unsure what to do, or what he was going to do. I was beyond terrified.

I felt as though he was trying to say something to me. He kept opening and closing his mouth like a fish, but no words were coming out. Then, out of nowhere, he vanished without a trace. Still frozen in place with my hand outstretched, I caught a glimpse of something on my bedside table that hadn't been there before. I reached out to pick it up, my hand trembling uncontrollably in the process. It was a business card for "Remove-All Removalists." I frowned, unable to recall where or how I'd gotten it. Studying it further, I couldn't help but notice how old and weathered it appeared to be. I could feel my brain ticking over and suddenly it was as though a light bulb had gone off in my head as I realised who the card belonged to. It had to be the long-lost missing removalist, the one who'd vanished trying to collect Agatha's furniture.

As I became further lost in thought, I was pulled back to reality instantaneously when a spectacularly loud crash sounded from downstairs, rattling every wall in the whole house. Leaping to my feet, I raced into the hallway, coming face to face with my sister. My parents' bedroom door flung open a few seconds later and out charged both my mother and father; Dad was half asleep and armed with a baseball bat.

"What the hell was that?" both Mum and Isabelle said in unison.

We all stood for a moment in silence, waiting for each other to do something, or say something. When no one did, we all moved forward and hurried down the stairwell, one after another, curious to discover what had happened. I presumed Noah slept through the ruckus, I didn't see him join us.

Splitting up autonomously to search the house, Mum began running around wildly switching on lights, which made me feel a thousand times better.

"In here!" Isabelle's voice called out a few minutes later, coming from the living room, "Just be careful, watch your step and stay as close as you can to the walls!"

Rushing to see what all the fuss was about; I rounded the corner in a wild hurry and was almost suffocated instantly by the swirling dust cloud that filled the room. Mum caught up with me almost at the same time, just about knocking me over as she charged past me to get to Isabelle, who was leaning against a wall over the other side, covering her face and swatting at the air in an attempt to clear the thick dust from around her.

I carefully crept my way further into the room, peering through the settling dust to the best of my ability, afraid I was going to trip or fall over whatever had fallen and caused the gigantic crash.

"Stop where you are!" Mum cried out suddenly. I stopped immediately in my tracks and waited, unsure what the panic was about. Squinting into the far corner, I could make out the shape of my mother, holding an arm across Isabelle's body. "There's debris everywhere and the floorboards are unsteady, someone is going to end up with a broken leg. Scott, would you get in here!"

Coughing loudly, Dad popped up beside her out of nowhere, presumably having come from the entryway on the other side close to where they were standing. "What in the world," he muttered as he began clearing rubble from beneath people's feet. As the dust finally settled and I could start to see clearly again, I let out an audible gasp as my hands automatically clapped across my face when I realised what was lying before me.

There was a giant, square-shaped hole in the centre of the loungeroom floor, which our couch had toppled into, and yet, it was what was inside the hole that horrified me beyond words. Laying there amongst the debris beneath the floorboards, was a shrivelled dead body.

Chapter Twelve

With my head involuntarily locked in place, I stared wide-eyed momentarily before glancing over to see how disgusted my mother was.

"There's a body in my floor," Mum whispered, almost inaudibly as she stared blankly into the vast hole.

Dad put his arm around her shoulder and stared down at the body in disbelief.

"It's disgusting," Isabelle murmured before screwing up her face, covering her nose and stepping backward.

I bent down very slowly and carefully, examining the edging around the hole with my fingertips, intrigued. It seemed like the cut out in the floor that had fallen away was much too clean of a shape to be just a random collapse, there were no rips or tears in the wood.

I was correct. As I checked underneath the edging, I noticed huge, thick hinges bolted into the underside of the wood. It appeared to be a large, old trapdoor of some kind that had concaved in upon itself for some reason. There were remnants of an old wooden ladder still attached near the top of the hole, and what looked like the rest of its pieces strewn along the floor at the bottom, as though it had simply rotted away and fallen apart over the years.

"It's an old trapdoor," I pointed out to my family. As much as I didn't want to, I bent further forward and took a closer look at the body. He looked slightly mummified and was curled up in a ball on the ground but I squinted and could make out a logo on the arm of his shirt. Unsurprisingly, it bore the logo for Remove-All Removalists.

"Oh, wow," I uttered, a little louder than I intended to.

Mum shot me a look that was both annoyed and confused.

I pointed to the dead man's chest and remarked simply, "There was a removalist who disappeared in this house thirty-odd years ago. I suppose we just found him."

She loosened her expression and sucked in her cheeks as she turned a pale shade of green, like she was trying to stop herself from puking. "I'm going to go make a phone call to the police," she muttered as she left the room through the arch behind her and a very pale Isabelle didn't hesitate to follow.

Dad sighed, glanced over at our other couch and appeared to think for a moment before he turned and crouched on the floor in the corner, drawing his knees to his chest and hanging his head in his hands. The poor guy seemed highly stressed. I felt extremely bad for him, I couldn't imagine what the repair bill for this kind of thing was going to be and that was just part of it. On top of that, there was the added stress of a long, drawn-out investigation ahead and proving to the cops that no one knew there was a dead guy inside the secret floor room beneath us.

The more I reflected on it, the more weirded out I was getting. Was it the ghost of this man I'd seen in my room just moments before the floor collapsed into the hidden room? I looked down into the hole again, trying to see the man's face. It was almost impossible to tell due to the level of decay and the position of the body, but from what I could see, they did share similarities. Why had he shown up tonight? Did he know that the floor was going to collapse, or did he make it happen?

I was taken by surprise when that same ghost appeared beside my father with a huge smile on his face. It wasn't a creepy smile, however, it was a genuinely happy grin. He gestured towards the floor at the decaying body and then held his hands over his heart. I wasn't entirely certain, but I guessed he'd found peace in the discovery of his body. In a way, I was finding it hard to believe what I was seeing and couldn't quite come to terms with how normal it was becoming to casually see ghosts pop up in the house. He waved at me briefly and gave a single nod as though saying thank you before closing his eyes, as though he was concentrating intensely.

Within seconds, I began to notice he was fading out, becoming more and more transparent the longer I watched. I started to smile, like his happiness was rubbing off on me and for a brief moment I felt peaceful. I quickly changed my mind, however, when the calm look on his face dropped and he became almost solid-looking again instantaneously. As though something had sucked him back to this reality, quickly and sharply. As I watched, both intrigued and mortified, he went into a spasm, suddenly dropping to his knees in apparent agony, and began to plead with someone or something that I couldn't see. I felt sorry for him and without thinking, started rushing towards the other side of the room, like somehow I thought if I got to him quick enough, I could help.

"Dad, look up!" I called out without hesitation.

Not watching my footing, I slipped on a loose, cracked-out floorboard and nearly went toppling into the giant void. My dad looked up towards me just in time and sprung to action immediately, leaping around the gap in just a few giant strides and grabbing my arm to help steady my footing. I jerked my head up and looked around him just in time to see the removalist guy vanish in a ball of fire, screaming in agony the whole time. I squealed very loudly in surprise, and my dad scooped me into his arms, hugging me tightly in comfort.

Completely freaked, I buried my face into his chest and tried to slow my breathing.

"What was that all about Livvie?!" Dad asked, a hint of fear in his voice.

"You didn't see him, did you?" I whispered, feeling somewhat crazy.

"Err, see who?" Dad mumbled, pulling me away from his chest and narrowing his eyes at me.

"I, uh, I don't know. I'm sorry. Don't worry about it." I muttered.

The police arrived within a short while and the body was loaded up to be taken away. They seemed to believe that our couch had been so heavy it had been straining the floorboards ever since we moved in and eventually caused the old door hinges to give way and collapse. Without a formal investigation, based on speculation only, the police guessed that the removalist had likely climbed into the trapdoor in search of something inside the hidden room below and the door, being extremely old and heavy, had fallen closed and gotten stuck, trapping him inside. It seemed as though there were an eternity of questions to go along with their paperwork, but eventually, the policemen carried out their duties and left us to, in their words, "get back to our evening."

After we all sat around in silence for half an hour, mostly just trying to shake the weirdness of the night off, Isabelle called it and went back to bed. My parents followed shortly after, and as much as I wanted to join them, I just stayed motionless where I was. I was mostly just too stunned to move. I didn't know what had really happened to the ghost, or how to comprehend it, and was fighting a never-ending battle with myself as to what I was supposed to do. Once the house started creepily creaking and squeaking excessively, I finally decided to head to my bedroom, just wanting to wipe the evening clean.

Unfortunately, that night as I slept, the horrors of my life at present settled in and ruined my dreams.

I was walking through a foggy graveyard and as I looked around, I realised it was night-time, possibly very late. I passed many tombstones and yet had the feeling that I needed to keep going, I was looking for something. Or maybe someone. Stopping once I had reached a line-up of the four Grayson graves, I was startled to see that Grace Maker was there also, standing beside her father's headstone at the end.

I started to ask why she was there, but she silenced me and said, "I came for the same reason you did. To see these graves." She gestured toward the Grayson family's tombstones, "I know that Matty told you I'm a Grayson too."

I opened my mouth, but once again Grace cut me short. She lifted her hand into the air and plucked a tiny knife, possibly a fishing knife once used to cut snagged lines, out of thin air. I noticed most of the metal was stained with blood.

"This is the knife Agatha used to hack herself up and spill her blood over the wall of that house. The reason the police never found this knife was because she kept it with her on the ghostly plane, beyond any living beings' reach. It is a very important object.

When the Grayson family moved in, she hid it in the house until they died. Then she took it once more, until the house had finished being examined by police. And then, well, the Murphys moved in."

Grace paused to laugh.

"I found this knife inside your mattress, Olivia. See, I bet Agatha figured that no one would find it there, but I was smart and watched her hide it this time. I believe it has to be some sort of power source for her, so it must be the key to her weakness. And now...."

Grace suddenly bowed her head down and when she looked back up, her face had changed.

Her skin was old, wrinkled and yellow-looking, her teeth were rotted and half of them were missing. Instead of silky, brown hair, she had wiry, grey straw flowing down her back. I started backing away, but she moved forward with every step I took backward.

She lunged forward and grabbed onto my shoulders, finishing the sentence she had started with vigour, "And now, we can destroy her!"

I awoke with a jerk, nearly rolling off the bed. The first thing I noticed was that sunlight streamed in through the window. The second thing I noticed was that I had broken out in a cold sweat throughout the night. Running a hand through my hair, I was disgusted to find that it was both damp and crispy in different places. I wanted to shower straight away before I had to get ready for school, but in this instance, curiosity had to come first. That dream had seemed so real and with what had happened to me lately, I figured anything was possible.

I bobbed down beside my bed and started pushing into the tough fabric of the mattress. I made my way along, feeling every side. I was bummed for some reason when I couldn't feel anything but springs on the inside of the mattress.

I started pushing harder, feeling deeper than the surface, and was almost ready to give up, but then, I felt it. My hand came into contact with a small, hard foreign object inside the mattress right near the foot of the bed. I slid underneath the bed and looked up at the underside of the mattress. Feeling the outline of the lump with my fingers, I concluded that it definitely had to be a knife of some kind.

The thought of not finding it had made me disappointed and yet, now that I had found a real lump in the mattress, a wave of anxiety shot through me. There was no way what Grace had said in the dream could have actually been true. I had to know for sure and wondered how I could possibly get the knife out of my mattress without wrecking it. My mother would kill me if she found out I'd torn open my mattress. But I told myself that I didn't have a choice, there was no way I could ignore it now. I just had to know if it was the knife. Perhaps it was something simple and more realistic, like a lump of dust bunny that had been there for a long time.

As quickly as I could move, I fetched my school scissors out of my pencil case and crawled back under the bed. I made a tiny slit in the fabric and stuck the scissors up inside it, afraid I would slice myself if I pulled the little knife out with my hand. I threw my head to the side just in time as the object inside the mattress fell out onto the ground. I rolled over onto my stomach and picked up what was in fact an old, silver knife that had been hidden inside my mattress. It was the kind fishermen commonly used to cut snagged lines and most of the metal was coated with dried blood.

Freaking out a little more, I hurriedly slid out from under the bed and examined it more closely. It was the *exact* same little knife I had seen in last night's dream, down to every detail. I stood up and threw it gently onto the bed before half running to my cupboard to get out my school uniform. This was too much to handle on my own, I was even more eager to get to school and talk to Grace than I had ever been.

Just as I was about to get dressed, a high-pitched, piercing scream-like noise sounded from somewhere behind me. My hands automatically shot up around my face, covering my poor ears tightly. Desperate to know where it was coming from, I whipped around on the spot to face the window, somewhat hoping I would just see someone standing there that I could clock over the head to shut them up. Thankfully, and strangely, the sound stopped almost immediately. Uncovering my ears slowly, I cautiously began to walk towards the window, certain that was where the sound had come from.

As soon as I reached the closed window, the curtains began to billow and fly around wildly. So much so, that they flapped out enough to hit me in the face and flew back in with enough force to create a heavy thudding sound against the wall. Staring at the window, on edge, I jumped as a whispering voice suddenly carried through the non-existent breeze.

"It's not what it seems." Then, as quickly as they had begun billowing, the curtains fell dead still against the window.

Frightened and confused, I stood frozen for several minutes, unable to do anything but breathe heavily. Taking an extra deep breath to regulate my lungs into a normal breathing pattern again, I pulled myself together and shook it off. The only way to get to the bottom of this was to get to school and talk to Grace, I knew it.

Darting across to my cupboard, I hesitated for half a second while I made a disgusted face at my ugly uniform like I had every day since the very first time I'd worn it. I forced myself to put it on and brushed my hair, deciding I would wear it in a ponytail today. Briefly looking in the mirror, I decided this look just wasn't working for me anymore, I was sick of looking like a jazzed-up nun. I hitched my skirt up higher on my waist and rolled the top band over and over until the skirt sat comfortably a few centimetres above my knee. I then used hairpins from my dresser to pin it in place.

Checking myself out in the mirror, I felt much more like my old self. To finalise the new style, I twisted the bottom of my shirt into a knot and released my top button. Posing seductively, I picked up my phone off the bedside table and snapped a photo. I captioned it, "Missing you," in a text message and sent it to Sam. Then, grabbing a pair of sneakers, my schoolbag and my phone, I hastily started to leave the room.

Until I remembered the little knife was left unattended on my bed, where my mother would probably find it. Feeling like I should keep it with me, I turned back to get it, shoved it into the bottom of my bag and took off out the bedroom door and down the stairs.

Once at the kitchen table, I slipped on my shoes and checked the time. Excellent, ten to eight. I had enough time to swallow breakfast before it was time to go. Choosing a deliciously ripe-looking banana from the fruit bowl, I peeled and ate it as slowly as I could manage, trying not to draw attention to myself.

They would think I was sick if they noticed how desperate I was to get to school. I mean, I had been caught wagging eight times the month before we had left. And suspended three times within six months a year before that. Although, that was when I had first gotten with Sam and my class rival, Sarah Taylor had been hitting on him. I punched her fair in the face the first time I had seen her take a liking to him. One would have thought she'd have learned her lesson. Thinking back, I realised I was quite ruthless back then, possibly due to Sam's influence. He had always been the initiator of the plans that got us into trouble.

Starting to get impatient, I tapped my fingers on the bench and swung my schoolbag back and forth as I waited for my snail of a brother. Noah ate his cereal so slowly that I could count every flake on his spoon before it reached his mouth.

It was a quarter past eight by the time we finally left the house and I was hyper with energy, not for school, but because I couldn't wait to see Grace. I needed to know if I was losing my mind, or if the dream had somehow been real. I needed some clarification from someone outside my house who knew what was going on.

I didn't even stand in the same spot long enough to see Mum drive off when she dropped me off at the front gates of Harriet Brown High School. Didn't really hear her say goodbye, or ask me to make friends, not enemies in her usual daily pep talk. I jogged across the oval towards my form room, hoping I was going to bump into Grace when I rounded the corner. I poked my head around the side of the building before turning the corner. No Grace.

The day passed by quickly and I soon realised after spending my whole lunch break walking around whilst eating that Grace Maker wasn't at school that day. I focused so much of my energy on finding her that I barely realised when people actually tried to talk to me. I was slightly disappointed, but more angry than anything else. Why was it that when I did want to talk to her about my house, she was nowhere around? She had offered help and told me that I would eventually believe her and want more information, but then when it came to it, she seemed to vanish without a trace.

I didn't listen to a thing the teachers said, nor did I attempt to speak to anybody else in class all day. In the good old days, I would have made quite a game out of getting other kids in trouble for speaking to me while the teacher was talking. Today, however, I simply stared at the clock all day, waiting for the next bell. It wasn't until my last period of the day that one of my classmates spoke to me, and what she said caught my attention.

Chapter Thirteen

"You're the girl who lives in the house of bloody walls, hey?" she asked, intrigued.

I didn't remember her name, but she was in more than one of my classes and I'd nicknamed her "The bimbo cheerleader." Her perfect figure and doll-like features gave the impression she'd just stepped out of a magazine. I didn't exactly know her, but I couldn't stand her.

"Uh, yep," I responded with a sigh.

She gasped and turned to the boy sitting beside her, whispering from a distance where I couldn't hear what she was saying.

Getting annoyed, I rolled my eyes, turned back to my math book and continued jotting down information from the chalkboard.

Within seconds, she was at me again. "My Grandpa used to work as a gardener for Mr Clayton back in the sixties. Is it true what they say? Is the manor really still haunted by Agatha Clayton?"

I didn't know what to say.

Thankfully, she didn't wait for me to speak anyway and blurted, "They reckon she did it you know. She's the one who killed her parents. It was all for their money. They cut her off when she left home and supposedly, there's a fortune hidden within the house."

I nodded slowly, unconvinced, "Okay…I mean, I heard a brief rumour about her being the murderer and all, but I've never heard anything about hidden money."

She leaned in toward me and said seriously, "Mr Clayton only told a few people about it, the ones he really trusted. Grandpa says the old Claytons didn't trust banks. They kept a large portion of their life savings in a giant vault and hid it somewhere within the house. Since there's no family of theirs left to claim it, they say if you find it, it's yours to keep. You could be rich!"

I chuckled and rolled my eyes. "There is no money. My mother is a neat freak. She's torn the house apart just to remove the layers of dust and grime that built up from the house being shut up for so long. Believe me, if there was a huge vault of money in the house, she'd definitely have found it by now."

The girl scowled and shrugged her shoulders, seemingly disappointed before turning her back to me, even going as far as to turn her chair sideways.

What a cow. What did she expect from me? An invite to come over and treasure hunt? It did make me wonder, however, if that was the reason the removalist had climbed down into the room under the trapdoor and gotten stuck. Perhaps he'd heard the money rumour also and was looking for the supposed vault.

When the school bell finally rang to signal the end of the day, I was the first out the classroom door and also the first to reach the school gates. I knew where I was headed before I went home.

Grace's house. She was wrong to think she could avoid me now.

It didn't take very long to reach Grace's neighbourhood at the pace I was going. She had to be home; I didn't know what I would do if she wasn't. I walked quickly down the street, towards the area where Matt had fallen off his skateboard when I had first met him. Coming to a halt suddenly, I glanced at the houses surrounding me on either side, realising I didn't actually know where the Makers lived, I'd been just going off where I'd met Matt. I hoped I was even in the right neighbourhood. The hairs on the back of my neck stood up when I felt someone breathe on me from behind. A strong hand clamped down on my shoulder and spun me around to face them.

I let out a big breath of air and cried out, a little hysterically, "Matt!"

He grinned at me. "Did I scare ya?"

"As if," I scoffed forcefully and hitched my bag back up onto my left shoulder, as it had slipped down onto my arm when I'd turned suddenly.

Matt nodded and replied sarcastically, "Oh, I'm sure. What are ya doing around here anyway? Looking for me?" He stuck out his chin, ran a hand through his hair and puffed out his chest.

I put on a disgruntled face, trying not to smile. "Ha, in your dreams," I said jokingly, "Look, I think you're a nice guy and all, but I'm going to be straight upfront and let you know right now that I have a boyfriend. I'm actually looking for your sister. She wasn't at school today and now I really need to talk to her."

Matt groaned. "She seriously wagged *again*? Mum's gonna kill her." He checked his watch. "Eh, it's only three-thirty. She never comes home straight away after school, even when she does go. She goes to the cemetery every afternoon. She'll be visiting her *real* family's graves right now."

I nodded automatically as my body went numb. Grace was at the cemetery, just as she had been in my dream. The dream that helped me discover the little Agatha fishing knife inside my mattress.

"Uh, Liv, are you ok?" Matt's voice sounded distant, my mind was half shut off, trapped in a whirlwind of fear.

With some effort, I gave my head a slight shake and focused on the blurry figure standing in front of me. Matt waved a hand in front of my face, looking confused. "You're a little pale."

I tried to grin normally at him but could only manage a weak smile. As he came back into focus, I couldn't help but admire how good-looking he was. I could so easily get lost in his brilliant blue eyes.

Feeling guilty, I spluttered, "I gotta go," and started to walk away at a fast pace.

"Hang on!" Matt called out.

I turned back, flustered.

He still smiled. "Did you maybe want some directional help? You were kinda walking the complete opposite way to the cemetery. I mean, I'd be happy to guide you if you'd like the company?"

I felt uplifted at the idea of Matt's company and found myself blushing slightly. Guiltily brushing it off, I said in a very calm, dull tone, "That would be great, thanks."

He nodded his head in a silent indication of the direction we should walk. We set off, propelling into a full-blown conversation about each other's lives. In all honesty, we probably could have gotten there a lot faster if we hadn't dawdled along at a less-than-productive pace. I found myself chatting away as though I'd known him for years and he reciprocated. It was about forty minutes later when I spotted huge iron gates at the end of the small street we'd turned into with a huge, rusted sign barely still bearing "Bellicose Cemetery." I picked up my pace, heading straight for the entrance.

Matt held back once we'd reached the gates, however, giving me a wave off.

"You're not coming in?" I asked, admittedly disappointed.

"Nah, honestly I'm a little over it," he shrugged. "I've tried more than enough times to get my sister to speak about whatever issues she holds inside about her parents, but she never talks to me anymore, she just blocks me out. I, uh, really did enjoy hanging out with you though. You can say no if you want, but do you think it would be okay if I grabbed your phone number? Um, just as a friend, of course, I don't want to make you or your boyfriend uncomfortable. I just feel like we get on pretty good and I don't have a lot of friends myself."

I tucked my hair behind my ear and thought about it for a moment, then nodded. I didn't see any reason we couldn't be friends, at this point in time he was more available than Grace was.

He passed me his phone and I punched in my phone number. He grinned. "Cool, I'll text you. See ya later?"

I smiled and nodded to him. Both he and I parted ways in unison and I turned back to the graveyard.

Graves were lined up in jagged rows beyond the gates and after standing at the entrance for a few minutes, holding myself up with knees that wanted to give way, I was stupid enough to walk right into the cemetery. I stopped briefly when I felt my phone buzz in my pocket, and smiled a lot wider than I intended when I answered the incoming call.

It was Matt's voice that chuckled, "Just checking I wasn't fake numbered."

I turned around and shook my head at him in the distance, grinning uncontrollably. Making a point, I laughed sarcastically before pulling my phone away from my ear and hung it up with my hand outstretched so he could see. Then I shook my head, turned back around and jogged further into the cemetery.

My head turned continuously as I walked through the rows of tombstones in search of Grace. I tried to call out her name a few times, but my throat was stiff, and my voice escaped in a tiny whisper. I didn't know for sure if ghosts haunted outside of houses, but I didn't want to find out. My legs seemed to have a mind of their own as they guided me through the graveyard; it was as though I was on autopilot and knew which direction I was supposed to be going.

It took no more than a few minutes for me to spot Grace kneeling by a large, plain white tombstone. I walked over anxiously, stepping as softly as I could on the dry, cracked ground, trying not to startle her. She didn't look up as I approached, but just as I was about to say hi, her head jerked up and she snapped, "What are you doing here?"

A little taken aback, I replied, "What do you mean what am *I* doing here? I've come to find you, since you clearly decided to start avoiding me! I need to talk to you about my house."

Her expression softened and she bit her lip as though she didn't know what to say next.

I didn't wait for her to give me an excuse and started talking, telling her everything I'd seen and heard over the past week. I explained the scratching, whispering, odd window curtains, the knife I found inside my mattress and the ghosts I'd seen. I told her about my discovery of the newspaper clippings in the shed, seeing Agatha and the possession I'd endured which nearly caused me to murder my brother. I went into vivid detail about the floor collapse and the removalist ghost being flamed away before my eyes. I even told her about the supposed money hidden in the house being the motive behind Clayton's murder. I assured her that I believed her story now and that I needed her help just like she'd said I would.

She didn't move the entire time I spoke, didn't get up or even make one, single sound. Her eyes were frozen open—it was almost like she had become a living statue before my very eyes and as I finished my long speech, I began to wonder if she was one. I therefore jumped slightly when she suddenly stood up to face me, stared into my eyes for a few seconds, then turned her head to stare at the tombstones again. The silence was driving me insane, but I decided to wait patiently until she answered me; I didn't want to push the matter. I stepped up beside her and focused my attention on what she was fixated on.

There were two identical white headstones sitting immediately beside each other, lined up perfectly in proportion. These were the graves of Mr Arthur Grayson and Mrs Penelope Grayson. Glancing to the right of Mrs Grayson's grave, I studied the smaller white headstone bearing the name, "Owen Grayson." The innocent little boy who had been brutally murdered in his sleep.

An awful image suddenly floated across my mind of a brilliant white tombstone bearing the name "Noah Murphy." I took a deep breath, shook it off and focused on the actual grave in front of me. Knowing whose grave would be on the left of Mr Grayson, I turned my head to look. But what I saw was not what I had expected at all.

My eyes grew wide as I absorbed the sight before me. The greyish headstone declaring Mary Grayson had a large crack running vertically upward through the centre from the point where it met the ground, like it was about to split in half. I wondered how I hadn't noticed it before; it had been right beside Grace and me the whole time and would certainly catch a passerby's attention.

I walked around behind Grace and stood directly in front of Mary's tombstone. Grace looked across at me and watched my every move as I passed her. I examined the spine-tingling sight before my very eyes. I couldn't help but wonder, if all the Graysons were buried on the same day, why was only Mary's tombstone broken? It looked like it had been struck by lightning. I was curious how long ago the grave had been destroyed, by whom, and why. I turned to Grace, pointed at the grave and choked out, "How long has this grave been this way?"

A single tear ran down her cheek. She flicked her dark hair off her face and replied, "It's always been like that, ever since I started visiting them."

I swallowed. There was something about Grace's tone that frightened me even more. Was there no caretaker for the cemetery? The headstone had been broken for possibly well over a year and no one had bothered to repair it?

We both stood in silence for a few moments and, deciding to move back onto the topic of my dangerous living situation, I was the one who broke it. "Grace, I don't mean to pressure you or whatever, but you told me to come to you if I needed help. And, well, here I am. I need your help. I don't want my family to get hurt, especially by each other."

She folded her arms and began to rock back and forth as though she was nervous. She bit her lip again and frowned. "But....," she said softly. "But to help you I have to tell you everything. *Everything*. Including who I really am. And I realised I'm not ready just yet."

I was confused. Didn't she know by now that I knew she was related to the Graysons?

"Grace—" I started.

She interrupted me by snapping, "Just leave it for now, ok! I'll come see you later, I promise." And with that, she turned on her heel and jogged away.

I stood still for a moment, lost in thought, and then turned and bolted after her, but it was no use. She had disappeared fast and by the time I passed a few rows of graves, she was nowhere in sight. I stopped at the gates to catch my breath, looking around just in case she was nearby. Once my breathing had returned to normal, I decided to give up for the day and go home. My mother would begin to worry if I wasn't back by four-thirty, which was now only a few minutes away.

By the time I reached the front lawn, I was exhausted, both mentally and physically. I just couldn't understand Grace. She seemed to be in a different mood and state of mind every time I saw her. I had a strong feeling there was something about her that just wasn't right, something more than just her birth family she was hiding from me. From deep inside my gut, I had the sudden urge to look up at my bedroom window and when I did, I could have sworn that I saw a girl duck out of sight quickly. Maybe I was imagining it? I shook my head at my own ignorance, I knew better by now.

I looked sideways at my brother's window and wasn't the least bit surprised when I saw the little ghost of Owen sitting in a ball on the windowsill, looking out onto the street, as sad and lonely as ever. I shrugged and kept walking towards the front doors, he didn't bother me anymore, how scary could a harmless dead little boy really be?

I yelled out a quick hello as I entered the front hall. No one responded; however, I thought nothing of it and made for the stairs down the end of the hallway. As I entered the kitchen, a whispering voice caught my attention.

Stopping in the middle of the room, I looked around slowly, waiting for someone to pop up suddenly. When no one did, I edged forward, hoping I hadn't heard anything in the first place.

"Psst!"

I whirled around in an almost complete circle and only just spotted a middle-aged woman's face partially poking out from the laundry room doorway.

I wanted to ignore her and go up to my bedroom, but she became more persistent and began tapping on the doorframe to get my attention. I was about to cross the room when she suddenly fell forward into view as though she'd been pushed from behind and cried out "Oh, no!" before starting to fade away. It was as though her whole body was being encased in a translucent, mist-like substance as she was pulled away into nothingness.

Barely visible, she called out, "Just remember, it's not what it seems!"

And then just like that, she was gone. I had a bad feeling about the way she'd vanished, like she'd been pulled away against her will.

I stood on the spot for a good few minutes, completely bewildered. Every time I started to believe things couldn't get any weirder, something was able to prove me wrong. First, I'd seen a ghost being destroyed in a ball of fire, and now vanish in some kind of weird mist. I was starting to really not like coming home anymore as it seemed that every time I did there was something freakishly unnatural lurking around the corner.

I shuddered. I couldn't get the new female ghost's face out of my mind. Who was she? I felt as though I'd seen her somewhere before, or perhaps it was her voice that was familiar. Either way, I had absolutely no idea what she was talking about.

After trying to make sense of everything for a few minutes, I decided there was no point dwelling over it and climbed the stairs to the second floor. The fact that she hadn't disappeared in a blazing fireball suggested to me that she wasn't gone permanently, so I knew she'd find me again at some point if she wanted to talk to me badly enough.

When I opened the door to my bedroom, the last thing I expected to see was my mother sitting on my bed curled up in a ball with her head in her hands. A little worried, I crossed my arms against my stomach and waited for her to say something.

When she looked up at me, I noticed that her face was tear-streaked and she was shaking horribly. Proof yet again that coming home was becoming a bad idea. Seeing me in the doorway, she got up and rushed over to hug me. My stomach dropped; I had a bad feeling that something was terribly wrong.

"Mum, what is it?" I whispered in her ear.

She pulled herself away from me and took a deep breath like she needed time to find the courage to speak. "Oh Liv, your father's been in a horrible car accident."

Chapter Fourteen

I held a hand up to the side of my forehead, in utter shock. "W…what? When? Is he ok?" I managed to stammer.

She nodded, patting her face gently with a tissue to wipe away fresh tears. "It was earlier this afternoon," she sobbed. "He's alive, but the doctors believe the impact caused some severe internal damage and, well, with the condition he's in at the moment, they told me he may never be the same again."

She burst into tears again and hugged me tightly.

I patted her on the back as tears pricked the corners of my eyes. "What happened?" I managed to ask her whilst fighting the urge to bawl like a baby.

Still holding me firmly, she had to take a few long breaths before she could reply. "He…he lost control of the car and hit a power pole. It crumpled and fell on top of the car, crushing it in upon itself. No one else was involved but your father almost died amongst the rubble. They only just managed to get him out."

I felt my jaw drop open involuntarily in disbelief.

After a moment of processing the situation, I cleared my throat. "Can we see him? I want to see him. Where's Isabelle and Noah, are they with him?"

Mum sighed, wiping tears off her cheek. "Isabelle picked Noah up from school and she's taken him to the park, I don't want him to know just yet. It's going to be a big shock. I'd prefer it if none of you kids see him while he's in hospital, actually. You'll be able to see him when the doctors let him come home."

I reached up to my face and with a single finger, wiped the few escaped tears from my own eyes whilst continuing to pat Mum on the back with the other.

This was all too much. I found myself suddenly very annoyed at my mother. Before I could hold my tongue, I unintentionally exploded in anger, "What the hell is wrong with you, why didn't you come get me from school? I don't want to wait; I want to see him," I demanded.

Mum looked up at me and raised her eyebrows. "Well, I just thought I'd spare you the pain while everything was still fresh and I didn't know if he was going to live. I've had a nightmare of an afternoon. You were better off at school. I'm sorry. We can go up to the hospital now if you really want to, but are you sure you want to go see him at this stage? He's pretty…beaten looking."

I sighed and with popping eyes, nodded sarcastically without hesitation before realising I was being bitchy. "Sorry, Mum, I didn't mean to get snappy with you, it just doesn't seem real."

She stroked the side of my face lovingly. "I know. How about we go now then, I'll grab the keys and meet you at the car," she sniffled.

A short while later, we parked up in the hospital car park and made our way to the ward where my father was being kept. I couldn't stop the horrifying images of what he might look like from filling my mind. I pictured a gruesome, battered, bloodied-up mess of a man's body. Like the leftovers of a beast's dinner or something. We entered the ward and I braced myself as he came into view. But I was slightly amazed, he didn't look anywhere near as horrific as I had imagined. Trust my mother to exaggerate. Yes, he was scratched, bleeding and cast up in many places, but for a man who survived a car crash, he looked pretty great. He even smiled when he saw me, and I raced over to give him a big hug, strategically placing my arms around him so I wouldn't press on his injuries.

"Wow, Dad, what happened? What went wrong with the car?" I asked him gently.

He looked down, almost guiltily, purposely avoiding my question. I turned to Mum, curious to see if she knew the rest of the story. She was looking out the window, avoiding any possible eye contact with me. I frowned, now a bit suspicious.

"Seriously, how'd you crash?" I asked firmly, directing my question back to my father.

Looking extremely ashamed of himself, he whispered "I did it on purpose. I wanted to crash the car."

I was gobsmacked. "You mean you tried to commit suicide?!"

"Shhh!" my mother chimed in from the background, looking rapidly around the ward to see if anybody was listening.

Dad nodded slowly with tear-filled eyes.

I shook my head, angry and completely shocked. "But why?" I could tell he was reluctant to answer and trying to pick his words carefully.

Finally, he said simply, "I've just had a bad week."

Liar. Furious now, I demanded, "Why won't you tell me the truth?"

He patted my arm and said, "You're too young to understand, guilt does strange things to a person."

Guilt? I was eager to know what he would have to feel so guilty about that he would try to take his life away. I crossed my arms and pursed my lips to let him know just how angry I was. I remembered a time when he and I could tell each other anything. We didn't keep secrets from each other, or at least that's how it used to be.

He must have known exactly what I was thinking because he quickly launched into an explanation after he saw my expression change.

"Look, we weren't going to tell any of you kids this, although I admit we did tell Isabelle—only because she's an adult now and technically has her own place…but anyway, your mother and I didn't *buy* our new house. It was willed to me."

"Scott!" my mother loudly exclaimed.

Dad looked up at her with zero regret on his face and said, "It's okay Margaret, she deserves to understand."

Unimpressed, my mother shook her head angrily and, huffing loudly, turned on her heel and left the room.

Turning his attention back to me, Dad continued. "My cousin, Arthur, used to live in that house a long while ago with his wife and kids. We used to be pretty close growing up. Hell, we were best friends right through primary school and were pretty inseparable through high school as well. When we were around sixteen, he had a baby with his high school sweetheart Penelope and after his daughter was born, I was pretty much the only friend he had left. He married Penny around the time I met your mother and they had a second child a couple of years before Isabelle was born. Your sister used to play with him, but I don't think she remembers Owen now.

Eventually, though, he moved away to Bellicose with his family after we had… well let's just say a bit of a falling out. He touched base every now and then and several times offered me a job at the company he worked for, maybe as a peace offering, but it didn't feel right at the time. I always just brushed him off, not wanting to be involved with his drama anymore and I certainly wasn't about to uproot our lives just to reconcile with him.

Anyway, he passed away a long time ago and I found out a few months after he died that he'd left me his house in the will. I just never had any incentive to move here until recently when his old company reached out and offered me a job here. Turns out, they remembered me. I only took it this time because they offered me literally three times what I was earning at my old job."

Dad paused for a moment and chuckled before continuing, "Had they done that the first time you kids would have grown up right around the corner from the Graysons. But now, every day of my life, I just feel so guilty that Arthur and I never got the chance to make things right before he died and ever since we moved into his old house…I've had vivid hallucinations of him. Not only that, but there's this one old picture of him and I—from when we were teenagers—that keeps appearing on my bed, even though I keep putting it away. I hate to admit it, but I'm frightened, it's like he keeps coming to me, trying to warn me about something…or guilt trip me, I don't know. I feel like I'm going insane, Livvie. I just couldn't take it anymore."

I was not expecting that at all. My father and Arthur Grayson were cousins. I was suddenly much more connected to the Grayson family than I'd initially thought. They were part of our family. Blood relatives. I didn't know what to say to my father in response. I should have used the opportunity to tell him everything I'd been experiencing, but I somehow felt that would push him over the edge. He seemed unstable on his own, he didn't need my crazy on top of his own ghostly apparitions. On some level, I felt relieved. I wasn't alone and I finally had a "why." A connection to all the strange happenings in the house. They were my family. My cousins.

After lots of hugs and many tears, Mum and I left the hospital to head home. Once there, she sank into the couch and pulled out her mobile phone to call Isabelle. I decided to go upstairs and have a hot shower to calm myself down and relax for a little while. Whilst I fully intended to head for the bathroom, my curiosity peaked when I reached the second-floor landing and noticed my parents' door hanging open. I only found it strange as usually, if they weren't in the room at the time, they always had it closed. I knew I was being nosy, but I couldn't help but investigate. I peered inside the room and immediately noticed a small, framed photo propped up on my father's pillow.

I picked it up and studied the picture. Though similar to the photos in the basement, I was still blown away by how young and shiny my dad looked, figuring he couldn't have been more than eighteen at the time it was taken. Sure enough, he had his arm around another young man, whom I assumed with confidence now was Arthur. Curiously enough, he looked familiar to me, and I found myself wondering if I had seen him in the house at some point. Although, aside from the removalist, I couldn't remember seeing any male ghosts, other than little Owen. I shrugged it off, figuring he looked familiar because I'd seen him already in the photos from Dad's hidden albums.

Considering all the weird and frightening events I'd endured myself whilst living in the manor, I couldn't blame my dad for feeling like he was going insane and I felt bad for him. Older people didn't seem to be able to cope with unexplainable things the same way that younger people could. I shoved the photo frame under my parents' bed in the hopes that it would give my father some kind of relief if it ended up lost under there. I then took one last look across the mattress and around the bedside tables, as though checking the coast was clear before leaving the room and heading for the bathroom. I needed a good, long shower.

The warm spray of water was wonderful and felt peaceful enough for me to close my eyes and forget the world for just a few minutes. I washed myself with a prettily bottled body lotion that wasn't mine, but it smelt so beautiful that I couldn't resist. I figured it was the soap that Isabelle used, as the smell reminded me strongly of her.

No amount of shampoo, soaps or hot water was able to wash my mind clean, however. I was still amazed by the fact that my father had not only known Arthur Grayson but was related to and had grown up with him. If Arthur had never moved to Bellicose, there was every possibility I would have been friends with the Grayson kids, my second cousins, growing up too.

I wondered if Isabelle did remember playing with Owen at all. Although, that was unlikely, she would have only been a toddler when they left town.

I turned the shower off after what felt like half an hour and grabbed a towel. Wrapping it around my torso, I tucked the corner into the material under my arm to hold the towel up and made my way towards the small mirror that hung on the wall above the bathroom sink.

The glass had steamed up heavily in the time taken for my shower, so I wiped a hand across it to clear a spot for my reflection. I squealed loudly when I saw a figure reflected in the glass, who was evidently standing behind me. I turned around and backed into the sink as I tried to figure out who the hell it was.

It was a young, teenage girl that stood in front of me, staring miserably into my eyes. The same girl, I realised quickly, whose face I had seen in the little mirror in the shed. I knew instantly she had to be the ghost of Mary Grayson. With chills running down my spine, I remembered that the bathroom was the place where Mary had been drowned by her father, so I shouldn't have been surprised to see her. Then, as quickly as she had appeared, she abruptly vanished into thin air.

Shaken, I grabbed a second towel off the rack and proceeded to wrap my hair up in it to absorb the excess water my hair liked to hold onto. I was slightly confused. Unlike her mother, Mary Grayson made no attempt to speak to me at all. Why then did she even bother to show herself to me? I shrugged it off, opened the door and headed down the hall for my bedroom.

Once there, I dropped my towel, put on my underwear, and started scouring my drawers in search of my comfiest pyjamas. Just as I had my hand clasped around a nightshirt, the hairs on the back of my neck prickled. I knew that feeling—I felt as though I was being watched. Bracing myself for whomever I was going to encounter, I pulled my shirt down over my head to quickly cover my torso, picked up my pants and turned around slowly. It was, however, not a ghost standing in my doorway. It was Grace Maker.

"What the hell are you doing?" I squeaked in a high-pitched tone as I threw my pants across my bare legs in a desperate attempt to cover them.

Grace closed her eyes and grimaced, apologetically blurting out, "Sorry! I didn't realise you were indecent." She clapped her hands across her eyes and looked down at the floor.

I took that moment to hurriedly pull on my pants and then said with sass, "Ok, I'm not half naked, you can look now. What are you doing in my room?"

Grace spread her hand open and peeked out from behind her fingers. Deciding it was safe, she uncovered her face and murmured, "Okay, we should talk. It's important."

"Oh, now you wanna talk? Are you kidding me?" A little annoyed, but curious enough to want an explanation on what was so important now that Grace needed to bust into my house and bedroom, I crossed the room, sat on the bed and waved my hand in an indication for her to speak.

She sighed and began to pace steadily back and forth along my bed, as though trying to decide what exactly to say. Stopping suddenly in front of me, she stared directly at my face and said, "Whilst I may not be one hundred percent ready to give you all the in and out details, you deserve to know the truth. I thought about it some more, and it turns out you don't need my help exactly, but I'm going to need yours."

She took a deep breath, exhaled, and said slowly, "So here goes. I'm not who you think I am. Well, no, actually I look like who you think I am, but who you think I am is not the person that I actually am."

I raised my eyebrows, taking a moment to try and make sense of her babble, but ended up more confused. Rubbing my left temple with my fingers I mumbled, "I literally have no idea what you're on about, but if you're smoking something trippy, you better share."

She sighed and began to roll her hands together, fiddling in a nervous manner. "Okay, maybe it will be easier if I just show you and we can go from there."

I waited for a few seconds, then nodded, I was nervous to see what she was apparently about to show me. She took a step back, took a deep breath in, hung her head forward and collapsed onto the floor in a slumped heap.

"What the heck, Grace!" I exclaimed jumping to my feet.

Once I caught up with what I was really seeing, I stopped dead still in my tracks. Grace's body was lying on the floor, seemingly asleep or knocked out, but where she had been standing just a moment before stood a transparent teenage girl, who had stepped out of her body as she had fallen. The same ghostly teenager I had seen just minutes ago in the bathroom.

Chapter Fifteen

"What the, what…who—*what* are you?" I spluttered, both confused and afraid.

She looked upset, even insulted, and motioned up and down her see-through body with her hands as though she had just performed a magic trick. When I didn't respond, her bottom lip dropped and she took a small step towards me.

"Oh no you don't!" I spat at her as I seized the closest thing I could find to threaten her with. I waved my hairbrush out in front of me as though it were a sword and moved a tiny step towards the closed bedroom door.

She looked down at the girl's body at her feet and then back up at me again. "Please don't try to run away, I don't want to hurt you," she said calmly.

The tone of her voice barely fluctuated and I couldn't tell if that had been meant as a threat or a genuine statement.

"If you'll just listen for a moment, I'll explain everything. No messing around, no jokes and no dancing around the truth this time," she said.

It was extremely creepy hearing the voice of the girl I'd gotten to know as Grace come out of the mouth of a ghost that looked nothing like her. I studied the body on the floor and felt somewhat more comfortable when I confirmed that her chest continued to move up and down, breathing away in her unconscious state.

I considered the ghost's offer for a moment and waved the hairbrush in a way that said, "Go on then."

She nodded, started pacing again, and began to recount her supposed explanation.

"I guess I'll just start at the beginning. The truth is, *I am* Mary Grayson. I used to live in this house, in this bedroom actually, eighteen years ago in 1987. I remember the day I died in vivid detail, like it happened just yesterday. Believe me, it plays over and over again in my head, on an endless loop. That morning, My father woke me in a panic, accusing me of murdering Owen in his sleep. Now, my dad wasn't the most patient man and lost his temper with me extremely quickly when I wouldn't confess, believing me to be a liar when I told him I didn't know what happened…and well, you already know what he did to me. But I swear I didn't do it, Liv. I couldn't murder my baby brother under my own power, I only ever protected him. Which is what I repeated to my dad, over and over again that day. I honestly don't remember anything about his death. I learned later, after my own death, that Agatha possessed me and wiped my memory clean.

Anyway, when I drowned, I remember a feeling of wonderful peace taking over my body and the next time I opened my eyes, I was standing there, watching over the scene as my father pulled my head out of the bathtub and dropped me with a thud onto the bathroom floor."

She stopped pacing and began to speak rather quickly, without taking a breath, as though she was afraid I would take off running if she didn't get to the point fast enough. Little did she know, I was now very much invested.

"It took me a few minutes to figure out what was going on, but I ended up realising that I had become a ghost." She paused and I stared at her as she started pacing again in front of me, tracing a smaller path whilst fiddling around with her hands and fingers.

I lowered the hairbrush slightly and took a moment to breathe and take it all in. Even after everything I'd already found out and been through, I was having a hard time processing her words. She stopped pacing and started talking again, but this time her words came out very slowly and she screwed up her face like she was struggling to remember.

"My mother, brother, and I, were all dead by the end of that day and for some reason, all became spirits unwillingly. We never even got the chance to move on, so much for the whole 'go into the light' deal, right? My father, however, disappeared after killing himself and we haven't seen him since. Mum doesn't even know if he became a spirit or just moved on instantly for some reason. Anyway, fast-forwarding to the important part. After I died, I remember watching as the paramedics saved Mum's baby. She spent the last few moments of her life stressing that they weren't going to get the baby out in time. Once she knew the c-section was successful, she slipped away. When she appeared beside me as a ghost, Mum freaked at first but was more worried the baby was now without a mother. Once she'd adjusted to the change, she was just relieved the baby had managed to survive and assumed that her newborn would be raised in the house by an adoptive parent until old enough to take ownership. But I knew that wouldn't be the case and I was right," she stopped for a moment to fold her arms. "They took him away from us."

"Him!" I gasped loudly.

Mary shot me a dirty, impatient look and I closed my mouth tightly waiting for her to continue.

"My mother and I tried countless times over several months to leave the house so we could see where he went and who he was given to. We wanted to follow and watch over him, but every time we tried to leave the house, we ended up being bungeed back like a rubber band. I soon realised that ghosts are only able to exist at the place where they died, and even then, the strength it takes to just make an appearance is rather draining.

It took almost five years of practicing, but eventually, I was able to stay out of the house for just long enough to track my brother down. As it turned out, he had been adopted pretty much straight away by a wonderful and well-known local television reporter, who had been trying with little success to adopt a child since her husband's death. By the time I found him, she had also adopted a second child—a baby girl two years younger than him, whom she named Grace. Seeing them together and how happy they were as a family, I admit, I got a little jealous in the moment and lost control of my ability to stay out of my 'death bubble'. I got sucked back to this stupid house in an instant and it took a long time to regenerate enough power and strength to leave again.

My first point of call, when I managed to leave again years later, was to look into the files on my family to see what had become of the house and our family belongings, I had been wondering why no one else had moved in. As it turned out, my father had willed the house to your father and the police were more than happy to abide by those instructions to keep their paperwork straightforward and move past our deaths as quickly and easily as possible. They had even covered up the tragedy as much as they could by handing my brother over to a desperate adoptive parent without any information on his family background, birth mother or birthplace, a condition of his adoption not many people would accept.

Whilst I am grateful that he went to someone who has truly loved and cared for him all these years like he was her own, he has no idea of who his real family is, or where he came from. I figured the only way I was going to be able to tell him who he really was, was to get out of this house as more than just a ghost and become a part of his life. At the time, I figured the easiest way to do that was to possess his adoptive sister.

Over the years you see, it just got more and more torturous being stuck here, you know. We know it's Agatha's doing, she feeds on our pain. We feel it. So, about a year ago, I gathered my strength, left the house and figured out how to merge myself into her body, like a live-in possession I suppose. Matthew Maker is my little brother, Liv, and he is the only one who is safe here, the only one who can destroy Agatha and bring us all peace. I've been possessing Grace this past year, trying to tell him but all he ever got from it was the idea in his head that it was Grace who was born the Grayson's baby."

I felt as though I'd been punched in the stomach. *Matt* was baby boy Grayson and all this time I'd been getting information from a dead girl playing puppeteer who'd been walking around and controlling sixteen-year-old Grace Maker's body. I had known right from the day I had met her that she was strange but this, this was just too much crazy.

"Please tell me you're joking," I whispered.

Mary shook her head at me. "No I'm not, but I'm desperate," she laughed softly.

I didn't even feel close to laughter. I just stared at her and waited for her to tell me it was all a prank. But she didn't. I slid down the wall near my bed and sat with my knees pulled up to my chest. Looking up at her I said, "So…wait, I haven't even really met Grace Maker? This whole time it's just been you? How does that work, does she know what's going on?"

She nodded slowly and shrugged. "Honestly, I have no idea. I think on some level she does, but I'm fairly sure she just thinks she's asleep and dreaming."

Curiosity was building fast within me, I felt there were still so many unanswered questions. There was however two linked questions that stood out more than the rest, so I asked simply, "Why is Matt safe here? Why is he the only one who can get rid of Agatha?"

Mary sighed. "Because…" she started but then trailed off into silence.

A second voice piped up, seemingly coming from nowhere. "Because I believe he can't be affected by Agatha's mind control."

I looked around, thinking I was imagining it for a moment, until the voice's owner popped up out of thin air beside her daughter. Mrs Penelope Grayson. She continued solemnly, "From what we've worked out, Agatha's spirit works differently to ours for some reason, maybe due to bad intentions or an evil soul, but for some reason, she can't just possess anyone she wants. Instead, she seems to use some kind of mind control to make them do her bidding. I believe Matt should be protected, though."

"I-I don't understand," I stammered.

Wheezing, she said, "I think it's a blood-to-blood connection of some kind. Agatha's mind control power seems to only affect anyone blood-related to her. See, Arthur…. he's really her half-brother. When he was fifteen, he discovered—not long after I found out I was pregnant with Mary actually—that he was conceived in an affair his mother had during the time she was a maid working for the Claytons. His biological father was George Clayton. He showed up on George's doorstep when he found out and basically tore their family apart, ending with Agatha walking out after she and George blew up in a huge fight. Later, when Agatha found out her parents had been murdered, she blamed Arthur and was hell-bent on destroying him and his whole family. In her eyes, if he hadn't shown up, she wouldn't have left, and they wouldn't have been alone the night they died."

I held up my hand to interrupt her. "Wait, do you think that's why she's after my family too? Just because technically we're blood relatives of Arthur's or something?"

Mrs Grayson nodded and said with a chuckle, "It's the only thing that makes sense to me, unless you think someone in your family was the cause of her parent's deaths too."

I nodded stiffly and waited for her to continue. She paused for a moment and held her belly, seeming to need a second to gather enough strength to talk. "Anyway, to add to the situation, the baby I was pregnant with when we moved here, well, he's not Arthur's biological son. I myself had a brief affair when my marriage began to faulter, not too long before we moved to Bellicose. Not only is my youngest son not a blood relative of Agatha, he was also born in the house, just like Agatha was. He's connected in ways even I don't understand. Therefore can and must be the one to banish Agatha's spirit and set ours free. I think."

"You think?" I spluttered, raising my eyebrows.

She stopped briefly to glance around the room, seemingly nervous. "Well, there's never really been a chance to test that theory, has there? I've only been able to piece together information from what I know and have researched over the years, where I can. Resources as a ghost are slim, you know. And I know that Agatha has always been frightened about Matthew finding out his real identity and coming home. There's an aura change throughout the house whenever his name is mentioned. We spend every day of our existence in hiding, trying not to stay out in the open too long. If we do, something starts to suck the energy out of us like a painful vacuum cleaner, making you feel like you're going to disappear into the abyss. It's the most awful feeling in the world. We get weaker every day and I know we don't have much time left. It's like she uses us like a battery recharger and soon, she'll have enough power to end your family too. Matty is the only one who can stop us from disappearing altogether, give us a chance to move on and save your family from ending up like ours."

Absolutely bewildered, I stood up slowly and collected my thoughts. "Well then, how does Matt supposedly banish her? You know this all barely makes any sense to me, so how are we supposed to convince *him* that any of this is even true? You're basing all of this off some theory you created." I was getting slightly annoyed now, the whole situation was ridiculous.

Mary suddenly decided to chime in, "Now you know why I haven't been able to find a way to tell him; he'll think it's just a made-up story coming from his little sister. I didn't think about that side of it when I chose Grace, but I didn't know what else to do. Do you remember that little knife that I helped you find in your dream?"

I frowned, "Well, yeah but how do you know about that dream…? I never told you I found the knife because of a dream, did I?"

Mary shrugged and said casually, "I gave it to you. The dream I mean. I projected it into your head. That knife is the same one she used to kill herself and is the key to releasing her spirit. It's an ancient, ritualistic knife she tracked down and bought when she was alive and trying to bring her parents back from the dead. She thought it had the power to release a ghost from the netherworld but, as it turns out, it does the opposite. That knife has the ability to trap the soul of a ghost from their remains. Call the blood spatter in the wall her remains I suppose, but that blood is what's keeping her connected to the house. Whilst the blood remains on the wall, her spirit is tethered to this house. Anyway, to get rid of her, Matt must take the knife and push the blade into the centre of the wall where Agatha spilt her blood. Trust me, I did a bunch of research on it when I noticed how protective she was of that knife. Agatha left a bunch of her old books in the basement.

If Matt can successfully plunge that knife into the wall, into her remains, it'll trap her spirit and essentially, banish her from this house, which in turn severs the ties she has over our souls. Think of it like putting a key to a lock. She'll be forced into oblivion, and we can finally cross over. We're all trapped here because of her in a twisted version of her unfinished business. As soon as you told me she tried to make you kill your brother, I knew she was getting stronger and I had to get a move on and tell you the truth. Don't you see, I don't have any memory whatsoever of being under her control when she used me to kill Owen, but you do. Obviously, her strength is growing. She will not stop coming after you until her revenge is carried out. She'll haunt you and possess you and then make it seem like you had some sort of fatal accident or family tragedy, exactly like what we went through. We've had a long time to figure all this out, you know."

I was trying desperately to keep up, confused about so many things. "Oh goody," I said sarcastically. "I'm glad you have this all figured out then. He's not going to believe me you know; this whole 'plan' is useless."

She sniggered and gave a cheeky smile. "Now, this is where you have an advantage over me. Do you really think it will be hard for you to convince Matt? You could probably say anything to him, and he'll believe it in a moment. I've seen the way he looks at you. Use his crush on you to your advantage."

I could feel myself blushing. "Crush? Yeah right, we've only just decided to be friends. I barely even know him!" I protested, making a disgruntled face, yet was unable to stop a smile from forming.

"Wait a minute," I said, realising something, "Isn't it a bit weird encouraging his attraction to me? Aren't we technically cousins or something?"

Mrs Grayson shook her head. "My husband was your father's cousin, but Matt isn't his biological son, remember? Therefore, you aren't related. Go ahead and bat your eyelashes as you please, it may help."

Overloaded with information, I took a deep breath and mumbled, "All I can do is try, I guess." Mary's face contorted with anger as she dropped her hands to her sides and balled them into fists before leaning forward and swooping towards me so fast that it was a painful blur.

Chapter Sixteen

Mary's popping eyes filled my entire view as she yelled at me, "If you want to end up like me, you'll 'try'. If you want to survive and save your whole frickin' family, you'll do better than 'try'!"

I barely had time to open my mouth before she narrowed her eyes at me, turned on the spot and dropped to the floor, instantly fusing back into Grace's unconscious body. It was the weirdest thing I'd ever witnessed. Possibly.

A few seconds later, Grace, or rather Mary encased by Grace, lifted herself up off the floor. I cringed as she turned to face me. I was so creeped out by the very idea of a ghost-filled human just walking around like normal. She shot me a snotty look and stormed out of my bedroom in a huff. I swallowed and thought to myself, what a hell of a mood swing!

Left alone with Mrs Grayson for the first time without fearing her, I remembered the creepy curtain incident from earlier that day and found myself asking, "So, since we've cleared everything up, any chance the creepy whispering thing can stop now?"

She looked at me quizzically. "Sorry dear, I don't know what you mean. I haven't been whispering to you." And with that, she smiled at me and vanished on the spot, leaving me alone with my thoughts.

Interesting. I crossed the room and flung open the door, hurrying down the hallway. I ended up in the kitchen and as my stomach started to growl, I realised why my body had led me there. Anxious snacking was very much needed at this point. As I checked the fridge for something, anything to satisfy my stomach, I found myself wondering where my mother had gotten to. I figured she was probably in her room now, hiding away. I was quite devastated myself, but I couldn't compare to how Mum must have been feeling about Dad's attempt at suicide.

My eyes fixed on a bowl of green jelly that someone must have decided to make at some point during the day. I grabbed the bowl and a spoon from the cutlery drawer beside the sink and lowered myself into a chair. I found myself desperately racking my brain for the right wording I was going to use to tell Matt who he was and what he had to do to save his whole family, and mine.

My mind wandered as I thought about what Mary and Mrs Grayson had said. There were still a few details that didn't make a whole lot of sense to me, but I figured they must know what they were talking about. They'd had eighteen years to figure it all out after all. For now, I had one simple job to do. Get Matt to come home and save us all. I felt like a complete idiot even thinking it, like I was supposed to be a featured heroine in some stupid horror film. I rolled my eyes as I wondered how my life had become so weird and so complicated so very quickly.

Isabelle and Noah came home not long after I'd polished off the bowl of jelly. The next few hours were a blur. None of us knew what to say and our actions towards each other became mechanical and robotic, like we had all been switched to autopilot. Mum avoided being near us at all. I considered texting Matt, but realised there wasn't much I would be able to say at this point without blurting out everything I really wanted to say to him, and those things definitely had to be said in person.

I was more than ready to ditch my family after dinner and hole up in my bedroom, so I trudged upstairs and allowed myself to collapse onto my bed. I couldn't stop thinking about Matt and was ashamed of myself for wanting desperately to message him rather than Sam. To make myself feel better, I text both of them goodnight. Sam in a loving way and Matt in a way that made it seem casual, like I was looking forward to hanging out some time, but not too eager. Then, for some reason, for the first time all week, I slept a peaceful, dreamless sleep.

The next morning, I woke up to the sound of dull yelling coming from down the hall. It sounded as though Noah was getting chewed out by Mum for the state of his bedroom. Feeling grateful for not being the target of her grief-fuelled rage, I stretched out in an effort to get myself vertical. Today I was going to focus on Matt. Or rather, focus on telling him who he really was.

I still wasn't quite sure how I was going to do that, but it seemed I didn't have much of a choice. Mary was obviously too chicken to give it to him straight. How in one whole year does a person not manage to tell someone a tiny bit of information about their birth?

Unfortunately, by the end of the week, I had more of an understanding of how time could disappear with no further efforts made. It seemed every time I had the chance to see him after school, he was busy, either helping his mother or already out and about hanging with mates. Finally, the weekend arrived, and I figured I didn't care what he was doing. I needed to speak with him and would have to just show up instead of asking first. Throughout the week, there had been several more incidents involving my family members getting hurt in seemingly random accidents and we'd been lucky so far no one else had ended up in hospital. Isabelle got burned when the stove caught fire after it had already been turned off. Mum smashed her head when she walked into the laundry and slipped in a giant pool of laundry detergent that was somehow spilt in the doorway. She was the only one home at the time.

I strategically decided to wear a short, pretty summer dress and styled my hair in such a way as to compliment it. Avoiding my mother at all costs, I slipped down the stairs and called out behind me as I headed for the front door, "Going to a mate's place, be home later!"

I made a beeline for the Maker's house, or at least the street I figured their house was on having run into Matt twice on it. As I strode along, I planned out in my head for the right wording to use to let him in on his family background without making myself sound crazy. There was no easy way to explain, so I figured jumping right into it would probably be the easiest way. I had nothing to lose anyway.

As I made my way down their street, I thankfully could already see him in the distance, bent over a beat-up old car's engine in what I presumed was the Maker's driveway. His shirt was off, making me less eager to talk to him. I could already feel stirrings of crush-like feelings awakening deep inside me, even though I knew I shouldn't.

He looked up just as I got to the end of his driveway and smiled, wiping his forehead free of the sweat dripping across it. Hitching his jeans up, he remarked loudly, "Hey Liv, what brings you here? Grace's inside if you wanted to see her."

I shook my head, "No, uh, that's okay." Closing my eyes for a moment, I braced myself and said, "I actually came to talk to you."

He looked happy for a moment, then slightly confused, but nodded, "Okay, what's up?"

I gestured to the street whilst checking over his shoulder towards the house. "Erm, did you want to go for a walk or something?"

He agreed, now with an on-edge tone and threw the rag he was holding into a nearby bucket.

Just as we were about to walk off, the front door of his house opened, and Grace Maker shuffled out. I was curious to see what kind of attitude Mary was going to have towards me today. I was still trying to wrap my head around it, the thought of a ghost walking around living inside an unaware teenage girl's body made my skin crawl.

"Oh, hello Olivia," she said seriously as she crossed the driveway towards Matt and me. "How are you today? What kind of interesting news might you be here to tell my brother?"

Matt frowned, even he seemed to realise something was weird about her tone. "Get lost Gracie," he piped up. He then put a hand on my shoulder and steered me towards the road.

I looked back just as Grace smirked and I could almost see Mary's face shine through her eyes during the stare-down she was giving me. I nodded at her as a sign of understanding and continued walking away with Matt.

We had gotten right to the end of the street before he broke the silence and asked, "So, what was it you wanted to tell me? Is everything ok with the boyfriend?" He sounded somewhat cheery now, like he was expecting good news.

I hated myself suddenly. Why did I have to give him the opposite? Figuring I'd start off with the simplest of questions, I asked, "Matt, did you know that you were adopted?"

He stopped walking and nodded. "Yeah, since I was like, eight. Why? How do *you* know about that?"

I was relieved. That was at least a foot in the door. "Let's just say I'm invested. And would I be right in guessing that you don't know anything about your birth parents?"

He began walking again, very slowly. "Not really. I mean, I've asked my mother more times than I can remember, but she swears even she was never given any information about them. It was a condition of my adoption, to take me without having any medical or family background records. I don't know who my parents were, but I despise them for that. I have always wondered what was so wrong with me or my biological mother that I was chucked away without a second thought about my future." He sighed and looked away from me, as though ashamed of showing me his true feelings.

I almost rubbed his shoulder in sympathy but didn't want to get too emotional with him in case he got the wrong idea. "And what about your sister?" I asked.

He shrugged. "I think Mum has all her records, but she has never shown them to either of us. She keeps that kind of stuff hidden away. I think she just doesn't want us to know who Grace's birth family was, considering she was pretty much born whilst her mother was dying, that's not exactly knowledge I reckon anyone wants to have. Although, I'll admit, Grace has been acting really weird this last year or so. Like, a whole different person. I reckon that's when she found out who she was because that's when she started going to the cemetery."

I grimaced, thinking for a moment about what to say next. I decided to try Mary's advice for the big "reveal" and began batting my eyelashes like an idiot, trying to look charming.

He frowned at me with a weird look on his face, so I abruptly cut the act, shook my head and said seriously, "So what if I were to tell you…that it wasn't actually Grace who was born a Grayson?"

Matt stopped, turned and stayed silent for a few moments before saying, "What do you mean?"

I repeated the question and before he could answer or say anything else, I added, "It was you."

He laughed nervously. "You're kidding."

I shook my head. "I'm sorry, I'm not. It was you, Matt. Not your sister. That's why *you* have no birth records. That's why no one wanted to tell your adoptive mother where you came from. You were born into the greatest tragedy this town has seen. And everyone wanted to wipe it clean."

He stared at me, pain swirling in his eyes. "You have no idea what you're talking about." He turned on his heel and began to walk away.

I grabbed his arm in an attempt to stop him, but was unsuccessful as he wrenched it out of my grasp.

Angrily, he snapped, "You know, I thought you were a pretty decent chick, but I guess I was wrong. This isn't funny. Stay the hell away from me."

A little hurt, I spurted out, "Matt, wait, your family needs you. My family needs you!"

He gave me a disgusted look and continued storming away. Well, that couldn't have gone any worse. I hurriedly chased after him at a fast walk.

He outran me by a mile, but I eventually ended up back at his house where I found him kneeling in a crumpled heap in the driveway with a hand on his head and the other wrapped around what looked to be a newspaper clipping. Grace was standing behind him with a hand on his shoulder, a saddened look on her face. I approached with caution and leaned over to see what he was reading.

It was a piece of crumpled page torn from an old newspaper. Observing closer, I realised it was the missing page from the article at the library about the Grayson deaths. Mary must have been keeping it in Grace's room all along.

Matt looked up at me with a mixture of disappointment and sadness on his face. I could see tears forming in the corners of his eyes. He brushed his hand across his eyes quickly and held out the clipping for me to see. "This is where you got your information?" he asked simply.

"No, not exactly. I mean, I was looking for it at one stage, but it was torn out of the papers at the library. I found out…from, erm someone at school." I glanced sideways at Grace, who appeared very guilty and stressed.

Matt held the clipping out further, indicating I should take it from him. I gently took the paper from his outstretched hand and read the cutout.

August 2nd, 1987

Bellicose has been left in shock following the deaths of four residents in the early hours of this morning. Further investigations are underway, however, it is alleged that Miss Mary Grayson,15,brutally stabbed her 5-year-old brother, Owen, to death whilst he slept, before being tragically drowned in the bathtub by her father. Further evidence suggests that an enraged Mr Grayson then attempted to murder his wife, Penelope Grayson, by throwing her through the kitchen window shortly before taking his own life.

Mrs Grayson, who was 38 weeks pregnant at the time, survived her husband's attack for a short while, and attending paramedics were able to stabilise her for long enough to deliver her baby, passing away moments after his arrival. The Grayson's infant, a healthy baby boy, is currently in the care of a foster family until a permanent home can be found. The Grayson family, Arthur, Penelope, Mary & Owen, will forever be in our memory. Further details will be released when forensics have completed a toxin screening on the bodies and put together a more conclusive list of events.

I felt awful for him. Grace and I exchanged glances before I looked back at Matt. He stood up, took the clipping from me, folded it up and tucked it away in his jeans. "My birthday is August 2nd, 1987," he stated softly.

I gave him an understanding half smile, reached out and patted his arm. He quickly pulled me into a tight hug instead, resting his head down on my shoulder.

One moment it was a hug of friendship, the next I could feel his arm slide down my lower back into a more romantic embrace. In a moment of weakness, I felt myself accepting his actions and embraced him back—until I realised what I was doing.

When I wiggled out of his grasp, he quickly apologised and casually stretched out his arms and shook out his hair, looking slightly guilty.

From behind him, Grace gave me a smirk and the, "I told you so" look.

"I should go," I said quickly, suddenly feeling uncomfortable enough to leave.

Matt looked somewhat disappointed, but shook my hand and said softly, "Thank you."

I smiled at him and began to head home.

Grace caught up with me and planted herself in my path, seemingly angry. "You haven't even made a dent in it," she whispered harshly, pointing her index finger at my face with vigour.

"Back off Mary, just let him process one thing at a time," I snapped back. "Even if you couldn't have managed to tell him about the supernatural stuff, you could have at least told him who *he* was ages ago! Would have sped up this whole process now, wouldn't it."

She pursed her lips, threw her hands on her hips and muttered, "Well taking it slowly *now* won't help any of us! You do realise Agatha is going to make another attempt on you at some point soon, right? Do you want to end up like me?"

I pushed her aside with the back of my hand and kept walking, calling over my shoulder to her as I powered forward. "You've had a whole year to tell him and haven't. I deserve at least the weekend."

Chapter Seventeen

Almost a week passed and by Thursday afternoon I found myself starting to wonder if I'd dreamt the last few weeks. Things had been extremely settled, to the point where I wasn't sure anything I'd seen within the house was real. No noises or whispers haunted me at night and no ghosts made an appearance, not even briefly. Not once had anything out of the ordinary haunted me. I hadn't seen Grace, or rather Mary wearing Grace, at school the whole week either. It appeared Mary wanted to avoid me. I'd even been to her house to try and talk to her, but conveniently every time I'd go, she was never home.

The only reason I knew the whole thing hadn't been an illusion was because of Matt. We'd hung out a few times now on the afternoons I tried to visit his sister and texted back and forth throughout the week. He'd asked me a few times if I knew any more information about his biological family and was persistent on knowing where I'd gotten my information from in the first place. I always just changed the subject and focused on happier things, things that didn't make the pit of my stomach hit the floor. I could understand his desire to know as much about his family as possible, but found I couldn't bring myself to tell him the twisted truth. That they were still in the house and needed his help to move on.

Since Mary had started avoiding me, Matt was the only friend I had. I didn't want to sever our newfound friendship by telling him that he had to save both his family and mine from a murderous spirit that was still currently living in my house. Perhaps I was being a bit selfish, but I enjoyed Matt's company too much to lose him. He was the only person I had to talk to outside of the house. No one else ever bothered to try and talk to me at school as it seemed everyone now considered me just the weird kid living in the severely haunted house.

I hadn't forgotten about Sam though and ensured all conversations with Matt remained strictly friendly. Although it wasn't the same as being able to see him all the time, I found myself calling Sam a lot more throughout the week though, perhaps out of guilt from talking to Matt so much. I was annoyed at myself for enjoying Matt's company more than I'd ever really enjoyed Sam's.

That evening, after a few mindless hours of attempting to relax in bed, I decided to take a bath once everyone else had gone to sleep. I felt like I deserved a little bit of time to breathe, finally feeling somewhat settled into my new life after a long transition period. That, as well as visiting my father every evening at the hospital had led to a very exhausting week, requiring a good, long soaking.

However, even though the house and spirits had finally given me a break, all that did was give me more time to do research in an attempt to understand how the ghosts operated and had a place in our world. Plus, there was a huge exam coming up at school I'd been dutifully studying for, thus my need to actually go to the school library in the first place.

Interestingly enough, during my free time, I had discovered that the little snippets I'd been seeing from the last moments of the Grayson's lives were called "Echoes." They could happen at random to anyone, but usually could only be triggered in the exact place where a violent, abrupt, or unresolved death actually occurred.

Laying back in a very full tub, I closed my eyes, sunk into the bubbles, and allowed my mind to drift off, blissfully unaware of the world around me. It was then that I felt someone tug on my foot, nearly pulling me underwater. Shocked, I gasped loudly and ripped my foot out of their grasp, looking around wildly to see who it was.

Grace was sitting at the end of the tub glaring at me with her arms crossed. "Seriously dude, what are you doing?" I said exasperated, covering my bubbled-up bare chest with my arms.

"So much for one weekend, hey," she remarked, clearly snooty and agitated. I sighed, rolling my eyes at her.

"Mary, in case you've forgotten, I didn't ask for the duty of telling Matt all of this stuff. I thought that was your job. Isn't that why you're still living inside his sister?"

Her eyes narrowed in at me even more and she muttered through clenched teeth, "Adoptive sister. And yes, yes it is. But then you came to town and spared me the responsibility. Once I found out your family was involved in all of this too, I knew it would be a thousand times easier for you to give him the news. How do you honestly think he's going to react if I step out of this body and say, 'Hey guess what, I'm your dead sister and you have to destroy the spirit who possessed me and my father, killing our whole family in the process before she possesses and kills your girlfriend's family too and then sucks all our souls dry.' Yep, you're right, that will go great. He hasn't seen any of us, or any ghosts for that matter. He would freak. At least you're alive, you can tell him in a normal way."

I rolled my eyes again, re-adjusting my body under the layer of bubbles to keep my exposed chest hidden. "Normal way? What don't you understand, there is no *normal* way. Sure, maybe you telling him would make him think he's going crazy, but if I break the news then he's going to think that I'm crazy. So, you tell me what makes more sense. And by the way, I'm *not* his girlfriend. We're just friends, I still have a boyfriend from my old life."

Mary appeared deep in thought for a moment, before standing up and declaring, "Fine! I can't stay here long, but I need you to realise that Agatha is getting more pissed by the day. Why do you think it's been so quiet? Why do you think she's left you alone? Why do you think you haven't seen my Mum or Owen around?

Because Agatha is gearing up. She's draining them, powering up and getting ready to go all out on your family. Considering she came after you first, I think she's going to follow the same pattern she did last time. The longer you wait, the stronger she's getting. She's sucking the souls out of my family, weakening them in preparation to take you and your father completely over. I've spent the last couple of days trying to find out what it means when a ghost vanishes in a fireball. From what I can tell, it's pretty bad—I think it means the process is complete and the spirit has been fully destroyed. When we die, if we earned a spot in the better place, we should get to step into a warm, white light. Ever heard of the phrase, 'Go into the light?' Even the bad ones don't go up in a flaming fireball, they just get sucked into a dark, black void." She crossed her arms and glared at me.

When I didn't move or respond in any way, she bent and splashed water in my face.

"Ugh, Olivia, time is running out! I know she's after my soul, I can feel her trying to pull me back to this house. It gets harder and harder every day to stay attached to Grace. Mum and Owen frequently move around, popping in and out from the ghostly plane so they dodge her and all week I've been trying to stay as far away from this place as possible, but I couldn't keep waiting for you to say something to Matt. We really need him now, before it is actually too late."

I held a hand to my cheek, attempting to get a grip on my emotions. It wasn't over. I couldn't believe I'd let myself think the nightmare had just gotten better, or better yet—gone away. I had a sudden urge to sink under the water and not return to the surface. "Okay, okay. I'll go see him tomorrow."

Mary looked relieved and nodded before looking around nervously, then left in a hurry. I wondered how she'd even gotten up to the bathroom without my parents noticing. She must have been extremely stealthy. I shrugged it off and slid out of the tub, grabbing my favourite towel from the wall-mounted rack and wrapping myself in it. As I then turned and leaned down into the bath to pull out the plug, my head swirled in a wave of extreme dizziness and filled with a terrifying scene.

I was sucked instantly into a parallel world, and as reality disappeared around me, I realised I'd felt something like this before. I could feel a large, firm hand gripping the back of my neck and a clump of my hair that was wrapped around their fingers on a second hand being yanked on every time they moved. I realised quickly that my head was being held down into the bath well as the water began to rise towards my face.

I could hear a distant voice yelling, obscured by the sound of the water splashing into the tub, and someone else was screaming and crying, but I could barely focus as waves of pain shot up through my neck and head. I started kicking and throwing my arms up around my head, attempting to free myself from the firm grip that had a hold of me as the water quickly filled up, nearing the tip of my nose. I could tell it was no use and felt my heart sink as I accepted that he was too strong for me. He pushed my head down further the harder I fought and within seconds the water began to lick my face.

Before long, I was unable to breathe and began to suffocate underwater. I gave one last burst of effort in a desperate final attempt to free myself before the world went black and in an instant my legs gave way and I crumpled into a heap on the floor.

Hitting my head on the side of the tub as the memory was sucked away and I became me again, I took a huge breath and cried out in pain. I knew instantly I'd been in Mary's echo, the memory of the last few moments of her life. I felt awful for her, the real experience must have been a thousand times worse.

I picked myself up off the floor, my body uncontrollably shaking as I attempted to stand up straight. Realising the towel had come loose in my struggle, I collected it from the floor and wrapped myself up again. I hated having to experience these moments and wondered why they kept happening to me specifically. Random my ass, I scoffed silently. I breathed in deeply, gratefully inhaling as much oxygen as I wanted and took a moment to calm down and stop shaking before leaving the bathroom.

As I edged down the hall in the darkness, an uneasy feeling swept over me. I knew I was being watched, again. Picking up my pace whilst checking behind me every now and then, I managed to trip on a slightly frayed and upturned section of the rug near the top of the stairs, falling forward into a kneeling position.

As I nursed my poor carpet burnt knees, a voice whispered from somewhere close behind me, "Bring the boy home now, before it's too late."

I flicked my head around as quickly as it would turn, but just as I suspected, there was no one physically there.

A thumping sound came from the stairwell, and I found myself whipping back in the other direction, trying to see what had made the noise. As though watching an old black and white silent horror film, I could make out a shadowy, masculine figure standing near me at the top of the stairwell. He was gripping the shoulders of a middle-aged woman, who was terrified beyond words. I couldn't see his face, but they were clearly in a physical argument, and he was shaking her viciously. Within seconds, the man pushed her down the stairs without mercy.

It felt like my heart was about to burst out of my chest at the speed it was racing, but I couldn't tear my eyes away as I watched her tumble down the stairs, inaudibly screaming. As though satisfied, the man began to turn around, with the intent of continuing upstairs. Even though I knew they weren't real, I froze momentarily as I expected him to come towards me, but instead, he vanished into thin air right before I got a glimpse of his face. I collected myself in a hurry and raced over to the stairwell, looking down into the darkness. The woman had, of course, vanished also.

Another echoed memory perhaps? My skin wanted to crawl off my body and slither far away from this house. I was almost too scared to continue walking back to my bedroom, but at the same time, I wanted to hide away safely tucked in my bed. The intensity of the echoed memories in the house were getting to be so frequent it was almost too much for me to bear. I wondered what would happen if they became so powerful, they became real, and I died in the same way. I was beginning to think Mary was right, the sooner I could get Matt here the better. He may not believe me, but I would have to actually try. I missed the peace and quiet the past few days had provided.

Turning around and tiptoeing down the hall, I tried everything possible to shake the bad feelings away and pretend I was fine. A loose floorboard outside my bedroom creaked loudly as I reached for the door handle. Screwing up my face, I waited momentarily to see if anyone had been alerted to the sound.

Seconds later, Isabelle appeared in her doorway, half asleep and rubbing her eyes.

"Oh, hey Belle," I said casually.

She peered down the hallway at me, stretching out her back. "It's like two in the morning, what are you doing?"

I shrugged. "Couldn't sleep so I went for a bath. Did I wake you?"

She shook her head and rubbed her belly before sniggering, "Nah, baby bladder. Had to pee."

I smiled as she began waddling down the hallway, heading for the bathroom.

I felt like I almost had to prepare myself to enter my own bedroom. For some reason, I was afraid to go to bed. I couldn't explain it, but something was holding me back. Then, there literally was something holding me back. A hand clamped down on my shoulder and forcibly spun me around.

Trying not to scream when I came face to face with her, I chose instead to jam my fist in my mouth. It was the same elderly woman I'd seen just before Mum told me about Dad's accident, the one who'd been smothered by the strange mist. The one I'd just seen in the echo on the stairs.

She smiled at me before patting my shoulder sympathetically and said two simple words, "Please, help."

When she spoke, I knew immediately why I recognised her voice. It was the same voice who'd been whispering to me all along, first in bed, then in the curtains. The voice I'd originally assumed was Penelope Grayson. I didn't know what to say to her, so I fell silent in the hope that she'd actually talk to me properly this time.

And that she did, in a hurry.

"I don't have much time. My name is Evelyn Clayton. You likely know of me as Agatha's mother. My husband, George, has already been destroyed, burned out of existence forever and I'm getting weaker by the hour. Please, you don't understand, my daughter isn't—"

She then suddenly screeched out an ear-piercing shriek as her whole body caught fire.

Completely startled, I jumped back in fear as I watched her burn before me. Swallowed in seconds by a ball of flames, the ghost of Mrs Clayton was gone. As though non-existent, the fire burned out the second it consumed her with no evidence left behind.

I fell sideways into the wall and rubbed my forehead, trying to make sense of what she had managed to get out, which hadn't been a whole lot of useful information. What could she have been trying to tell me? Obviously, whatever it was, was enough to ensure she was gotten rid of immediately. I wondered if anyone else had heard her scream. No one had come running, so I figured probably not.

Coming around, I reached out again for my door and took a step forward, only to slip, stumble, and fall headfirst into the wall. Nursing my now sore face, I looked down to see what I'd slipped on. It was a pool of blood, collecting on the floor as it ran down the wall. The wall beside my door was bleeding.

Chapter Eighteen

Completely freaked, I gasped and stumbled backward, only just managing to catch my balance. Staring mesmerised and unsure what to do, I was a little surprised when Isabelle toddled back up the hallway, oblivious to my terror.

"Night," she muttered as she passed by.

How could she have possibly missed it? There was a puddle of blood pooling on the floor and a fast-moving trickle running down the walls, which was slowly filling it up. Unless, of course, there was nothing to see. Maybe I was imagining it, or hallucinating. "Please be an illusion," I whispered. I closed my eyes briefly and when I opened them, I got my answer.

The walls and floor were as clean as a whistle. I was starting to get annoyed with myself. Why? Why was I seeing things that weren't even there? I hadn't found anything in any book about hallucinations involving blood pouring from walls. I asked myself if it was Agatha toying with me, or if there was more meaning behind it.

The next afternoon after school, I messaged Matt asking if he wanted to meet up to hang out. I had to get out of the house anyway since Mum had hired a repair company and they had a whole team of tradies out fixing the hole in the living room floor and I couldn't stand listening to the banging, clanging and machinery noises any longer. Thankfully, Matt seemed eager to hang out with me and I couldn't help but feel bad for the information I was about to load him up with. But it was time to get this over with, to do or die. Maybe literally.

We agreed to meet at Mirsey Park, which was just down the road from the high school. If you could call it a park that is. I had heard others call it, "Misery Park," which was much more fitting. It consisted only of a barbecue, a set of two swings, a picnic bench, and a single metal slide no one could use because the sun roasted it all day long.

When I got there, Matt hadn't arrived yet so I made my way across to the swing set to wait for him. Swinging back and forth slowly, I breathed in the fresh air and used the spare time to decide exactly what I was going to say to him. He came jogging around the corner not long after I'd started swinging higher, a huge smile on his face as he waved to me.

"Hey, you," I called out as he got closer, planting my feet into the dirt to bring the swing to a halt.

He grinned even wider and slid into the swing beside me. "Hey! So, what's the hot gossip? I kind of got the impression there was something wrong; you seemed a bit, er, stiff when you asked if I wanted to meet up."

I gave him a half nod and stared at the chain holding my swing up for a few moments, temporarily finding myself unable to look him in the eyes. I sighed.

"Yeah, I actually do have something important to tell you and I'm pretty sure you're not going to like it. You may even think I'm crazy, but just bear with me, okay?"

He frowned and gave a half-hearted shrug. "Okay…"

I closed my eyes for a moment and braced myself. "So, here's the deal. I know your hidden birth identity is new information to you and all, but you obviously know all about the manor you were born in, right? You grew up already knowing its history, even though you didn't know you were a part of it. Well, the truth is—"

I was cut off by the sound of Matt's phone ringing.

He politely looked at me as though waiting for permission to answer it.

Sighing, I indicated he should take the call with my head and waited in silence.

He apologised, got up and walked a few metres from me before answering the phone.

After a few minutes, he came back with a slightly concerned, yet annoyed look on his face. "That was Mum. I'm sorry, I've gotta go. Grace wasn't at school today, hasn't been home this afternoon at all and Mum didn't even see her before school this morning. She has to go into work and she wants me to be home in case Grace shows up."

"Oh, okay, no worries," I mumbled, getting up in preparation to leave.

"You can come with me if you like?" He smiled. "I mean, you still have something to tell me, right?"

I nodded, grateful I wouldn't have to start all over again another day and we set off down the street for his house.

Upon our arrival, Matt walked me into the living room and made a break for the kitchen, insistent on pouring me a drink. It was the first time I'd been inside the house. Every other time I'd come around, Matt and I just ended up hanging out in the garage or lounging on the banana chairs on the front porch. I walked around slowly whilst I waited, looking at all the family photos on the walls of Matt and Grace growing up. I couldn't help but adore how cute he was as a little kid.

Out of the corner of my eye, I noticed a large wedding photo was the central attraction on the TV stand, which peaked my curiosity, as I knew Matt's adoptive mother was widowed.

For an old photo, it was very well cared for and the top of the frame itself was even engraved with the words, "Forever and always, Mr and Mrs Maker." Picking it up gently, I smiled at the happy couple and couldn't help but feel pity for Matt's mother. She had obviously loved him very much.

Matt came back into the room holding two glasses of what looked like bright red juice and offered one to me. I wasn't overly keen on drinking it considering it looked identical to the blood that I'd seen running down the walls at home, but I was thirsty. I placed the photo back on the stand and took the glass from him graciously.

"This is your Mum?" I asked, gesturing towards the photo.

Matt nodded his head, "Yeah, her name is Lynne. That's her late husband, Peter. She still refers to him as Dad when she talks about him to me and my sister. I never met him of course, he passed away before she adopted either of us."

I gave a slight nod and asked, "She never remarried?"

"Nah she's never even been interested in dating; says he was the love of her life. She doesn't talk about his death though, I mean, I know he was murdered, but I've never known the details."

I studied the photo again, particularly Peter Maker. There was something about his face that was familiar, but I couldn't figure out what it was.

"Anyway," Matt piped up from behind me. "Didn't you have something to tell me?"

"Uh, yeah. I really do." I said, disappointedly. For a moment I'd honestly forgotten I wasn't there for a social visit. Matt sat on the couch and motioned for me to join him. I took a seat a few cushions over from him near the other end of the couch and, placing my glass on the coffee table, tried to pick back up where we'd left off before.

"Ok, so, the manor you were born in. Well, the truth is, I live there now. I don't know how much you've looked into the house's history, but before your parents bought it, it was owned by a woman named Agatha Clayton. Do you know anything about her?"

Matt's facial expression dropped instantly. He appeared disappointed and I could almost see the cogs in his brain ticking over and over like machinery. "Oh no, it's all true, isn't it? What people say about the place…they reckon Agatha possessed the Graysons—uh, my biological family—they say she's the reason they all died that day."

I felt as though a weight fell from my shoulders. At least the house's well-known reputation made this job easier than I was expecting it to be. I nodded, stretching out to pat his arm. "So, you believe the manor is haunted then?"

"Oh definitely," he remarked with a firm nod. "I've seen weird stuff involving that house with my own eyes. Like, there was once, just a couple months ago actually, I rode past and saw a pale little boy sitting on one of the upstairs window ledges. He was not human, hey. And I swear I've seen shadows of a woman in the downstairs windows. Plus, the front door opens and closes by itself all the time. At least it used to."

He leaned back slightly and made a face. "I can't believe you live there. That house has been empty for so long and from what I've heard, for good reason."

"Yeah...," I said slowly. "Well then, I guess it's a good thing you believe in ghosts, because here's the kicker. I need you to help me get rid of one. Agatha's ghost is the reason the house is still so haunted. She's pure evil and wants to hurt, well actually, kill, me and my family and from what I'm aware of, apparently, you're the only one who can destroy her, Matt."

He stared at me without blinking for a long while before finally uttering, "I'm confused."

"Look, I know it sounds weird but just remember, I warned you before that you'd think I was crazy, but if you believe the legends, believe Agatha's ghost is real and that she killed your family then please believe that you can destroy her. If you don't get rid of her, they think my family is going to end up exactly like…well exactly like the Grayson's."

Matt didn't even try to speak. Instead he stared off into space, as though waiting for something.

I tried to wait, figuring I should let him process at least that much. I was extremely relieved that he was still sitting with me at this point, that he hadn't thrown me out of his house. Yet.

"Who's they? I don't get it," he finally piped up. "So, you're telling me that the ghost of Agatha Clayton really wants to kill you? Why? Just because you moved into her house?"

"Oh, wait, there's more," I said regrettably. "The spirits of your biological family are trapped in the house. I know this because I've seen and spoken to them. That's who I meant by 'they.' They've been, uh, helping me understand the whole thing myself I suppose."

His facial expression reflected his utter shock perfectly, which was exactly the way I expected him to feel. "R…really?" he asked quietly, a look of pure confusion on his now pale green face.

I nodded sincerely. "Matt, your mother came to me when I first moved in, begging me to bring her baby home. At the time, I thought she was talking about Grace. Until I found out later on that you were the one who was born there. She mentioned something then about her baby being the only one who was safe in the house and the only one who could destroy Agatha and bring everyone peace. I didn't understand at the time what she meant. Not until recently."

I watched Matt closely, waiting for him to blow up or at least react in such a way that would cause him to run off, but he never faultered.

"I was supposed to tell you the whole story last week when I came around, the same day you found out the truth about your birth, but I couldn't bring myself to do it. So, here it is, I'll tell you everything I know."

He raised his eyebrows and stared at me quizzically.

I took a deep breath and began to tell him everything, breaking down all the information the way it had been relayed to me by both Mary and Mrs Grayson. I did, however, leave out the details about Mary possessing his adoptive sister Grace, figuring it was unnecessary for the time being and not my duty to disclose. By the end of it, he'd become an extreme shade of white and seemed incapable of moving anything but his lips.

"So, not only has my whole life been a lie, but now I find out that the truth about my life has also been somewhat a lie. Do you know who my biological father is?"

"I'm sorry, I don't know. Your mother didn't say."

He looked up at me, sullen. "You've *really* spoken to my dead birth mother?"

I nodded.

He dropped his head into his hands. "Right."

I let him think for a few moments and moved in beside him, trying not to be pushy. He eventually looked up at me and we stared at each other for what seemed like forever before he finally decided to talk again. "You know, this might sound odd, but I feel like I've always known on some level, deep down."

I tilted my head at him and frowned, surprised.

"I, uh, I used to have this recurring dream," he said. "It only stopped a few weeks ago. I always thought it was a silly nightmare. Now, of course, I'm not so sure. In the dream, I'd be running around that manor surrounded by a bunch of ghosts who would stand in the background and yell at me as I ran down the hallway bearing a knife. There was something chasing me, but I'd never see who it was and all I could think about was getting to the living room and plunging the knife into the wall. I could never make it, the figure that was chasing after me always caught me and I'd wake up. Curious, huh? I, uh, I hope that isn't how it would go down for real."

I smirked. "Dreams always make the worst of a situation. Like I said, you and Agatha were both born in the house and don't share a blood connection. According to your mother, you should be immune to her. Bet your dream doesn't incorporate that fact. Hey, you know there's a good chance the dream came from Mary, your older sister. She's the one who told me most of this stuff. It sounds like something she'd do, as a sort of preparation so you would be more accepting when it came time. She gave me a dream too, which helped me find Agatha's knife. She's been watching over you ever since you were born, you know, she's very protective of you."

He smiled. "I guess my family never did stop caring, did they? My whole life I grew up thinking I was just abandoned in a ditch somewhere, left to die or something. To know what I do now really changes everything. I was never actually unwanted."

I shook my head and gave him a warm smile.

We sat still for a few minutes, deep in thought. Breaking the silence suddenly, he sniggered, "Well I guess one positive thing to come out of all this is, at least you and I didn't end up being related."

I giggled, leaning my head on his shoulder. "Yeah, but I still have Sam. We've been together for years and I don't intend to just give up on that."

He nodded and put his arm around me. "I know, I know. I'll settle for friends. So, what now?"

I frowned. I'd been so focused on how Matt was going to react that I hadn't thought about the next part yet. "I don't know, I guess maybe we start fresh tomorrow. Did you want to come over or something to map out the house and we'll work out a plan from there?"

"Sure, sounds like a good start," he agreed.

We sat quietly with each other for another ten minutes at least before I decided to leave, finally feeling a sense of accomplishment. On the way home, however, I decided to swing past the library to borrow a few books on ghosts and the supernatural world. There had to be something in one of them that could offer a more guided explanation. I couldn't stop thinking about what Mary had said about her family hiding, coming back and forth from the ghostly plane.

That evening, after I finished my dinner, I helped clean up the kitchen while my mother was on the phone with the hospital. We'd finally received the good news that my father was healed enough to be discharged as of tomorrow. We were all so relieved and celebrated by kicking back with a large bowl of pineapples and ice cream, our traditional family dessert favourite and a movie. Noah, of course, practically inhaled his dessert and took off to his room, unwilling to watch any, "boring girly films."

However, since my mother had chosen the movie, it ended up being a weird old classic I'd never heard of and I almost fell asleep several times throughout. The only thing that kept me going was thinking about getting up to my room to scour the new batch of books I'd borrowed. Thankfully, Isabelle was the first to call out Mum's terrible movie choice and as they got into a heated debate about what movies should be considered "good" classics, it gave me the perfect opportunity to sneak away.

I soon knelt on my bed, able to reach out onto my bedside table, picking up and poring through the small pile of ghost lore books in search of something, anything, I'd missed the last time I went looking for answers. This time, I did find an overview of the difference between good spirits and bad spirits and their limitations. The book touched base on the fact that evil spirits, the ones who were violent in nature or were corrupt with bad intentions were unable to physically enter the body for ghost possession. I understood it to be somewhat similar to the theory that vampires were unable to enter your home without permission. At least in certain lore anyway. I shook my head at myself and sighed. Great, now I was thinking about vampires being real.

I skipped ahead, trying to find any section about different ways ghosts could move on. Thankfully, there was one. I learned there were three ways ghosts could pass on.

The first was a good soul being offered a better place in the light, an eternity of peace. That one was obvious. The second was also straightforward, a bad soul being forced to go into the darkness and tortured for eternity. The third, however, was something different entirely and as I read about it, I wondered if this was the same book Mary had read. The theory was, spirits with unfinished business who remained earthside could be absorbed by other spirits and never get the chance to move on at all. With determination, another spirit could learn how to strengthen their own essence by draining other spirits, like a clogged drain slowly pulling water through a filter until finally the blockage is pulled through. When the process was complete, the spirit would burn up in a blazing ball of fire, ceasing to exist as their soul was fully absorbed. If the receiving spirit collected enough souls, it was theorised they could live again.

Gobsmacked, I knew immediately this was what Agatha was trying to do. I pictured the removalist ghost, remembered when his body was discovered how he first started to move on peacefully into the light, then ending up on fire before vanishing altogether. And Evelyn Clayton, she'd tried to tell me something before she was sucked away by flames as well. I felt a little more in the loop now, comprehending at least what the flames meant. Those ghosts had been fully absorbed, would never get the chance to move on properly. I was torn between wanting to read more, or just sleep so I could get to the next day quicker. I folded down the corner of the page I was on and put it back with the other books on my bedside table, figuring I could always continue in the morning. I laid down, terrified now with the knowledge that Agatha wanted to be resurrected. Rolling over, I had just closed my eyes when I felt a droplet of warm, sticky water hit my neck.

Worried, I opened my eyes and stared at the ceiling. I lifted my hand and touched the wet spot on my skin, reaching out with my other hand to flick on the lamp in order for me to see what was on my fingers. It wasn't water; it was a droplet of blood. I panicked and sat up, somehow immediately knowing where it would be coming from.

I was unfortunately correct. The little hole in my bedroom wall had begun to drip blood.

"Mary!" I whispered desperately, hoping somehow, she would come to my rescue. My voice cracked as fear took over. "Mary, what do I do now!"

And suddenly, the wall was no longer dripping blood, it was pouring blood. I tried to hold my palm over it, but the blood managed to slip between my fingers and run everywhere, all down the wall, all over my arm and bedding. I swiftly gave up on the idea of stopping the flow and jumped off my bed, intending to run downstairs. I didn't know where I'd go, but I knew I had to get far away from this room. I quickly realised this was the wrong call.

Laughter rang out through my ears and a familiar, rasping voice hissed viciously, "This time, no one is going to interrupt me!"

I turned in every direction, with my hands flailing helplessly in the air, as though I thought I could fend Agatha off if she tried to control me. Then it hit me, as strongly as it had before. She was taking over me. And there was absolutely no way I could stop her.

Chapter Nineteen

I wrestled with myself as my surroundings began to erase, floating off to the place where I knew I wouldn't be able to control my own actions. The world around me disappeared as a wave of calm forced its way through my body. This time when I reached the white room, however, I was ready and raring to do whatever it took to get myself out. Racing over to the wall closest to me, I placed a flat hand on it and closed my eyes. I then began slowly walking, feeling my way along, perhaps looking for some kind of switch or button. If this was *my* brain, then I had to be able to trigger something to get out somehow.

While this theory made sense, upon circling the room twice, I found that no such switch existed. I cursed at myself. It wasn't going to be easy to regain control. I stood still for a moment and focused, forcing the little window into the view from my eyes open.

My hand swept through the kitchen drawer, pushing aside egg flips, tongs, and wooden spoons as I searched for the large knife that I had used the first time I attempted to dispose of the small Murphy boy.

I tried not to worry as I pulled my attention back to the chamber within my brain that was still controlled by me, the part I was stuck in. I knew there wouldn't be much time left now and I wasn't even close to figuring out how I could overpower her. Panic worked its way through my mind and a burning feeling began to creep up my throat. As annoying as Noah could be sometimes, I loved my brother and definitely didn't want him to die. Especially not this way. He was supposed to die in his sleep as a very old man someday, years after me so I didn't have to suffer the loss. I swallowed in an attempt to rid the flaring feeling and stared down at the floor. I told myself to stay focused. Crying wouldn't change the outcome and I couldn't give up yet. I was livid with myself for ignoring the seriousness of the situation. I shouldn't have taken so long to talk to Matt and make a plan to destroy Agatha. I jumped when the window opened again suddenly, forcing me to see the stairs leading to the landing on the second floor. It was like she wanted me to see my actions.

I moved up the stairs, knife by my side, as fast as I could. Trying to leave no room for interruptions this time.

I let a soft "no" escape my lips and concentrated as hard as I could to close the viewing window again. I needed to think of a plan without distractions. I wondered if Mary's spirit would be able to get to me if I called to her. But even if she could, what could she do? How would she be able to help me? She'd watched her own brother die at her hands and didn't even remember it. She wouldn't be able to help me get back in control over my body when she couldn't manage it either.

After searching every inch of the floor on my hands and knees and discovering that it was as blank, clean, and smooth as the walls were, I finally gave up. Slowly and sadly, I dragged myself over to the perfectly made-up bed and slumped myself onto it. Tears poured down my cheeks as I realised what was about to happen. I hoped with every inch of my body that by some miracle my mother, or even Isabelle, would come to check on Noah within the next sixty seconds. Otherwise, there was no hope anything would stop her this time. Since we'd become more settled in the new house, my mother had stopped checking on Noah every night at bedtime and I had the feeling Agatha knew that. There wasn't even the slightest possibility that Dad would come home from the hospital at this time of night either.

Perhaps it was my imagination from wishing something would happen so badly, but the sound of a car door closing from somewhere outside on the street echoed through the house, causing my puppeteer to stop in her tracks for a second or two. Upon listening and deciding it was nothing important, she, unfortunately, continued walking my body across the landing. The view of my little brother's room jerked into my head and as much as I tried to push it out, it stuck in the front of my mind. She was forcing me to see what she was about to do.

I crossed the room, heading straight for the little boy who was sleeping peacefully in his bed. I raised the knife above my shoulder and prepared to plunge it into his chest.

Suddenly, my hands dropped down. Not into Noah's body, but rather down by my side instead in a startled manner. The sound of excited voices carried up the stairs. She had stopped due to interruption. for the second time. Within an instant, I was being sucked back into my own body again. Upon return, I slumped heavily onto the carpet as my knees buckled out from under me. I could never quite get used to that feeling.

Collecting myself as fast as I could, I tossed the knife under the bed and sprinted towards the door. Slipping into the hall, I ducked into my bedroom just as the voices got to the landing. For a moment I could have sworn I heard Sam's voice.

A knock sounded on my door a few seconds later and my mother's voice bounced chirpily through the wood, "Guess who's come to see you, sweetheart!"

My heart started to race as the door swung open. It was him! Sam's smiling face greeted me warmly as he held his arms out, waiting for my embrace. I let out a squeal of excitement and rushed forward to hug him. Looking over his shoulders as I tucked myself into his body, Mum gave me a grin, turned and made her way back towards the stairs.

We stood for what felt like ages, cuddling and talking, catching up on the past few weeks. He complained about what it was like back home without me and how lonely he'd been. I took in every detail of his face while I listened intently. Gosh I'd missed his distinct chiselled jawline and unique shade of hazel eyes.

"How long will you be staying?" I eventually blurted after the rush of excitement from seeing each other was over.

He shrugged, "A week or so, I guess. Maybe longer if you want me to.
I asked Mum to tell the school we went on holidays."

I fell into his chest and squeezed. "The longer the better."

I wondered if my mother had a plan for where Sam was crashing, so I cut the hug short and darted towards my open bedroom door. At our old place, he was allowed to sleep on a mattress in the loungeroom when he stayed overnight, but I felt uneasy knowing how dangerous that area was in this house and hoped she would let me set him up on the landing at the top of the stairs at least.

Calling down the stairs I yelled, "Hey Mum, where is Sam sleeping?"

Mum's voice replied, much closer than I expected. She must have come up to bed as her voice rounded back to me from her bedroom. "I'm sure you're capable of working something out. Just be safe, you two."

I blushed and turned back to Sam, a wicked grin on my face. My mother knew I wasn't exactly the nun type, but this was the first time she'd ever acknowledged it. Letting Sam stay overnight in my bedroom was a very clear sign.

He chuckled and turned towards the bed. Instead of happiness, he let out a disgusted cry and whipped back around to stare at me. "Why is your bed soaked in blood?"

In all my excitement to see him, I had forgotten that the damn hole in the wall had covered my blankets in a pool of very real blood. The strangest part about it was that the wall itself was now completely clean. As though wiped of every trace where the blood had come from, the stained wall, hole and drip marks were non-existent. All that lay before us was a pool of blood on the bed and blood-soaked bedding. As if that didn't look bad enough, the little fishing knife Agatha had used to kill herself was displayed on my bedside table—the tip stained red with fresh blood.

"I-I didn't do that," I stammered.

He looked me up and down intensely, as though trying to scan me with his eyes, and stayed silent for several minutes. "Didn't do what?"

I sighed. I was going to have to tell him something. I passed by him and started to gather the ruined bedsheets into a ball, racking my brain for an explanation that didn't sound crazy but also didn't drag him into the twisted situation I was currently in. Unfortunately, there wasn't any. Figuring I needed to let him judge for himself, I decided upon telling him the whole story, knowing if he was going to stay with me he would eventually find out anyway.

I threw the balled-up blankets and sheets into my wash basket in the corner and pulled him down onto the bed. He flinched but allowed me to sit next to him. I'd never seen him so edgy around me. With all the havoc we had caused together in past years, I'd never have expected him to not trust me. Launching into a long, well-detailed story, I began to tell him *everything*.

Once I'd gotten through the whole story, I waited for him to process the nightmare of my new life. He had gone pale and looked as though he might pass out. I took that as somewhat of a good sign, it meant he believed me to some extent. "So, let me get this straight," he finally piped up, springing up off the bed to his feet. "There's literal ghosts stuck in this house and you're like, what, friends with them? Well, except one of course who wants to kill everyone. And some Matthew dude, who is of course related to the so-called ghost family, is going to remove the killer ghost by stabbing that knife—" he pointed, "—into the blood-stained wall in the living room. Then all the ghosts can cross over happily ever after and your family can live here in peace."

I swallowed and frowned at him, a little hurt. I wasn't sure what to make of his attitude, wondering if he was making fun of me or actually trying to get on board with the plan.

"Well, long story short and without the sarcasm, that sounds about right, yes," I said quietly.

He nodded repeatedly, like a bobblehead who'd been hit way too hard. "Yeah, Liv, I don't know what I'm supposed to make of that. Are you trying to be creative about breaking up with me to be with Matt or something?"

I felt insulted. My mouth fell open in disbelief. "Is that really what you think?" I asked angrily.

He turned around in a huff, throwing his hands in the air and gestured wildly while he spoke. "You have never been a damn ghost buster Livvie! You don't do supernatural crap and you've never believed in ghosts. We used to laugh at people who said they'd seen a ghost. Yet you come here and get involved with some guy and all of a sudden it's all ooh look at my spirits and cursed house."

I was livid, he hadn't listened to me at all and had just taken a few pieces from the story to compile his own evidence and make it about another guy, which was completely unlike him. I realised suddenly that the long-distance relationship had really begun to take a toll on us.

"You're such a knob, it's not even about Matt at all, Sam!" I exclaimed, frustrated "We aren't even that close, it's not like I hang out with him outside all of this. You have no idea the kind of nightmare I've been dealing with living in this place. It took a while for me to believe in it, trust me. It's a really weird situation and somehow, I just got landed in the middle of it. I spend half my time wondering what the next thing to go wrong is going to be, or who the next person's death I get to experience in an echo will be. It hasn't been all sunshine and lollipops with Matt!"

Sam sighed, looking somewhat guilty for his outburst and apologetically pulled me towards him.

As he embraced me, he stroked my hair, kissed my cheek and said, "I'm sorry, you know I trust you. It just hasn't been easy being apart. I've been waiting for you to fall for someone else and want to move on. I just don't understand though. Why exactly is this Agatha spirit woman after your family? If Matt is safe because he's not related by blood, then how is your family a target?"

I pulled my head back. "Well, I'm related to the other Graysons remember, but I've been wondering the same thing. It doesn't make much sense to kill us all off just because we're cousins, especially since Dad wasn't close to Arthur anymore. If I had to guess, I think my father knows something more than he's letting on, about why her parents were killed or who did it. He has to mean something more to Agatha's vengeance. That's why his kids are on the list to be wiped out just like Arthur's were."

Sam nodded in silence. I could tell he still didn't understand or even believe me fully, but it meant a lot that he was trying to be there for me anyway. I patted him on the arm and briefly left the room to get fresh sheets from the linen cupboard. When I came back, Sam was sitting on my naked mattress turning the knife over and over between his fingers. "Why does it have to be Matt who kills her?" he whispered, "What if I do it instead?"

I gently tossed the sheets down onto the bed and leaned forward to take the knife from him. "I don't know exactly; I only know what they told me. It's something to do with the fact that he was born here and is part of the Grayson family, but is able to resist her mind control because he's not blood-related or something. So, she shouldn't be able to stop him like she can everyone else. I don't really understand myself, but that's the running theory anyway."

He shrugged and got up to help me make the bed. "That's kind of stupid. I don't reckon he is the only one capable of ending this crap."

I had a bad feeling that he was making a mental plan to get rid of her with the idea that he could attempt it himself. I didn't know what would happen if he tried, but figured it wouldn't end well. I felt guilty, knowing I shouldn't have told him anything. I didn't want him getting involved and ending up hurt, or worse.

I placed the knife onto my bedside table as we finished making the bed and shortly after, I snuggled down under the covers. I patted the space beside me, inviting him to join me under the blanket. Though I was no longer in the mood for getting loved up, the second he leaned in and kissed me, lustful feelings took over my whole body instantaneously and we sank into the bed and spent the next hour catching up on all the intimate time we'd missed being apart. We later fell asleep in each other's arms.

The next morning, I awoke to an empty bed. Worried, I shot upright, hurriedly scanning the room for him and only relaxed when I heard a loud variety of voices coming from downstairs, one of them clearly Sam's. Everyone must have been enjoying an early breakfast together and I'd had such a good sleep I was missing out on it. I leapt out of bed and made a break for the kitchen, excited to have a somewhat normal day with my boyfriend—like the good old days.

Everyone shouted loudly with vigour as I entered the kitchen. Smiling faces greeted me from all around and I could see why. My father was sitting happily at the head of the table, covered in bandages and only one cast left, but for the most part looked fantastic. He seemed happy at least, which is what really counted. I couldn't have timed my arrival more perfectly, settling into a chair to enjoy the hot breakfast my mother had just finished plating with my whole family, like we'd used to do all the time on weekends. We all laughed, talked and shared stories about our week, passing and swapping a variety of food options across the table.

I watched Sam chatting away with my parents and found my mind wandering, like I wasn't really able to pay attention to what he was saying anymore. It was strange to see them being so nice to him, considering I knew they both thought he was a bad influence on me. Suddenly, I found I was picturing Matt talking to them instead. I wondered what my parents would think of him. He had such a sweet nature compared to Sam, who was admittedly a little rough around the edges. I frowned to myself as Sam came back into focus, a guilty weight in the pit of my stomach. Thinking about someone else meeting your folks surely wasn't a good sign of a healthy relationship.

About halfway through our meal, a loud knock sounded at the front door. No one budged, instead looking around in confusion at each other. A little bummed at the interruption, I announced, "Ok then, I'll get it," as I made for the front entry.

Chapter Twenty

Opening the door with a grimace, my attitude quickly changed when I saw who was standing there. Matt stood on the doorstep, his skateboard at his side, with an immensely happy look on his face. Without thinking, I gave him a brief, excitable hug before realising what I was doing and pulled back. I found myself suddenly unable to say anything at all. What would Sam think of Matt being here? Especially after I'd told him that we didn't hang out with each other and weren't really close.

Looking uneasy now, Matt broke the silence. "Sooo, how's about that action plan we were going to get together and work out?"

I cringed autonomously and he looked curious. "Oh no, I'm sorry, I completely forgot you were coming today. It, um, might have to wait," I muttered. I could tell he was confused. I stepped back slightly, intending to turn and check over my shoulder before I said anything else and instead bumped into someone who'd snuck up behind me. It was Sam.

"Matt, I presume," Sam said wearily.

I nodded.

Matt paused, thought for a moment, his eyes flickering between me and Sam and said, "Ah, this must be the boyfriend? I'm sorry I don't mean to be a bother. I just wondered if maybe you had kept any of my family things? Grace mentioned that the back sheds were never cleaned out after they died, so I was hoping they may have left some stuff behind that I could have. That's the only reason I came over."

Damn, he was a quick thinker; I was impressed by how effortlessly he'd come up with that. I looked to Sam to gauge his reaction. He had gone a little red in the cheeks but seemed to have stopped himself from saying anything snarky.

"Oh, uh, sure," I agreed, opening the door a little wider. Sam crossed his arms, obviously irritated. "Come on Sam, he's not here for me, he's just here to collect his stuff." Sam raised his eyebrows and I corrected myself quickly, "Uh, that is, his family's stuff I mean, from the back shed."

Both he and I stepped aside so Matt could come inside. I motioned down the hall with my arm, so Matt knew which general direction to go. As we walked towards the back of the house, I noticed Matt's eyes darting around in every direction he could, taking it all in. He seemed in complete awe of everything. I assumed it was the first time he'd ever been inside; he would have had no means or reason to ever come up before and avoided it like everyone else in this town.

My family all looked up as the three of us passed through the kitchen, exchanging glances and smirking at each other. Had I missed something? If I didn't know any better, I'd have said they were recently gossiping about the two boys behind my back.

I led Matt out the back door and down to the shed with Sam following closely behind us. Opening the door, I noticed the boxes containing the Graysons' stuff were all stacked neatly in a line against the far wall. I was surprised my mother hadn't scrapped any of it yet during her cleaning rampages. We'd sorted it out and filtered out the rubbish, sure, but the piles of actual belongings were still there and simply stacked neater than before rather than removed entirely. Perhaps that was more so due to laziness, however, the dump was over half an hour out of town and Dad was hardly available to run it out.

"Wait, they kept the Graysons' stuff all this time?" Matt asked, sounding surprised as he bent down to sift through the partially open boxes.

"Yeah, that's why you came to grab it remember," I said firmly, sliding my eyes back and forth and tilting my head in Sam's direction.

"Oh, right, yes of course. Thanks," he said appreciatively, staring into my eyes with a warm glow and genuine smile. I found myself getting lost in his eyes and smiling back without thinking.

I shook myself free of his gaze and helped gather some of the smaller boxes into one simple stack that would be easy for him to carry. An old stainless-steel mug with the name Arthur glazed into it started to fall off the side of one of the top boxes and both Matt and I reached for it at the same time, brushing our hands together and successfully stopping the mug from falling. I wanted to pull my hand back, but found myself enjoying the touch of his skin at the same time.

Sam piped up from the background, stepping in between Matt and me. "I think it's time for you to leave now mate. You've got your things, no need to hang around since you guys aren't really friends and all, right."

"Samuel, don't start," I groaned.

Matt placed the mug back on top and made a face as though he was about to speak, but decided against it and said a quick goodbye before hoisting up his triple stack of boxes and heading back towards the house.

I waited until he was out of earshot before angrily whispering, "What the hell was that for, he's done nothing wrong."

"If you don't care about him, then it shouldn't bother you," Sam retaliated, irritably. "In fact, I remember a time when you'd beg me to get rid of guys who took an interest in you by doing the 'hard ass boyfriend' thing. In less than five minutes I could clearly see that he has a thing for you, Liv, and coming from my perspective—it seems like you feel the same for him."

I wanted to say it wasn't true, but the longer I spent with Sam, the more I was realising that we had definitely drifted apart. He wasn't acting like the same person I used to know and love. Or maybe he was exactly the same person, but I wasn't into his attitude anymore. Sam looked at me and his expression softened as he waited for me to say something. As though my mouth had a mind of its own, I spoke without a filter. "Maybe you're right. That's it then, I guess you should leave if you're happy to just give up."

He looked slightly hurt but understanding at the same time. He ran a hand down my arm, gave a half nod, and said softly, "See, I knew this was going to happen. Too much has changed. I guess I'll just go home."

I should have felt like crying, but instead, I smiled. Not in a rude way, but as a form of agreement and I knew he understood. With nothing more to say, he turned to leave and I just stood there like an idiot, unsure of exactly how I was really feeling about letting him go. "Wait!" I exclaimed and he stopped in his tracks momentarily. "I don't want to break up, surely we can figure this out once all of this ghost drama is over."

He pursed his lips tightly before uttering three simple words under his breath, "We sure will." He then continued inside, much faster than before. I watched him for a moment and let my brain tick over and over for several minutes before gathering my strength and forcing my legs in the same direction. I had to catch up with him. I couldn't leave it on that note. I had a bad feeling he was going to do something stupid.

I'd barely made it through the door when I heard a bloodcurdling scream echo through the hall. I started sprinting hurriedly towards the direction it had come from. I heard something collapse heavily to the floor and another shriek ring out again before I'd rounded the corner into the living room.

My sister was standing frozen in terror over a curled-up figure on the floor. Blood was pooling around the seemingly lifeless body and my heart sank when I realised it was Sam.

I screeched out his name as I rushed forward and dropped to my knees beside him. I barely noticed as the area around me filled with people—the rest of my family members, all of whom had run in to investigate the source of the scream also.

Tears poured uncontrollably down my face as I rolled Sam onto his back to examine the damage. Blood was spurting from his slashed chest cavity and quickly soaking through his shirt as he clung to the space around his heart. I was no doctor, but judging from the wound I guessed it had been punctured.

I pressed my own hands against his in an effort to add pressure to the wound and stop the bleeding, but I knew it was hopeless. I heard my father in the background making a phone call to the emergency services, sounding as distressed as ever. I wondered if he knew what had happened. Sam was still alive, barely, and began attempting to speak to me. I patted his arm and stroked his face as he sputtered out, "I tried."

Confused, I started to ask what he meant but he slowly dragged an arm towards me and opened his hand into my lap. Agatha's little knife rolled out of his palm just as he gave his final breath. I was beyond devastated as the reality of what had really happened sunk in. He'd tried to be the hero and she had gotten the better of him.

I scooped up the knife and hid it hastily and discreetly in my pants pocket before losing control of all my strength altogether, laying down across his chest and wailing incessantly. I could hear my family in the background, babbling loudly yet incoherently, but I could tell they were trying to make sense of the situation and were completely freaking out. A hand clasped around my shoulder and attempted to pull me upward. I resisted for a moment, but when they pulled stronger, I relaxed ever so slightly and allowed myself to be lifted away from Sam's body.

Upon turning and coming face to face with Matt, I broke down even more and buried my head into his shoulder, almost missing what he said. "I was halfway down the front yard when I heard the scream. What happened?"

I pulled away from his chest, breathing in deeply to gain control over my emotions and glanced over his shoulder at my parents, making sure no one was within earshot or paying direct attention to us. "She killed him Matt. She got rid of him for trying to get rid of her."

He looked surprised. "*Agatha* attacked him?"

I nodded and caught a flicker of fear in his eyes briefly before I buried my head against his shoulder again. He held me tighter and continued to hug me until my eyes became so swollen I eventually stopped crying.

Emergency services showed up at our door some fifteen minutes later. Sam was one hundred percent dead long before their arrival, yet they still thoroughly examined him from head to toe to make sure there was no sign of life. I couldn't help but glare at them with folded arms. How dare they take so long to arrive at the scene. Some emergency services this town had; it had taken long enough for my father to convince them there was a real reason for them to come to our house to begin with.

I began to get choked up again as I watched them load Sam onto a stretcher in a zipped-up, tarp-like black bag.

In shock, my whole family watched and waited, every member slumped across the lounges, silent and shaken. Two police officers soon made their way through the front door and introduced themselves shortly after Sam's body was loaded into the back of the ambulance. They made a point of speaking thoroughly to each and every person, collecting pieces of information from everyone's point of view.

I didn't know what I was supposed to say to them when they directed a question at me. How could I pretend to know nothing about how he died? I may have been able to tell the truth about not seeing anything go down, but in the end, I still knew exactly what happened to him. All I could do was stutter and deny knowing anything at all. I could tell that they were suspicious though, judging from the questions they were throwing out. I knew what they must be thinking, one of us murdered him. Most likely me—the somewhat ex-girlfriend. I had the guilty knife in my pocket after all, which they hadn't searched us for thankfully. It seemed like a long while later that the interviews ceased, the police left, and everything was quiet once more.

Our living room was sealed off with bright yellow police tape pending further investigation from authorities at a later time, forcing the family to gather in the kitchen. Mum made chicken and salad sandwiches for everyone as a late lunch and we all ate in silence. Isabelle took two bites and left the room, her eyes almost swollen shut from crying so much. Pregnancy hormones combined with being the one to discover Sam's bloodied-up body had left her in an excessively overwhelmed state. Mum encouraged Noah to go and snuggle up in bed to watch a movie, kissing his forehead and following swiftly in Isabelle's wake. I thought about doing the same and wondered if my parents would let Matt come up to my bedroom if he wanted to stay with me.

"I think I'm going to retire to my bedroom as well," I announced. I stood up but before I could even take a step, Dad lunged out of nowhere and pulled me in for a quick, comforting cuddle, his wrist cast bashing me in the face as he stroked the hair out of my eyes before letting go.

Matt hung awkwardly in the background for a moment before politely asking, "Do you want some company?"

My father's head snapped in his direction instantaneously like an eagle locking in on its prey. Looking him up and down with seemingly harsh judgement, he took a heavy step towards him and surprisingly, thrust out his hand, offering a handshake. "I don't suppose there's anything wrong with offering my daughter some *friendly* company in her time of loss, but one wrong move and you'll be next in the body bag."

Matt looked worried, then slightly relieved and shook his hand graciously before we made a beeline for the stairwell.

"That door stays open!" Dad's voice carried from behind us.

I rolled my eyes. Like I could even think about that.

Wanting nothing more than to melt into oblivion and vanish for a while, I slumped down onto my bed. Matt sat beside me, leaving a respectable gap, and put his hand on my shoulder before running it up and down my arm in a motion of comfort. I knew he didn't mean anything by it, but it didn't stop me from feeling guilty. I stood up and crossed the room, facing the wall and covered my face with my hands.

Matt apologised softly.

I turned back to face him and lowered my hands, fighting as tears began to prick the corner of my eyes again. "Don't be sorry, you didn't do anything wrong," I said quietly. "My head is just all over the place. Sam and I, I think we were kinda in the middle of breaking up…"

"Oh, I'm sorry to hear that."

Even though he sounded sincere, I scoffed.

"No, really," he said. "I only went through a breakup myself a few months ago. It sucks. What happened? I thought you guys were pretty steady?"

I sighed. "We used to be, but too much has changed. I've changed. But mostly it was because he…well, because *I* realised I have feelings for you."

Matt sat up straight, moving on the spot like he was unable to sit still suddenly. It was like he was about to burst and wanted to speak, but I could tell he was trying really hard not to say anything.

I exhaled loudly in frustration and began to pace, pulling the lighter Sam had given me out of my pocket and throwing it across the room. "Ugh! He was supposed to be leaving, he was supposed to just go home, but instead he had to try and be the hero. He had to try and destroy her. And for what, to prove himself to me? It's my fault he's dead and I just don't know if I can deal with that!"

Matt took a deep breath and stared at me, now emotionless. "Ok, but for starters, you didn't know he was going to do that, did you? Think about it for a second, do you actually think you could have stopped him from going after her even if he told you his plan? You are not responsible for his actions, Liv. It's not your fault."

I couldn't stop the tears from building in the corners of my eyes this time, so I pressed my back against the nearest wall and slid down to the ground burying my face into my knees. "I sorta did know, he mentioned something about it last night. I brushed it off. I should have hidden the knife as soon as he told me he wanted to go after her. I should have done more to make him realise how dangerous she was."

A few seconds later, warm arms surrounded my curled-up body. Letting myself fall, I rolled my body to the side and collapsed wholeheartedly into Matt's welcoming arms. He held me as I cried for what felt like half an hour whilst stroking my hair.

For the first time in weeks, I felt truly safe. After I'd wept myself dry again, I looked up into his face and said, "Don't leave me alone, ok? I can't handle ghosts right now."

He nodded and held me a little tighter. "Never."

For just a moment, I forgot about my pain, leaned up and kissed him on the cheek. He did not hesitate to then lean in and kiss my forehead, simultaneously moving one of his hands from my head to my waist and pulling me in tighter. "Liv, this might be the wrong time to say this, but I have feelings for you too."

After that, Matt and I spent a while in each other's arms, happily cuddling in a warm embrace and soaking up each other's company. He held me firmly against his chest with such a comforting grip that it made reality just melt away. We sat and talked for what seemed like hours, forgetting where we were and the absurdity of the world around us.

While I was happy to finally admit to Matt how I felt about him, and to have him express those feelings back, I was also weighted with a guilty conscious knowing that I'd only just lost my boyfriend. Pretty much ex-boyfriend, I had to remind myself, which made me feel so much worse, knowing we were mostly undecided about breaking up when Sam had marched off into the house. I blamed my own stupidity for his death, knowing that if I'd just accepted how I felt about Matt and had a proper conversation with Sam about everything that had been happening at the new house sooner, he might never have come to Bellicose to see me and would still be alive. It really was all my fault. The more I allowed myself to think about it, the angrier I became and the quicker I remembered that we were still in deep trouble.

Standing up with as much energy as I could muster, I announced bravely, "Right, that's enough wallowing. We need to fix this mess and get rid of that bitch as soon as possible."

Matt stood up also, placing a hand on my shoulder with a gentle amount of pressure as though he was about to push me back down. "No, *I* need to destroy Agatha. She can control you, remember? I have to be the one to go after her, or you're going to end up like...um, end up hurt."

A little frustrated, I nodded. "Well, what do you think we need to do first?" I asked.

He shook his head slowly. "Well, the first step would be to get your family out of the house. I feel like it'll be safer if no one's home, it only puts them at risk. Plus, they'll get a bit freaked if they see me running around your loungeroom wielding a knife, won't they? So, when's the next time they will all be out of the house at once?"

I thought about it for a moment, then sighed as my heart began to ache once more when I realised the answer. "I suppose they'll all go to Sam's memorial service. But we don't have a time or date for that yet and she's only getting more dangerous by the day. The longer we wait, the more chance there is that she's going to hurt someone else. I mean as it is, I've nearly stabbed my brother in his sleep twice now because of her. Plus, how can I explain to my family why I'm not attending his memorial."

"Yeah, that's good actually."

I raised my eyebrows.

"Well, no it's not good but you know what I mean, it'll work," he reassured me. "They'll do something small for him tomorrow. They always hold a courtesy memorial service down at the church the day after someone dies of non-natural causes, like a pre-funeral goodbye out of respect. Since Sam didn't live in this town, I imagine it will be kept private for your family only before his body is picked up to go home. So, we just have to wait one more day."

I wished I could have hope, but instead I was left with an empty pit in my stomach. She'd killed Sam in pure daylight and it was always worse at night.

A knock sounded on my already open door, for courtesy reasons more than anything else, before Mum poked her head in. Her face was a shade of white I'd never seen before and her eyes bloodshot. I didn't think she was coping very well with Sam's mysterious and sudden death in our house.

"Matt, will you be staying for dinner?"

Oh no, had the afternoon wasted away already?

He looked at me as though seeking approval, then back to my mother and said simply, "I'd love to."

She nodded and smiled before bustling back into the hall. Matt then pulled out his phone and sent a text to his mother, letting her know he wouldn't be home for dinner. I checked the time over his shoulder. It was four p.m. I took a deep breath and collected my lighter from the floor, stroking it like it was a token of some kind. Just then, a shrill cry sounded from the end of the hallway. My sister's room.

I sprinted out into the hall, with Matt closely following, and almost smashed into my mother as we pelted towards Isabelle's bedroom. She was standing at the foot of her bed and had bright red blood trickling down her legs.

"The baby!" she wailed as she stumbled, wobbly and disorientated into Mum's outstretched arms.

Chapter Twenty-One

"What happened?" Mum shrieked.

Isabelle was so stressed she was hyperventilating. "I don't know, I don't know! I just started getting pains across my belly and I thought I might be starting to go into labour, but then it got sharper and then...there was just blood everywhere!"

"Ok, honey, we have to get you to the hospital right now. It's a little early for this baby to be coming naturally," Mum said calmly but firmly as she placed her hands around Isabelle's belly, feeling for the baby's movements. "Everything is going to be fine."

My dad swept past me and burst into Isabelle's room just as she and Mum were making their way out of it. Without needing an explanation, he looked at the situation before him and sprung into action, scooping Isabelle into his arms and carrying her effortlessly down the hall. Mum pulled out her phone, calling the hospital ahead of time and letting them know what to expect. I felt helpless, turning into Matt's body for much-needed comfort. Why was this happening now? Could it be just a coincidence?

As if answering my question, I heard a faint sound in the background, like a laugh or light chuckle. Matt must have heard it too, as his head also darted up. Standing at the foot of the bed, right where Isabelle had been moments ago, was Agatha.

"What the hell do you think you're doing?" I spat out angrily.

Agatha shrugged without empathy, smirked, and then vanished into thin air. My heart began to race a little more as I looked back to Matt. "Do you think she hurt the baby on purpose?"

Matt said nothing at all for a few moments before he responded, seemingly stuck in a trance, his eyes fixated where Agatha had disappeared. I realised this was probably the first ghost encounter he'd ever had and didn't blame him for being a little freaked out. But, overall, he handled it like a trooper. "Nah, she wouldn't, I'm sure the baby is just fine. There may be an opportunity here though; I know it's not under the best circumstances, but I think I should use this time."

Slightly confused, I wondered what he meant for a moment before I caught on. He might have enough time to destroy Agatha while everyone was at the hospital. My heart sank a little when I realised Noah was probably still in the house. "I'd say go for it, but I don't think my brother would have gone with them."

Matt nodded, quickly dashing down the hall to search for Noah. We ran all over checking the bedrooms, bathroom, kitchen and even the backyard but there was no sign of him anywhere. I concluded that he'd gone along with them to the hospital after all. Which meant we really did have a window of opportunity. I felt around my pocket and passed the knife to Matt as subtly as I could manage, hoping *she* wasn't watching us.

Matt and I headed back towards the living area as silently as we could, basically tiptoeing in order to be as stealthy as possible. I hung back in the doorway as Matt advanced cautiously towards the cursed wall. I watched with angst as he reached into his own pocket and drew the small, very important knife.

Holding my breath, I waited as fearful as ever, hoping he would go undetected until it was too late for her to stop him. In the blink of an eye, Matt gasped as the hand he was using to hold the knife twisted out of control and came flying back at him, like he was trying to stab himself. I knew it wasn't him doing it, so I was both scared and confused. We had all believed Agatha's mind control couldn't affect him. If she could, we might have lost all hope of actually defeating her.

Familiar cackles of laughter rang out through the area and as Matt continued fighting the battle against his own arm, I rushed into the room to try and help, nearly getting slashed in the process as I grabbed onto his wrist.

"No, stay back, Liv!" Matt cried out, but I refused to let go of his arm and managed to steady it momentarily. The force behind it was incredibly strong and I was suddenly grateful for all those times I'd arm wrestled my father over the years.

A few seconds later, an invisible force collided with Matt and me, knocking us off our feet and into the closest end table, causing the knife to fly out and clatter across the floor as Matt smashed his wrist into the legs of the table.

Before we could do much more than roll over, a firm voice demanded, "You leave my son alone!"

I knew that voice. Materialising, Penelope Grayson bent and offered her hands out to help us off the floor.

Matt was in awe. "M-mum?" he stuttered, gawking at her.

She smiled, stroked his cheek with her thumb and turned to stand guard in front of us with her hands now on her hips in a firm stance.

Agatha appeared, as gruesome as ever, smirking at Mrs Grayson as she faced her in a standoff. "Grew a spine, Penny?" she rasped through clenched teeth. "It's ok, I got what I wanted anyway you fool." Swooping past us, she collected the knife off the floor before I even thought to react and vanished once again.

"Oh great," I muttered under my breath.

Matt must have been as worried as I was. He whipped around on the spot and started visually searching for Agatha, his eyes almost popping out of his head as he nursed his wrist.

The front door suddenly clicked and I realised that somebody must have come back from the hospital. Matt froze on the spot and Mrs Grayson vanished quickly, leaving the room ghost-free once more.

"Hi, Dad!" I exclaimed loudly, adjusting my askew shirt straps as he rounded the corner and came into view.

He scanned the room with narrowed eyes and a suspicious look on his face as he proceeded to guide Noah into the house with a firm hand on his shoulder. "What's going on?" he asked with a no-nonsense tone.

"Nothing special…we were just about to put on a movie." I said, in the most convincing manner I could. "How's Isabelle? Is the baby ok?"

Dad sighed. "Well thankfully, the baby is alive. They said something about a ruptured placenta and they're prepping her for a caesarean now. Your mother stayed with her and Carl is on his way, but master Noah here was flipping out too much to stay up there so I had to bring him home."

I was relieved, to say the least. If Agatha had caused Isabelle's placenta to rupture, she'd lost that game. Isabelle and the baby really were going to be fine. I was not relieved however that my father had returned home early and had a sinking feeling Agatha would be relentless now she had her knife back. Matt had to finish what we'd started and it had to be today.

"Say, Noah, do you know what always cheers me up? Going to the park! Maybe Dad could take you there instead? You don't wanna be stuck at home do you?" I looked innocently at my Dad and grinned.

"Say, Olivia, do you know what cheers me up? Cold beer and a TV blaring a good old-fashioned sports game. You know you could take him yourself if you weren't trying to get rid of me so you could continue playing some sort of weird, animal sex games in my living room."

"Wait, what? Oh, no. Matt and I aren't like, together. We've never even gotten close to doing anything like that!" My mouth hung open in disbelief and I glanced sideways at Matt to see his reaction, noticing immediately he wasn't confused at all about my father's suspicion, having gone slightly red in the face instead. By his feet lay the lamp that used to sit on the now sideways end table with a snapped leg. We must have knocked it off when we'd fallen into it, along with partially upturning the new rug my parents had bought to cover up the mismatched, repaired floorboards.

Matt patted the top of his head to flatten his hair and gestured to me using as little movement of his chin as he could manage, as though I should do the same. Reaching up quickly, I soon realised my hair was in all kinds of disarray. To my father, it probably looked like there was a different reason we'd been rolling around on the floor.

Dad released his grip on Noah's shoulder and gestured upstairs with a frown. Noah hung his head, seemingly disappointed, and toddled off up the stairwell, whilst Dad gave us an extremely stern glare before marching down the hall towards the kitchen, presumably to get his beer. Great. My dad thinks I'm a whore.

Matt pulled me back into focus by picking up the end table and lamp, placing them back where they had sat previously once he carefully readjusted the snapped leg to support itself. As the adrenaline began to wear off, my body began to vibrate and as I went to kick the rug back into place, I realised I was still a little shaken up from the struggle with Agatha. I couldn't help but feel doomed. She had the knife back now and even worse, she'd caught Matt trying to stab it into the wall. She knew what we were planning to do to her and we had no way to destroy her, no way to get the knife back. I wondered if Mary would be able to help us again, she'd managed to steal it from her once before.

"Matt, we've got to go up to the bathroom and call for Mary. I don't want to leave the house to go get her now that my dad is back and that's the only place I reckon she'll appear to us. She might be able to help us before Agatha has a chance to do anything else."

We strolled down the hall as casually as we could, with Matt questioning why Mary's ghost would be out of the house in the first place. I ignored him and powered forward as stealthily as possible. Even though I doubted my father would be hanging around in the kitchen, I didn't want to get caught heading upstairs. He'd surely think I was just taking Matt up to my bedroom for a quickie now that he thought we'd been having sex before and there's no way he'd let that happen.

Knowing Agatha had every opportunity to strike again at any moment, hurting someone else in the process, made my stomach twist.

Just as I thought it, a horrified gasp sounded from nearby. Matt was standing at the foot of the stairs, staring up at the balcony landing, a terror-stricken look on his face. I looked up towards the second floor, tracing his gaze. Agatha, wielding her special little knife, was hovering outside my brother's doorway. Apparently, she no longer cared about framing me now she had her knife back.

At almost the exact same time, Matt and I took off, thundering up the stairs. Once at the top of the stairwell, I halted suddenly, frozen in fear as I realised Agatha had vanished once again. I waited rigidly for Agatha to appear before me, to take over my body again.

Matt, seemingly braver, moved forward and scoped out the surrounding area by the doorway.

My father must have been curious about all the racket, because he was with us a few seconds later. "What the hell is going on around here? Did you adopt a rhino while I was gone?" he demanded.

I didn't know what I was supposed to say to him exactly, falling silent and wishing he would just go away before Agatha decided to show herself again.

Matt shrugged and also refused to say anything.

Noah broke the silence by wandering down the hall right into the middle of the three of us, apparently having come back from the toilet. He stopped suddenly in his tracks at his doorway, looking around at Dad, Matt and I, all positioned in a semi-circle surrounding his bedroom. "What did I do?" he asked softly.

Unfortunately, at that moment, it seemed Agatha was done waiting. She appeared directly behind my brother, grinning wickedly, with him completely unaware of her presence.

"It's you!" my father whispered.

I only had a moment to be shocked, unable to dwell on his words for long because Agatha held her little knife up for show and announced loudly, "I'm tired of playing mind games now, some things you just have to do yourself."

Noah's mouth hung open in fear as he started to turn around to see where the horrifying voice was coming from.

Agatha lifted the knife in preparation, but before she'd quite had the chance to plunge it downwards, my father lunged towards her and my brother, forcefully yelling out, "Hell no!"

Noah was propelled onto the floor as Dad pushed him down and swiped for the knife, slicing his hand open as he blocked her continued thrust from coming into contact with any part of Noah's body.

Agatha let out an almighty cry, presumably out of anger and grabbed my father by the neck, throwing him sideways into the closest wall with the strength of her whole body, causing him to end up in a collapsed heap on the floor. Without hesitation, I darted to Noah's side, helping him up off the floor and pulling him behind me so he was out of the way. But Agatha didn't even seem to care about Noah anymore, all of her attention was now directed at my father as she stood mightily in front of him, waiting while he picked himself up off the ground. Dad didn't even try to get away from her, instead choosing to pull himself into a sitting position at Agatha's feet.

"Why now?" he asked, defeated.

She glanced towards the knife in her hand and shrugged. "This was taken away from me a long time ago. I have it back now. I'm at full strength again, unburdened by the possibility of being defeated."

Out of the corner of my eye, I noticed Matt motion at me silently, gesturing to Noah's doorway. I nodded and slowly pushed Noah backward, ushering him until he was just inside the safety of his room.

"Stay in here, buddy," I whispered to him. "You'll be safe. Lock the door and don't come out for *anything*."

Noah glanced over at Agatha with a frightened look on his face before turning back to me, tears welled up in his eyes. Surprisingly though, he didn't argue and shut the door in my face gently.

Agatha and Dad hadn't noticed this at all, too engulfed in each other. My father was now on his knees, at Agatha's mercy. I watched with confusion as Agatha's ghostly figure flickered in and out momentarily before disappearing altogether for several solid minutes. We all waited with anticipation and looked around at each other, fearfully wondering what was going to happen next. Just as I was beginning to think she was going to stay gone for a while, she reappeared again with a wobble, almost in the exact same place.

As though she was seeing him for the first time in a long time, she squealed in my father's face, pointing her index finger at him and jabbing the air with every word she spoke. "You! It was you! How dare you! I want to hear you admit it!"

I couldn't help but notice how different she suddenly sounded. Instead of the usual gurgling nails type rasp, her voice had become quite feminine and meek.

Without thinking about it too much, I interrupted, suddenly curious about what she was accusing my father of. "Dad, what did you do?"

He rotated his head slightly to look at me, a sincere, gloomy expression on his face. "It wasn't really me; I didn't think about what I was involved in. I just helped cover it up."

My heart sank. Looking back and forth between Agatha and Dad, I somehow knew exactly what he meant, what I'd suspected all along, but couldn't bring myself to actually believe. Agatha stood her ground in front of him, waiting for him to spill the truth, a truth she apparently already knew but needed to hear out loud.

Her expression softened and for the first time in her death, I saw her as an actual woman, with emotions and everything. "I was there," she said simply. "I'd come back that night to see my parents. I don't even remember why, maybe to reconcile with my father. I just remember coming home and walking up to the door with dread in the pit of my stomach. Just as I was about to knock, I heard struggling and scuffling inside so I made my way around to the side windows and peeked inside. All I saw were the backs of two men, bent over the lifeless bodies of my mother and father on the floor. I remember almost screaming, but managing to hold myself together long enough to duck down and hide in the bushes. I waited and waited, just so I could catch a glimpse of my parents' killers. Do you know whose face was the first I saw?" She stared directly at my father, seething, waiting for him to make eye contact.

When he did, she spat, "Yours."

Chapter Twenty-Two

Tears began to form in my father's guilt-ridden eyes as he looked back at me, clearly in a world of emotional pain. "It's not as bad as it sounds, it...it wasn't like that," he insisted.

Suddenly having difficulty holding myself up as the reality of the truth hung in the balance, my knees buckled and I felt Matt's hand clasp over my shoulder in support. Perhaps too aggressively, I demanded, "Then what was it like, Dad?"

"Arthur Grayson was the one responsible for their passing," he said flatly before quickly launching into an explanation. "I told you how my cousin Arthur and I were still friends through high school, yes? Well, when he got Penny pregnant, he insisted on needing cash to support them. Said he wanted to start this whole amazing life with them and refused to let his child grow up in a financially challenged family, like he did. After many days of begging, Arthur's father promised to get him a job at the company where he worked, which he did, but then his boss—George Clayton—changed his mind last minute, insistent he was only allowed to hire staff over the age of eighteen due to his insurance policy. You may have heard his name; he was the original owner of *this* house back in the sixties or seventies and the founder of the same company I work for now."

Dad paused, as though allowing time for me to connect the dots properly, then continued more solemnly than I'd ever seen him. "Anyway, Arthur was never the most well-tempered man, even as a teenager. Upon being told he wasn't getting the job after all, he chucked a tantrum, ended up in a fit of rage and marched down to the office to scream at Mr Clayton, which ultimately got his father fired.

What he wasn't expecting was to then find out that Mr Clayton was, in fact, his biological father. After being fired, Arthur's dad lashed out at him and let slip that it was a good thing he wasn't his real son after all, that he'd married his already pregnant mother and raised Arthur as his own child to spare him the pain of inevitably being rejected by his stuck-up biological father, but now regretted doing so after the way it had turned out for him. Arthur of course stormed out and went to see George Clayton at his home later on to find out if he knew he'd gotten his maid pregnant and had a son. I don't know exactly what happened when he showed up to confront him, but all he ever told me about that conversation was that he was shot down as harshly as a person could be, that George knew he existed but never wanted him because he was just the product of an affair George wanted to forget. Angry that his mother's husband was right, Arthur confided in me for support and before long, he'd hatched this stupid plan to rob the Clayton's manor.

He figured George Clayton owed him some kind of compensation and called it an 'easy payout', claiming that stealing a large sum of money from him would set him and Penny up for their baby's future without impacting the Claytons at all. Apparently, Arthur's marital father had accidentally mentioned once whilst drunk that his boss was a stupid idiot asking for trouble because he didn't trust banks and kept his family fortune locked in a vault inside the basement of his mansion.

He asked for my help to steal the money for a percentage and I'll admit, for some stupid reason it seemed like a great idea at the time and I agreed. Just remember, we were young and I didn't think about the severity of what might happen, assuming I wouldn't even have to bear the consequences if any should arise. It was just stealing some money after all."

"Dad!" I interjected. I now understood the saying "the apple never falls far from the tree."

He looked severely ashamed, but held up his hand to silence me before I could say anything else and powered on.

"So, Arthur studied Mr Clayton and his wife for a few weeks to learn their schedule and see if there were any routine patterns or regular events they attended so he could figure out the best time to break in undetected. Saturday nights turned out to be exactly what we wanted. Like clockwork, Mr Clayton would disappear down to his man cave in the shed to watch TV for a few hours whilst his wife went to her weekly book club with her friends. One Saturday evening, we prepared and loaded up with all the necessary gear, breaking into the house whilst Mr Clayton was watching his program out in the shed.

Everything went smoothly with getting into the house and sneaking into the basement. Unfortunately, after the vault being in the basement theory turned out to be a bust, we tried the laundry, kitchen, living room and even the bathroom, but there was no sign of any kind of vault or money. Arthur began to get frustrated and became louder by the minute, no longer attempting to suppress any sound he made. He burst into the main bedroom, slamming cupboards and throwing things around with me following closely, trying to get him to calm down or we'd be caught. That was the point where everything went wrong. To both of our surprise, Mrs Clayton sprung up in bed.

It was just pure bad luck that Arthur had chosen that particular Saturday. We had no idea she had stayed home from her book club that evening, sick. We all panicked, she screamed and tried to run out of the room, throwing objects at us as she raced into the hall. Everything just happened so fast. Arthur tried to grab onto her as she ran onto the landing…this landing…and she fought him every step of the way.

He missed her once, but the second time he managed to grab ahold of her wrist just as she reached the stairwell. I stood by the railing like an idiot, too stunned to do anything. Arthur was yelling at me to grab her and as he tried to tighten his hold on her body, they argued, she struggled, pulled free, and went tumbling down the stairs. All it came down to was a bad landing and she was gone. She must have hit her head and died, just like that.

By this point, George Clayton had heard the ruckus coming from the house. He burst in through the back door just as we had gotten to the bottom of the stairs and caught us standing over her. He flipped out, charged at Arthur and they fought. I don't think Arthur knew his own strength and as the fight got more serious, he slammed Mr Clayton into a wall as he beat into him. What he didn't realise, was that there was a large picture hook with a broken tip on the wall right where George's neck was slammed. George Clayton died almost instantly. It was traumatising to watch the light leave his eyes.

Arthur broke down a bit as he caught up with the seriousness of what happened and he begged me to help him clean up any trace of fingerprints so neither of us could be associated with their death. We did a top-notch crime scene clean up, thoroughly wiped the bodies over, vacuumed and mopped all the floors, and cleaned any surfaces we thought we might have touched."

I couldn't believe it, my dad was as good as a criminal. I opened my mouth to speak, but realised he was still talking.

"I remember watching the news piece on it, waiting to get caught, knowing if we did, I'd likely be imprisoned also. Surprisingly, though, we got away with it. I didn't even know until the news reports circulated that they had a daughter. Arthur failed to mention that part to me and when I found out, I remember feeling a thousand times worse. Despite it all though, Arthur and I remained friends for several years after. Like I said, Isabelle used to play with their little boy.

Then one day out of nowhere, Arthur came around to inform me that he was moving to Bellicose and taking possession of the Clayton's manor. Because the Clayton's daughter passed away years earlier, as the last technical heir to the property, the property passed to him. It had taken years to clear the legal blockages withholding the property, but it was eventually put in his name after DNA proceedings cleared. He was more determined than ever that the vault of money we never found must be hidden in a secret compartment inside the walls. I told him he was insane; we argued and didn't speak for a few days.

When I saw a story on the news that Bellicose was holding a memorial on the anniversary of George and Evelyn Clayton's daughter, Agatha's, death, suspicions triggered in my head and I accused Arthur of killing her too, to gain the ability to claim the house. We got into a massive blue, Arthur moved away and I never saw him again. I'll never be able to forgive myself for being involved in the Clayton's deaths. But I promise you, I did not kill those people."

The landing fell silent. Even Agatha seemed deep in thought. She glared at my dad for several minutes before muttering, barely audibly. "I have never ever known the truth. That's all I've wanted for thirty-one years."

Dad looked somewhat relieved, but still caught in a moment of uncertainty, didn't move a muscle. We all waited, on edge, unsure of what Agatha's next move was going to be. I didn't know what to think, was it over now? Would she give up on her warpath of revenge on my family now that she knew my dad didn't actively plan to murder her parents?

Then, out of nowhere, appeared the man I recognised as Arthur Grayson himself, or at least, his ghost. He looked ever so slightly older than the photos I'd seen of him and I was amazed at how alive he seemed. He was by far the least ghostly-looking spirit I'd seen out of the lot of them. His skin was almost completely a pale flesh colour and the transparency of it only occurred in light flickers that came and went when he moved.

My father didn't appear the least bit surprised to see him, and I felt somewhat less victimised as I realised he was just as used to seeing ghosts as I was.

Arthur smirked at Agatha with folded arms, tapping his chest with outstretched fingers where a seemingly fresh stab wound remained obvious in his skin. "And all this time," he sneered, "you've kept my family hostage over that? Why didn't you just talk to me when I first moved here before you made my daughter kill my son? You were the one who lured me here in the first place! You are the true murderer here!"

Agatha looked taken aback. "Liar! What the hell are you talking about? You were the one who killed your daughter due to your own temper tantrum! That had nothing to do with me and you know it! I just wanted to avenge my parents. Our poor father! You want to accuse me of being a murderer, yet you've killed more people than I have! You were responsible for my mother's death, and our father's death; you killed your own wife. Oh, and let's not forget, you killed *his* father."

She pointed a long, bony, transparent finger at Matt.

I let out an audible gasp.

"What!" Matt exclaimed.

Arthur's facial expression changed from an annoyed glare to a snide smirk in half a second. "Oh, that's right. Yes, yes I did," he sniggered without remorse.

Tension built by the second and before another word was spoken, Penelope Grayson popped up beside Matt suddenly, resting her hand on his shoulder. Matt jumped a foot off the floor before he realised who it was.

"*You* murdered him?" she said. "Oh, Arthur how could you?"

Matt's eyes bounced around, darting from Arthur to his mother, to me, then back to Arthur before blurting out, "Seriously? Anyone care to tell me who my father even was?"

Arthur glared, seething, at Penelope and narrowed his eyes at her as though waiting for her to answer. Like a parent waiting for a child to confess to something they'd done wrong when the parent already knew they'd done it.

Penny sighed, turned to face Matt and said, monotoned, "Peter Maker."

I couldn't believe it. It was like being inside a television snippet from a courtroom drama scene. I suddenly understood why the picture of Peter I'd seen in Matt's living room had looked so familiar. It wasn't because I'd seen Peter before, it was simply that Matt was a spitting image of him.

Matt was frozen in disbelief, hunched over slightly like he'd been punched in the stomach, obviously trying to wrap his head around it, but he configured himself faster than I assumed he would. "So, you're telling me that my biological father was my adoptive mother's husband?"

Penny nodded with a guilty grimace. "He was transferred temporarily to my office when we still lived in Armistice to help with a case both of our departments were working on and we were assigned together as partners. Arthur had been, well, mean and distant at the time because he was so obsessed with his fight to claim the Mason Manor and Peter and I got along like a house on fire. As they say, the rest is history and one thing just led to another. Aside from our fling, he was a good man; we were both so ashamed of our actions and decided not to keep in touch when he went back home. We agreed to lose each other's phone numbers and said we'd go on with our lives like nothing had happened. When I found out I was pregnant, Arthur knew right away that the baby couldn't have possibly been his, but I told him it was a random one-night stand and I didn't even know the man responsible. He only found out the truth after we had moved to Bellicose and we happened to run into Peter."

Arthur chimed in suddenly, "Yeah and then later when I found out you lied to me, I almost bloody killed you on the spot. But I chose to get rid of the source of the problem instead. You can't help but lie, can you Penny? See, I discovered Peter knew about the baby, knew it was his. You told him that much before you 'lost contact' with the guy. See, he came around not long after we moved here, looking for you, asking all these questions but persistently dodging mine. So, I threw a few punches and we fought it out. When I'd beaten him an inch from his life, he let slip that you and he were unconditionally in love and both planning to leave your marriages for each other, had been for some time. Know what the cocky prick said then? That he was glad he was going to take you away from me because he could give you and the kids a better life than I ever had. So, I got rid of him. In my opinion, he had it coming."

"You bastard!" Matt spat, clearly fuming as he made a fist and lunged in Arthur's direction.

Penelope and I both instantly reacted. She grabbed his arm as I threw out my palm against his chest to hold him back.

"You're the bastard, boy!" Arthur raged back at him before redirecting his anger towards Agatha. He seemed to be on a power trip now, pissed off and holding his head high as though he was proud of his past actions. "That's it, I'm done with pretending—I tell you what Agatha, here's some cold, hard truth for you now. Killing your mother may not have been my intention, but killing our father was. I saw that hook on the wall when we were fighting and I jammed him into it for my own satisfactory justice. I deserved more from him, I deserved what you grew up with."

Agatha's calm side was well and truly buried in that moment. I watched the flickering skin on her face become a brilliant shade of red. Her anger reached bursting point and she lashed out, spear-throwing her knife swiftly across the room at Arthur. Which of course went straight through his non-solid figure, plunging itself into the wall behind him.

He let out a chuckle, gesturing towards my father. "Well now, I thought all this time it was him you were after? I mean, how do you know for sure he isn't responsible too? I mean, we were in it together after all. Maybe he's the one who pushed your mother down the stairs and I'm just covering for him."

I could see Agatha was done with his taunting by that point. She zipped across the landing in a flash, pulled the knife out of the wall and lunged at Arthur, blade first.

He waved his arm at her with minimal effort and sent her flying sideways towards my father instead. Dad leapt backward out of her reach and only narrowly avoided being hit by the knife. Agatha stumbled, losing balance as she missed hitting a solid target, but picked herself up quickly and flung back around to face Arthur, clearly getting frustrated.

Suddenly though, it was like she was unable to control her actions. She began twisting and turning rapidly, seemingly fighting her own knife-wielding hand. At first, I was confused, until I looked over at Arthur.

He was lightly waving his hand back and forth; the same direction Agatha's arm twisted each time. It appeared as if he was controlling her arm, the same way a conductor directed a choir. How had he become more powerful than her if she was the one supposedly sucking all the power from the Grayson and Clayton spirits? It didn't make any sense. I didn't have time to dwell on the matter, however, as Agatha stumbled and started swinging the knife wildly towards my father's chest.

Adrenaline took over and I automatically tried to jump in his direction. Matt pulled me backward at the last second and I turned back just in time to see the blade pierce Dad's shoulder blade.

He cried out in pain and threw his hands up in an attempt to pull it out. Still fighting for control over her actions, Agatha tripped over her own feet whilst throwing herself backward, as far away from my dad as she could get. It appeared she was trying her hardest *not* to hurt him.

From the other side of the landing, Arthur scoffed loudly.

"What's your problem?" Dad spat at him angrily, finally managing to pull the knife free. He let it fall with a clatter to the floor and pressed a hand to his shoulder in an attempt to stop the bleeding.

Arthur scowled, looking at him with disgust. "What isn't my problem, Scott? You were supposed to back me up, man. You were supposed to be there for me. I was all alone hiding a huge secret! I tried contacting you every week after we left. Every single week. You just ignored me! I needed my best mate back. You just stopped caring. Even when my family fell apart and my marriage fell apart. And where were you? Living some cherry pie life! I couldn't get you back here until after I was dead and even then it took mind controlling your boss to reach out with a high-quality job offer."

Apparently completely fed up, Arthur lunged forward in one sweeping movement to collect the knife from the floor. As though attempting to distract my father, Arthur quickly motioned as though he were throwing the knife at me without actually letting go of it. It worked. Within the split second my father was distracted turning to block me, Arthur lunged forth and plunged the knife straight into his chest. I screamed as Dad toppled backward into the railing, nearly falling over the banister. I barely had time to react, the next part happened so quickly. Arthur smirked and gave one final push, shoving both arms out in front of him rapidly, causing my father to topple helplessly off the balcony.

Looking smug and unempathetic, Arthur vanished into thin air as I screamed out uncontrollably, consumed by emotional pain. The next few seconds were a blur. Distraught, I broke down into tears and raced clumsily down the stairwell, throwing myself over my father's lifeless body sprawled out across the floor.

Chapter Twenty-Three

Matt was by my side not even five seconds later, kneeling beside me and patting one of my shoulders in comfort. I turned to embrace him, watching as tears began to form in the corner of his eyes before burying my head into his chest and weeping uncontrollably. I barely even noticed when Grace came wandering into the room.

All I heard was a few soft footsteps before a familiar voice stated softly, "I'm so sorry, Olivia. This was never meant to happen."

I sniffled loudly and pulled my head up as I wiped my face briefly, focusing in on Grace's face. I began to stare at her so deeply in fact, that I could swear I was looking beyond the surface and into her soul, for it was Mary's eyes I could see that stared back at me with genuine sorrow.

The longer I stared at her, the more my blood began to boil. At first, I didn't think twice about why she was there, too overcome with grief to care why she'd suddenly decided to show up. But then, Matt asked what she was doing here and I felt the anger set in, compressing the sadness within. "You were supposed to help!" I snapped at her, standing up with weak, shaking legs. "If you had just pulled your act together and told Matt the truth before we even got here all of this could have been avoided!"

She didn't move a muscle, which irked me even more. As calm as ever, she replied simply, "I am truly sorry for your loss, but you know as well as I do that this wasn't my fault. Redirect your anger towards the person who did it."

I lost control of my emotions and marched at her, intending to slam her into the nearest wall and punch her stupid face, however—almost as if he was waiting for me to snap—Matt grabbed me around the waist and pulled me back in order to thwart my outburst.

Letting go once I'd settled down, he took a step towards Grace and pointed at her in confusion. "Hold on, if I'm the Grayson's long-lost baby, how did you get involved in all this?"

A wave of silence washed over the room for several minutes before she finally answered, "I'm involved because I'm your sister."

Matt raised his eyebrows at her for a moment, then said slowly, "Yeah, my adoptive sister? I already know that."

"No," she said brusquely, "your biological sister. Well, half-sister if you want to get technical, I suppose."

Matt looked stumped, not understanding at all. "What do you mean, did Peter Maker knock someone else up?"

Mary rolled her eyes with a sigh and once again, allowed Grace's image to falter, obviously deciding stepping out would be the quickest and easiest way to relay the truth to Matt.

Panicked, Matt dove for her with outstretched arms, attempting to break her fall. Until he realised Grace's body was on the floor and a ghost was standing in her place.

Sticking out her palm for a handshake, Mary flashed Matt a fake smile and announced chirpily, "Mary Grayson, your deceased, biological half-sister. Pleasure to make your acquaintance."

"Oh." Matt stepped back quickly, his eyes popping out of his skull. He didn't blink for quite a while, clearly struggling with what he was seeing. "Err, hi," was all he could manage.

Mary nodded, pulled back her hand and smiled for real. "Look, long story short I've been possessing your adoptive sister Grace for about a year now, trying to figure out a way to tell you the truth about all of this so you could come home and make things right. I failed, obviously, and Olivia picked up my slack."

Matt gave a half-assed nod and turned his attention to the balled-up body of his unconscious adoptive sister on the floor.

"Oh, don't worry, Grace is just fine," Mary said. "It's just that the longer I'm in her, the longer she's wiped out for when I step out. She'll be awake in maybe four hours or so, I'd say, with no real memory of the possession. It'll come across a dream in her mind. For now, we need you to focus on destroying Agatha's spirit. You're aware we are all bound by her, stuck and unable to move on while she picks us off one by one, right?"

"Actually Mary, I'm not so sure that's accurate," I mumbled, remembering the moment Agatha had avoided stabbing my father after learning the truth about her parent's demise.

As though she'd been listening, Agatha suddenly made an appearance beside Mary, causing her to flinch so hard she disappeared momentarily before reappearing beside Matt. To our surprise, Agatha simply bent down over my father, pulled the knife out of his body, and offered it handle first to Matt.

"Do it if it makes you feel better," she stated casually, in her soft feminine voice. "All I wanted was to know the truth about how my parents died. I can move on now."

Matt hesitated, but graciously took the knife and thanked her.

I stared at Agatha in disbelief. "You're frickin' kidding, right? All of this, just to turn around and say you're ready to go now? After you tormented me, killed my boyfriend and destroyed their family?" I gestured toward Matt and Mary. I could feel myself getting overwhelmed again and had to take a few deep breaths while I waited for Agatha's response.

Agatha hung her head for a moment, then looked up at me with a genuinely bewildered expression. "Uh, I know I've made some mistakes, but I didn't do any of that stuff. The only person I killed was the fake 'removalist' guy. He was just some low-life thief who was snooping around trying to find my family fortune. I *may* have tweaked the bolts on the trapdoor so when he got in, it fell shut on him and locked so he couldn't get back out. But really, he deserved it, so that was his own fault."

Mary piped in from the background, "I'm sorry, what?" She turned to look at me with desperate eyes. "She didn't kill your dad, then?"

I shook my head, "No, actually that was the work of your ill-tempered father."

Mary turned back to Agatha, amazed. "Wait, so then, you didn't use some fancy mind control to overpower me and make me kill Owen?"

Agatha scoffed, seemingly insulted. "No silly, I'm not exactly a maternal person but I'd never hurt a child! I mean yes, I did possess you—but just to see what I could do. I wanted to see what I was capable of and practice for when I got ahold of my parents' killer. I hoped if I got strong enough, I'd be able to avenge their deaths by making their murderer commit suicide or something. I swear, the last thing I did with you on the night your brother died, was put you to bed. That was also the only time I've ever managed to do something like that."

Mary shook her head and gripped the sides of her face, like she was trying to remember something desperately. "If you didn't do it…I don't understand. Did I kill my brother? How could I do something like that without any memory of it?"

Agatha shook her head and shrugged, "I'm sorry, I really don't have an answer for you."

It was like time paused for a few moments, with everybody unsure of what to say or do next. I shook my head, not willing to accept Agatha's sudden claim of innocence. "But, you possessed me? You tried to strangle me the first time we met and then tried to make me kill my brother. More than once, I might add. You've tortured me and my family since the moment we got here—physically pushing my mum down the stairs and rupturing my sister's placenta. Causing accidents that hurt pretty much everyone in some way or another. Not to mention all the bleeding wall illusions and mind tricks along the way." I slowed my speech as Agatha began to shake her head continuously, but I was adamant about stating one last painful fact. "You killed Sam for trying to destroy you…?"

Agatha frowned and rubbed her face, seemingly deep in thought. "Sorry, I didn't do any of those horrible things. Well, except maybe cause the blood illusions. I swear though, all I ever wanted was to find out why my parents were killed and who was responsible."

Agatha took a moment to kneel down beside my dad and patted his chest with sympathy, as though she felt sorry for him. I flinched as she touched his body, caught in an automatic reaction fearing that she was about to hurt him. Until I remembered he was already gone, and no one could ever cause him pain again.

"I admit, for the first few years after I died, I enjoyed messing with people," she said. "But I only did a few simple haunted house tricks, like making lights flicker and spooky moaning noises when kids came to the door, that sort of stuff. That's all. Most of the time, I just sat in a ball and cried.

After my death was the first time in a long time I felt truly alive and free, as odd as that might seem. The freedom doesn't last long however. It becomes exhausting moving things around and don't even get me started on how much energy controlling people consumes. I ended up severely drained every time I tried. I only possessed Mary once when she was alive, for less than an hour and I couldn't even imagine having the strength to possess anyone now. I thought dying was supposed to give me the power to catch my parents' killers and sick revenge on them without consequences. But during my whole spiritual existence, I've mostly been just fading in and out for long periods at a time and sometimes even find myself with patches of missing memory, much like you I suppose, Mary. Except for me, years go by at a time without me even noticing. In fact, when I appeared on the landing tonight right in front of your father, that's the first time I've managed to come back to this plane of existence for years.

As for the bleeding walls…that wasn't actually my doing, per se, I think it was part of a spell. When I was alive, I started messing around with witchcraft books. I remember there was some kind of ritual involving a blood-to-blood spell. The book said something about the walls of the house of death bleeding as the illusion of secrets revealed themselves. It might surprise you to know that I didn't take a lot of notice when it came to the side effects of messing with that stuff. I was too depressed to care. At the time, I didn't think it even worked, but I guess that one did, after all, just not the way I intended. And well, that's that, I haven't even been around to hurt anyone."

"How is that possible!" I exclaimed, gesturing at Mary with disbelief as I became gradually more annoyed at Agatha, speaking faster than before out of frustration. "They said you've been keeping them here, that they've been drained of their energy or whatever. I've seen two spirits disappear in a ball of fire myself! Your Evelyn—Mum—she said your dad had been destroyed before she was sucked out into non-existence herself…" I trailed off as I realised something. Agatha's mother, Evelyn, had been trying to tell me something the whole time. She kept saying it's not what it seems.

Agatha raised her eyebrows "What is it….?"

I stared at her, unable to speak as my mind began to tick over. If Agatha truly wasn't involved in anything that had happened since we'd moved in, then what was going on? I'd seen her several times and yet she now claimed she hadn't done any of the things I'd seen her do….and been drained every time she'd ever tried to do anything. Drained. It was the same word Mary and Mrs Grayson used to describe how they'd been suffering during their time trapped in the house. So, if not Agatha, who was draining them?

Mary crossed her arms as though something I'd said irritated her. "Mum did say we were only guessing, it's not like anyone gave us an instruction manual you know," she said. "We assumed Agatha was to blame after I told her she possessed me. I certainly didn't kill my little brother on my own will. Nor would my father murder me on his own accord. We figured she was the reason we got stuck here and why we've gotten so weak, particularly those who stay within this house. Every time we see her around, our spirits become drained that little bit more."

Agatha scowled at her and protested in a shrill, frustrated manner, "I haven't done anything to you people!"

Mary shook her head and shot her a dirty look, but Agatha didn't retaliate, looking insulted and falling silent instead.

I studied Agatha's face, trying to determine if she was being genuine. In the end, someone had to be responsible for Owen's death. Sam's too. Surely Agatha was lying. It had to be some kind of trap.

Matt took a small step back, loudly addressing both of them with his hands in the air in a surrender-like pose, as though he expected a fight to occur. "Ok, so I think we can agree there's been some kind of misunderstanding."

When nobody responded, he relaxed a little and spoke directly to Mary. "Maybe no one is forcing you guys to stay trapped, it could just be some kind of placebo effect. You've believed so intently all this time that Agatha was the reason you couldn't move on, so it really happened. You probably feel so drained here because it's been such a long time. Hanging around in the living world as a ghost isn't exactly supposed to happen, it's not natural."

I was impressed. For someone who'd only just officially gotten on board with the whole idea of ghosts, he was outdoing me in handling the overall situation. Whilst he made a good point, I was still uneasy about his logic and couldn't help but wonder if there was something we were missing. It surely couldn't be so simple. Something didn't feel right.

I could hear Matt's voice again suddenly and realised my mind had been somewhere else momentarily. "I think we can all agree, it's time to end this. After all this time hating each other—and blaming each other, I think you all deserve some peace. Agatha, if you're telling the truth and you truly want to move on, I suppose you can prove it by letting me release your soul. None of you deserve to be stuck here."

It was the first thing I'd heard in a long time that made sense. Mary looked down at Grace's unconscious body and then up at me and smiled. I could tell she was going to miss being around, even if she didn't really belong here.

In unison, we all started making our way towards the living room, Matt led the way with Mary and Agatha following closely behind, leaving a large gap between each other however. I dragged my feet at the rear of the line. With the prospective nightmare ending, I still couldn't shake the feeling that something was about to go wrong.

It wasn't until I stood in the living room, perfectly opposite the wall where I knew the bloodstain was hiding that I finally started seeing a light at the end of the tunnel. The eager Grayson spirits, Agatha included, surrounded me in the living room as Matt and I reached the cursed wall. Mary had disappeared briefly and returned holding Owen's hand, which was the way they continued to stand and wait for their long overdue peace.

Matt raised his arm towards the wall, his hand clutching the knife tightly, but hesitated when Penelope Grayson appeared beside him, smiling warmly into his eyes.

"Thank you for coming home," she said. "Please forgive me, my baby boy, things were supposed to be different. If I had realised what my husband was truly capable of, I would have swept up your brother and sister as quickly as I possibly could and left him to be with your father the second I had the opportunity. I just didn't take it in time."

Matt's bottom lip trembled as he nodded, remaining silent. For a moment, I couldn't tell how truly upset he was, but then his facial expression softened and a single tear rolled down his cheek. I felt bad for him and crossed the room to place my hand on his shoulder, comforting him as he'd done for me every time I'd needed him.

"Let's hope this works then," he said. "I guess it's not too late for you to go be with him." Matt stopped and turned around, asking with a hint of confusion in his voice, "Agatha, do you know exactly what I'm supposed to do here?"

Agatha smiled calmly. "The knife is the key, it knows what to do. It came with one of my ritual books. It's known as a soul blade and was designed to tether any spirit it draws in from blood remains it encounters. Basically, when I killed myself with it, it cursed the blood on the wall when it spattered to ensure my spirit was stuck to the house.

All the instructions for it were in that one particular dark arts book it came from, though I don't know where that ended up. I used it because I didn't know how the afterlife worked exactly and I had to make sure I stuck around in spirit form long enough to find my parents' killer and bring them to justice. I'm pretty sure—from memory—to end the curse you need to touch the wall to activate the blood then it should be as simple as connecting the blade with the blood, giving instructions and it should sever the spell. You can choose to release me or destroy me. I honestly won't stop you from doing whatever you think is the right thing to do. If the Graysons believe I'm the reason they're trapped, once I'm gone, they should be released automatically as well."

Matt shrugged, took one last look at his mother and stroked the wall with an open hand, revealing the bloodstains within. He braced himself, pulled back the knife and thrust it with force directly into the centremost point of the stain.

"Err…," he turned and grimaced at me, as though waiting for permission.

I nodded and he gave me a half smile in response.

"I feel like such a dweeb, but here goes. Release Agatha's spirit!" He said each word loudly and clearly, like he didn't want to mess it up and give the wrong instructions.

As creepy as ever, it was as though the wall groaned in response, a loud grumble echoed throughout the room before a cracking noise sounded from deep inside the house as the stained area started to crumble away. It was quite a sight to see.

Matt grabbed my hand nervously as we both turned towards the ghosts to watch what would happen. Agatha was the first to change. Her appearance rapidly transformed from raggedy and worn-looking, becoming the beautiful, lovely young woman I'd seen in the newspaper photo when she was alive. As her spirit found peace, she began to fade away and I noticed out of the corner of my eye that the handle of the knife began to glow an eerie green colour. The fainter she herself became, the brighter the handle glowed.

"Thank you," she whispered as she faded completely into the next plane of existence and the knife handle went dull once more.

Strangely enough, a minute or two passed by, but nothing at all happened to the others. I figured once Agatha was out of the equation, they would all just fade away into the light without an issue like Agatha said. But Penelope, Owen, and Mary all stood, waiting nervously and becoming increasingly upset the more time passed.

"Why haven't we moved on yet?" Mary asked, frustratingly gesturing to the entire room.

"Don't look at me, you were the one with all the answers," I responded bluntly, shrugging. "Maybe she really didn't have anything to do with you being unable to move on. It's up to your own willpower now." I waved my hands around wildly. "Command the light to appear to you or something."

Matt turned back towards the wall, tapped on the knife a few times, then stared back at his family. Mary frowned and looked at her mother, as though desperate for an answer. Penny just shook her head in despair.

"Ok, well I don't know what to do now. If you can't voluntarily leave, there has to be another reason you can't move on," Matt stated, plucking the knife from the wall and clasping it tightly.

"It may have something to do with me," a snide, rasping voice commented from the opposite side of the room.

Everyone turned toward the doorway in unison, though I didn't really need to look. I knew exactly who the voice belonged to.

"Agatha?!" Penelope gasped.

Chapter Twenty-Four

I was rattled, shaken, completely thrown off by what I was seeing. "You see her too, right?" I murmured to my left without looking.

"I thought she was gone?" Matt whispered to me, like he hadn't even heard me ask him first. I didn't know how to reply to him, I'd thought the same.

"Ha!" Agatha let out a single loud blast like a foghorn before suddenly bursting into a fit of laughter. The worst part was, the laughter itself didn't belong to Agatha. Though it visually appeared to come from her mouth, the voice clearly belonged to a man. "You should have just seen the looks on your faces! Ah well, it was great while it lasted. You all just couldn't leave well enough alone, could you? You had to go and send her off."

Unfortunately, I was quickly able to distinguish who the voice really belonged to, anticipating a similar situation to Mary's voice projecting from inside Grace's body. Before I could question what was happening or why, Agatha lifted a hand to her face and snapped her fingers, instantaneously transforming into Arthur.

"Arthur?" Penny shrieked.

"It was you," I said, my voice barely louder than a whisper. "You've been posing as her this whole time, haven't you? You're the real reason they're stuck here! You're the one who's been trying to kill my family…and *you* killed Sam."

"Arthur? Is that true?" Penny asked in disbelief as Arthur tilted his head and smirked at me, raising his arm slowly to robotically wave at me. In doing so, he instantly triggered a memory and all I could picture was the dark figure I'd seen looming in the shadows of the window the very first day we'd moved in.

"Sure is, my darling and you aren't going anywhere; you don't deserve it. You are so naïve and stupid aren't you, Penny? I mean, come on, think really hard. Your deaths weren't Agatha's fault at all, were they? She didn't care about any of you, she didn't even know you. By the time we moved into this house, her spirit had practically gone dormant. I made my own image scarce so you'd believe I was long gone, but it was always me in her place. Well, except before, when I decided to swap with her out on the balcony. Ah, the look on her face when she saw Scott was priceless."

Mrs Grayson seemed too astounded to respond, so Matt snapped, "What the hell are you talking about?"

Arthur rolled his eyes and began to pace. "My entitled sister literally just told you all that she didn't hurt anyone. How brainless are you people? How can you not put two and two together? Agatha had nothing to do with the famed 'Grayson tragedy,' it was just a necessary part of me righting the wrongs in my life.

Let me tell you a little story. You see, children, I decided to fight for my rights to this house after an intense dream I had one night. In the dream, I saw all of George Clayton's money still hidden in this manor, tucked away in a secret vault within the walls, which was activated by a hidden latch. I knew then that the money had to be real, it wasn't just a dream, more like a vision I was being shown. I wasn't about to let anyone else find it, so I did a little research and when I discovered the house was still vacant after my sister's untimely death, I was more determined than ever to come here and claim it.

Once my heritage was proven and I finally won the right to be here, every night when the kids and my *whore* of a wife went to bed—" Arthur stopped abruptly in surprise when Matt raised his hand casually—as though he were in a classroom—before boldly announcing:

"I'd just like to point out, my mother is not a whore, you pushed her away. She didn't have an affair; she had an opportunity for real love. You're a pathetic excuse of a man for how you handled that situation."

Arthur's attitude quickly changed from smug to plain pissed off. I gasped as he moved in a single swoosh, coming face to face with Matt before grabbing at his throat and pushing him backward, causing him to slam into the wall behind him. He appeared pinned and unable to move or speak.

"No, let him go!" I screeched. Before long, Matt was choking and gasping for air. When blue and purple bruises began appearing on his neck, I knew Arthur must be pressing down quite hard on his throat, strangling him. Knowing there was nothing I could do, I could feel my heart racing uncontrollably. I couldn't pry away ghostly fingers no matter how solid they appeared. Then an idea hit me. I knew I'd never be able to physically make him let go, so opted for distraction instead.

"Arthur, you evil son of a bitch, how stupid are *you*?" As quickly as I could move, I wrenched the knife out of Matt's clasped hand and held it out in front of me, threatening Arthur with it.

He just laughed. "Foolish girl, you can't kill me with a knife!"

"Wanna make a bet?" I turned around, placing the tip of the knife against the wall instead. "I bet there's some bits of you left on this wall too isn't there?"

Even though he laughed it off again, a flicker of fear licked his face. I knew then that I was right, he knew exactly what the blade was capable of. I drew my hand back, preparing enough force to push through the plaster.

Matt dropped to the ground a millisecond later as Arthur released him, at the same time the knife flew out of my grasp and into Arthur's hand.

"Doubtful. But I don't think I'll take any chances," Arthur said.

It was then I lost hope. He had the only thing I knew of that could potentially destroy him and clearly Matt was not immune to his power at all like his mother thought he'd be. As though he'd read my mind, he grinned, pointed at me with the tip of the knife, then at Matt before gesturing to the lounge nearest where we were standing. I reluctantly sat down, but Matt stood his ground, glaring at Arthur with as much hatred as I'd ever seen.

"Do you have a death wish?" I asked as I yanked down on his arm, forcing him to sit beside me.

Arthur raised his eyebrows and continued his story triumphantly. "Now where was I? Oh yes. So, after the rest of my family went to sleep each night, I slowly searched and stripped the entire house, room by room—checking every nook and cranny in existence for any evidence of a secret vault. One night though, Owen must have heard me rummaging in the basement when he was in the kitchen getting a glass of water and came snooping. I'd had a bad day, was already cranky and lost it. When he started nagging and asking questions about what I was doing, I threw out my arm in frustration, pushed him backward and lost his balance. He tripped, first over his own feet, then the uneven ground, and fell heavily on a sharp piece of stone sticking up out of the floor. He unfortunately hit his temple directly and there was nothing I could do to save him. If there's one person in the world I never meant to hurt, it was him."

For a moment, the smug, careless attitude faded from Arthur Grayson's face and was replaced by genuine sorrow as he stared across the room at his son, who appeared just as solemn as he listened to his father recount his death.

"But it did set a plan in motion, something I wasn't willing to do before that happened," Arthur went on. "Whilst I'd been trying to find the vault, I discovered an old book. Some sort of spell book for the dark arts. I believe it belonged to Agatha. In it, there was a ritual to gain immortality. The catch? Die, then in spirit form, absorb thirteen Souls of the Unfinished."

I must have pulled a strange face, as Arthur paused to chuckle before continuing slyly, "Basically, spirits suffering from having their lives stolen. Murder victims. Only once all thirteen souls have been collected can you then resurrect, not only alive, but immortal. I felt like I finally had a new purpose, like I was being given a second chance at life, a fresh start for myself, without the burden of family betrayal. My little boy was dead and I had nothing else to live for, so I figured why not give it a go. I wasn't about to go down in history as the man who murdered his whole family, however, so I came up with a tragic, historic ending for my family.

I grabbed a knife, took Owen upstairs, put him in bed and posed his body to make it look like he'd been stabbed to death there. Then I covered Mary in his blood while she slept, wiped my prints off the knife and placed it in her bed. The rest is *history*. Unfortunately, however, after I took my own life, I wasn't counting on my spirit going dormant for seventeen years. I only realised when I appeared one day in the living room and discovered how much the house and neighbourhood had changed. Nevertheless, the plan was back in motion and I knew if I was going to get away with what I had to do, I had to keep everyone believing it was Agatha behind the attacks, including my own family. Kept the focus off me, see. So, I disguised myself to look like her and continued absorbing the souls as planned. That's why I brought my dear cousin back here. After the Claytons, who better to absorb than the family of the man who betrayed me? Soon, I shall live again, powerful and incapable of suffering any more pain!"

I was astounded. Agatha never really was the evil one. Arthur was and ensured she'd gotten the blame all along.

He sniggered and held his arms out in front of him, showing off his semi-translucent skin. "See how wonderfully human I look after consuming just a few souls? I'd have more by now if certain family members of mine would stop hiding." He shot a dirty look toward Mary and Penelope. "It takes long enough as it is to fully drain a soul without added games. Now, if I could just find that money, I'll finally have finished what I started this all for."

"What is wrong with you?" I snapped uncontrollably, standing up to make a point. I couldn't listen to any more of his power-hungry speech. "You're insane, do you not realise that? Agatha was right, you're a murderer and you've managed to blame everyone else along the way for what you've done. Over *money*. How do you know it even exists? So, what, your adoptive father told you George kept money in the house, but what if he didn't? You've never seen it, nor has anyone else. Hardly anyone even knows about it. It's likely just a rumour that spread because the Claytons were rich!" I closed my mouth quickly as I realised my outburst had further pissed Arthur off.

Matt must have realised it too, as he quickly stood up and stepped in front of me, as though intending to protect me should Arthur try anything. Just as Arthur was about to raise his hand, a small, meek voice from the hallway cut through the room like a knife.

"What's wrong with Dad?"

Poking his head around the doorframe, Noah's eyes grew wide as he observed the living room full of ghosts. He stopped in his tracks and dropped the handheld game console he was clutching as his hands went limp from shock.

Arthur smiled wickedly. "He really is a mini, albeit blonde, Scott, this one—isn't he?"

Noah screamed as Arthur lifted his arm towards him with outstretched fingers. I'd barely blinked when Penelope threw herself in front of Noah, simultaneously flicking her arm out with force in Arthur's general direction, somehow managing to use her own power to knock Arthur backward. She looked surprised, as though she didn't even know she was capable of doing so.

Pushing my brother out into the hallway, she screamed, "Go upstairs, run!" Before turning back and smiling in triumph momentarily.

Arthur phased out and suddenly reappeared inches from her face. Her smiling expression quickly turned to fear as he placed a hand on her shoulder and grasped it as tightly as he could. At first, her spirit appeared to fade in a swirl of the weird, mist-like substance I'd first seen Evelyn Clayton disappear in, but as we watched in horror, the mist became brighter and thicker, and she went up in flames in no time as he began to suck the essence out of her soul. As I observed the pain on her face, it took me only a second to remember that the knife might be our last hope at this point. He'd tried to hide it, but he had seemed afraid of it—like he knew it might actually be able to destroy him. I wondered if it was at all possible that he had really used the exact same knife, the soul blade, Agatha had to kill himself. It was worth a shot, I just needed to get the knife back from him first.

I watched Penelope burn and thought about the other spirits I'd seen being destroyed, or rather absorbed in the house—which gave me a decoy idea to try. I figured I might be able to use pain as a long enough distraction if I could burn him too. I'd seen plenty of movies depicting the idea that if you burned the body, or the remains of a body, the ghost would be destroyed. Though his ghost was probably protected because of the soul blade, I hoped Matt and I might be able to hurt him just long enough to reclaim the knife back in order to kill him. I took a mini step closer to Matt and muttered under my breath, "We have to burn it."

Confused, he whispered back, "Burn what?"

I could see Penny's spirit blazing up fast and I knew I wouldn't have time to explain in full detail. "Just grab the knife when he lets it go!"

I leapt toward the wall, pulling out my lighter from my back pocket. Arthur seemed to know instantly that something was up, as he immediately let go of Penelope and turned towards us. She fell to the floor, gasping heavily as her spirit outline slowly came back into full focus. It was too late for Arthur to react. I clicked the lighter just once and held it directly to the bloody area on the wall.

"No!" Arthur cried out, attempting to reach us before the flames took.

Thankfully, the wall caught alight easily. Flames whooshed up, getting fiercer by the second and I was forced to jump out of the way due to the intense heat. As Arthur's spirit began to burn and blacken, he screamed and dropped the knife just as I'd anticipated allowing Matt time to dive in and collect it from the floor. He looked over at me and seemed to instantly click onto my plan.

Arthur threw himself towards Matt in a desperate attempt to grab him, parts of his body almost completely blackened out and other parts on fire, all the while moaning in agony whilst he swung his body weight around. Like a gymnast on steroids, Matt pulled a few classy manoeuvres and dodged him, racing to the wall with minimal effort.

Chapter Twenty-Five

Using one arm to cover a portion of his face and breathing heavily from the heat of the burning wall, Matt didn't hesitate to get the job done and with great force, jammed the knife into the centre of the bloodstain, yelling as loudly as he could whilst choking on the billowing smoke, "*Destroy* Arthur's spirit!"

The handle glowed once more, building up, becoming brighter than ever. The flames billowed across the whole wall, enhancing the colour in the knife as it shone an epic shade of green so brightly it reflected throughout the whole room, bouncing off every surface it found.

I squinted my eyes to avoid being temporarily blinded and looked back at Arthur, watching with satisfaction as he screamed and writhed, dropping to his knees and tearing at his face like it was the source of his pain.

Little did I expect an explosion-like effect to occur as the wall weakened and succumbed to being burnt out by the flames. I was knocked off my feet in an instant as the blazing wall shattered outward and came crumbling down, landing on top of Matt who had also been propelled forward by the impact. As we crashed to the floor, I raised my head just in time to see Arthur's ghost disintegrate into dust.

It was like an automatic switch had been flipped. All three of the Grayson ghosts began to fade instantaneously, the blockage preventing them from moving on having been removed.

"Thank you!" Mrs Grayson said gratefully, holding her hands to her cheeks in disbelief as she vanished peacefully in a warm white glow with tears in her eyes.

Mary smiled, mouthed thank you, and grabbed ahold of Owen's hand as they both faded out.

From the floor, I glanced up at what was left of the wall. Surprisingly, the flames miraculously burned out once they reached the edges of the famed living room wall, as though there was an invisible fire blanket blocking either end from going any further through the house. I was in absolute awe and found myself suddenly thankful that I used to be a firebug. Keeping a lighter in my back pocket had become a bad habit for me and for the first time, I'd done something good with it.

I smiled to myself, and Matt smiled back, assuming I was smiling at him. I suddenly realised I was still lying semi-on top of him and rolled to the side swiftly. Matt chuckled nervously and stood up, reaching down to offer me a hand up off the floor. I allowed myself to be lifted and was pulled immediately into a tight hug as soon as I became vertical.

"What a nightmare. I can't believe it's actually over," Matt muttered, wrapping his arms tightly around my body. "Kinda gonna miss my ghost family though, would have been nice to get to know them better."

I giggled and closed my eyes, taking it all in. Out of nowhere, Matt suddenly interrupted my peaceful thoughts by gracefully pushing me away from him slightly, grabbing the back of my neck with his palm and pulling me into him, planting a generous kiss on my lips. Though a little taken aback, I was surprised that I didn't even want to fight him, feeling like it was exactly what I was supposed to be doing at that moment.

Matt let go of me seconds later, gasping loudly. "Liv, look!"

A little dazed, I turned to see what he'd spotted and found myself looking at an unbelievable sight. "No freaking way."

Among the rubble, sitting on the floor inside the destroyed, ashen wall, was a large, grubby silver vault.

"You've got to be kidding me. I don't believe it!" I immediately rushed towards it, stepping inside the wall, wondering if it was just a figment of my imagination. Matt was right behind me, looking as stunned as I was. The vault was quite decently sized, about half the height of a person, as long as a bathtub and had a giant steel, coded wheel lock on it.

"We need bolt cutters!" Matt exclaimed dashing out of the room, I assumed on route to the shed. I knelt beside the metal bank and ran my hands along the edging, winding down from the prior events in awe while I waited for his return.

The money that Arthur Grayson had his heart set on, that he had killed for, was, in fact, real and truly hidden *inside* the house the whole time. Inside the walls. I stood up and turned to the rubble of the wall, examining the wreckage. It appeared there used to be a secret latch built into the wall, possibly attached to the back of a painting or something similar, that had been sealed over at some point, whether accidentally or on purpose, presumably when they'd cleaned up Agatha's death. There was no way of accessing the latch mechanism after it had been sealed into the wall, which was apparently how it had stayed hidden every time the house was searched.

I bent down and sifted through the pieces of metal that made up the highly advanced locking system, admiring the effort George Clayton had gone through to preserve his fortune and found myself wondering if Agatha had known about it the whole time.

Tapping on the side of the vault by the control panel, I couldn't help but notice how thin the metal was, despite the sheer size of the vault overall. I jumped when a shadow crept across the floor and breathed a sigh of relief when I looked up to see Noah's innocent little face staring down at me curiously.

"I'm scared, Livvie, I don't understand. What happened? Dad's dead, isn't he?"

I felt bad that I'd completely forgotten about Noah and didn't have a clue how to explain what he'd just seen, let alone how Dad had died. "You know what, it's just been an unbelievably bad day buddy. How about you go and get ready, and we'll go up to the hospital in a minute. Then I can talk to you, Belle and Mum at the same time."

Matt returned with the bolt cutters a few minutes later, attempting multiple times to cut off the lock. It was too strong.

Fiddling with the alphabetic buttons on the password control panel, Matt frustratingly exclaimed, "What on earth could the password be?"

After trying a few common number combinations, I studied it for a moment, trying to tap into my old, lawbreaking brain. Like revisiting a dream, I remembered the time I'd been caught ripping off a shop with Sam. We had used a series of tricks and distraction tactics over an hour-long process to slowly cover up the cameras in a bag store, enabling us to walk out with several expensive, name-brand handbags which we later tried to sell and got sprung. That was the closest I'd ever come to being formally charged. Sam and I managed to get away with doing one hundred hours of community service each instead. I could hear my dad's voice in my head when we were found out, pretending to be cross and yell at me for my mother's sake but also secretly congratulating my advanced skills and clever tactic later on when she wasn't listening.

In a eureka moment, like I suddenly had the password handed to me, I smiled and placed my fingers on the buttons, punching in the word "Agatha."

"Oh, come on, how did you know that?" Matt whined, bewildered as the vault door made a beeping sound followed by a series of clicks.

I shrugged, "Simple, she was the only heir he cared about and before Arthur caused their big fight, they were a close-knit family. Like me and my dad. Anyone with half a brain could have figured it out."

Even though the password released the lock, the door was so tightly sealed from being unopened for so long that it was almost impossible to pop open, but both Matt and I put maximum strength into it and the door flew open once the pressure gave way. Inside, there must have been hundreds of thousands of dollars worth of green bills.

"Our reward?" Matt joked.

I laughed, but couldn't help feeling guilty about keeping it. "We have to get rid of this, don't we?" I said regrettably.

Matt looked shocked. "What? No way, we earned it, Liv. Besides, no one really knows about it and no one's left to inherit it." He paused while I mulled it over. I sighed and nodded, knowing he was somewhat right but the idea of keeping it still felt wrong. He tilted his head and spoke using his hands. "You're technically related to the Claytons, right? So, if you think about it, it's not really stealing, is it?"

Was I though? Maybe on some sort of distant level if I were to break it down with a fine-tooth comb. That didn't make it mine. I must have still been making faces, because Matt continued to stress his point. "You know, if you destroy this money that would be the single-handed, most stupid thing anyone has ever done. And if you turn this in to the cops, there will be a never-ending series of investigations done on this house and your family. I'm sure, given what's happened here, you don't want that kind of attention."

I grimaced. He had convinced me. "True. Ok, we have to hide it somewhere for now then. I have to get up to the hospital, I have to tell Mum, well you know…tell her what happened to my dad."

He agreed and helped me cart the vault up to my bedroom where we stuck it in the corner behind the door, disguising it by covering it up in a pile of clothing. For such a giant vault, it was surprisingly lightweight. Thankfully, my mother had given up cleaning my bedroom years ago so I knew it would be safe there until I could figure out what to do with it. I then called out to Noah and we all went downstairs, intending to go up to the hospital.

As we passed through the kitchen, a brand new wave of grief hit me when I saw my father's body lying on the floor.

"Gracie!" Matt exclaimed, suddenly remembering his adoptive sister being abandoned in a heap on the ground when vacated by his biological sister's ghost. Upon feeling her pulse and placing a hand on her forehead, Matt breathed a sigh of relief, nodding at me. "She's a bit warm, but she's just unconscious. I think we should take her home first. If she wakes up in her own bed it'll be heaps easier to convince her the possession was all a dream."

I agreed and helped him place her in the back of Dad's car where we then drove her to Matt's place, positioning her in a comfortable pose in her bed.

Once Matt was convinced she would be alright, we made our way to the hospital. Aside from needing to update my mother on what had happened back home, I was curious to see if there had been any progress on Isabelle and the baby's birth. I found Mum sitting out in the waiting room and feared the worst. "On no, is the baby ok?" I asked fearfully.

"Oh, she's just fine!" Mum said happily, standing up when she heard my voice and giving me a quick hug before sitting back down and pulling Noah onto her lap. "It was a bit touch and go for a while there, but they're both doing great now. Isabelle named her Maggie, a modern tribute to my name I guess. Carl just got here so I came out to give them a bit of family time."

I breathed in relief and pulled her in for a huge hug, unintentionally pushing Noah out of the way as I did so. He chose to stand beside Matt out of the way instead. When Mum pulled back and I didn't let go, she must have known something was wrong. "Olivia, what is it?" she asked, a hint of slight panic in her voice.

It took all of my strength, but I sat her down and explained what had happened to Dad in as much detail as I could, leaving out the ghost-related bits. I told her that he'd simply had a relapse-type episode and thrown himself off the balcony, impaling himself during the fall with wood chunks from the broken banister. Given that he'd tried to commit suicide a couple of weeks prior, it was an easy, gentler explanation. Despite being given an alternate, less horrific version of the truth, she still crumbled into a million pieces at the news, literally falling to the floor on her knees. Not that I expected any different. I helped her up and held her tightly while she wailed, comforting her to the best of my ability. Seeing her so shattered caused me to break down and burst into tears, like I was reliving the feeling of losing Dad all over again.

We went to Sam's funeral three days later, then a few days after that, we attended my father's. Weeks passed, and we all suffered in silence as we grieved. Some days alone, some days together. Matt was by my side every step of the way and I reciprocated, being there for him the day he told Lynne, his adoptive mother, the truth about his biological parents and the affair her husband had to make his existence possible. In a way, she finally got her closure and the long-awaited answer as to why her husband had been murdered and who had been responsible. She cried at first, angry she'd been betrayed by Peter in that way, but ended up absolutely thrilled to find out that she'd raised her husband's son all those years.

Luckily for me, Matt somewhat followed in his mother's footsteps, adopting and raising a child who wasn't biologically his. As it turned out, the passionate night Sam and I had spent together the day before he was murdered resulted in a beautiful little surprise for me—a baby daughter. About eight weeks after my father's funeral, not long after Matt and I officially decided to be an exclusive couple, I found out I was pregnant with her—much further along than could have been possible for Matt to be the father. He never skipped a beat, taking her on as his own immediately, quite happy to honour Sam's memory. He insisted we name her Samantha Penelope.

In the years that followed, my mother sold the manor, taking Noah and moving back to Armistice, just a block away from my sister and her husband, whilst Matt and I moved in together, choosing to stay in Bellicose to her dismay. Shortly after Matty and I got married, we bought a large home outright using the cash from the vault, a couple of houses down from the Mason Street manor in order to raise our own children, a boy and girl we had in addition to Samantha. Whilst neither of us wanted to live in the once haunted manor, we decided to stay close to keep an eye on it to ensure the next family who lived there would stay safe. Because every now and then, I could swear I saw figures in the windows.

ABOUT THE AUTHOR

Kirra Michelle Tomkinson is an Australian author born in 1994.

Her three passions in life are her family, animals and writing.

Please feel free to follow her author page on Facebook :
(K.M. Tomkinson books).

Thank you for your support.